BEST GAY
EROTICA
2 0 0 1

BEST GAY EROTICA 2001

Richard Labonté,
Series Editor

Selected and
Introduced by

Randy Boyd

CLEIS
PRESS

Published in the United States
Cleis Press Inc., P.O. Box 14684, San Francisco, California 94114
Printed in the United States
Cover design: Scott Idleman
Book design: Karen Quigg
Cleis Press logo art: Juana Alicia
First Edition
10 9 8 7 6 5 4 3 2 1

Six legs, two hearts, my family
for Asa & Percy

TABLE OF CONTENTS

Foreword
Richard Labonté

After five years and several thousand stories, one might become numb to the arousal power, either physical or intellectual, of written porn.

One has not.

It's an enduring delight, really, to encounter the varied ways in which writers of the porn form (mainly men, but a few women, too, submitted work for this edition) play across the spectrum of gay male fantasy fulfillment. Nothing is taboo, no fetish unrealized, no pleasure is off limits: In a "best of" anthology such as this, where there is no set theme, it's a broadband world, with room for everything from heavy petting to heavy whipping, a tongue in the ear to a fist up the butt, serious tit play to sensual mind-fucking. Some vanilla here, some shit there, the stink of sweaty pits, and the scent of sweet breath—writing, in short, with many flavors.

This year's sixth edition of the *Best Gay Erotica* series, my fifth, sees the return of several repeat performers to its pages, among them Simon Sheppard (1996, '97, '98, '00), Bob Vickery ('98), Ian Philips ('99 and '00), Thomas P. Roche ('96), Andrew Ramer ('97), Larry Townsend ('99) and, from 2000, Matt Bernstein Sycamore,

Karl von Uhl, and Dimitri Apessos: Welcome back. Of course, Felice Picano is a veteran, too, with a distinguished three-decade career as a popular writer and critic, and with a stint as BGE judge in 1999, though this is his first appearance as a winner.

I'm also pleased when new names appear, with their first published work ever (Eddie Moreno), or for the first time in *Best Gay Erotica* (Jaime Cortez, Marshall Moore, Sandip Roy, D-L Alvarez, Doug Harrison, Marc Almond, Michael Stamp, Sean Meriwether, Jesse Grant, Michael V. Smith, and Barry Webster). New blood is invigorating, and I see the series as a place where the table of contents should offer a few surprises, rather than a roster of regulars; that's why I've enjoyed working with this year's judge, Randy Boyd, and past judges D. Travers Scott, Felice Picano, Christopher Bram, and Douglas Sadownick, all of whom understood that the goal each year is to uncover provocative sex writing that is as literate as it is lusty, and that "best" is not merely pedigree. This year, as in past years, more than half the selections are original bests, as picked by Boyd from among the 47 stories he was sent for judging (culled from 313 that I considered, 106 of which were submitted by writers, 207 of which I'd bookmarked in the preceding 12 months while skimming magazines and anthologies, reading novels and nonfiction books, downloading Web pages, and attending a few readings).

As ever, the winners range widely in tone and type, starting with the sly, wry insider attitude of Bob Vickery's "writergod" tale, "Knowing Johnny," which plays cleverly with a central conceit of professional porn: that it's fantasy, after all, and not real life. But could it be? Why the hell not! Erotic writing offers readers the chance to enter vicariously into a story, to take its sexual energy and to play with it (with oneself, of course). But what if the characters could step out of those same stories...

That playful element—maybe it doesn't happen quite this way in real life, but it should—also imbues "Gymnasty" by Jesse Grant, where a good-humored jock fantasy comes to pass, and the harsher but no less cock-teasing "Bear Basher" by Thomas P. Roche, where the consequences of an apparent gay bashing go very, very...right, and the satisfying payback tale "Heart" by Simon Sheppard, where revenge is sweet, and the rowdy, bittersweet "AIDS Is Over" by Karl von Uhl, where the sex itself, joyous and unbridled, is as much political act as it is physical release. On the other hand, real life is in fact the essence of two selections: Marc Almond's wistful, straightforward sex-club vignette series "The Show Palaces" and Sean Meriwether's self-voyeuristic hustler suite "For Hire: A Date with John," both of which immerse the reader in sex-charged settings: naked reporting, the erotic as personal memory, not as writer's fantasy, also inviting vicarious participation.

While I haven't quizzed the authors on how precisely their stories hew to their personal experience, enticing autobiographical elements appear in a number of this year's picks: "Just Another Night at the World's Greatest Gay Diner" by Dimitri Apessos is a charming account of a quick encounter that reads like a first-person pick-up; "Warm-up" by Matt Bernstein Sycamore, a more intense sexual snapshot, hums with the pleasure of the pursuit and that same sense of "this happened"; in "Knot of Roads," D-L Alvarez explores the pent-up frustrations of a kid who knows that survival lies only in escape (it's a preview of a work-in-progress charting the author's central California childhood); Doug Harrison reports on a fierce rite of passage, with unflinching honesty and exciting expertise, in "'You Need a Boy'"; Sandip Roy cruises and loses in the sauna, where "Prolonged Exposure May Cause Dizziness"; and Eddie Moreno wraps his love for music, his passion for the man who got away, his faith in family, and his unabashed sex play into the solid, sizzling package of "Woof. Yea. Uhuh. Yea, That's It. Uhuh. Yeaaa."

There's poetry, too, in the charged prose of Andrew Ramer's spiritual ode to enduring physical love, "When We Are Very Old," and in Jaime Cortez's paean to fleshy fruity pleasure, "Five a Day," two short-short stories whose metaphors ask that the reader's imagination merge with the writers' visions.

Erotica is of course a genre all its own, but there's double the fun when it's meshed with another, as it is in three of this year's works: Michael Stamp's shaggy-dog "Never Trust a Pretty Face," with its Depression-era hardboiled-detective main character, who comes a cropper when confronted by a most devious villain; Larry Townsend's historical "The Hittite Slave," set in ancient Egypt, where careful scholarship informs an unflinching story about circumcision; and Marshall Moore's adroit "The Future of the Future," where the Internet becomes deliciously interactive in a story that would be quite at home in a broad-minded science fiction magazine.

The fantasy inspired by good sex writing can take on absurdist tones, too, as in Barry Webster's "Body Symphony," in which a certain Russian composer finds inspiration in consummation, and in Ian Philip's "Foucault's Pendulous..." where a certain French philosopher is both intellectually and sexually dominant: two stories whose "what-if?" element borrows imaginatively from real personalities.

There's a romantic side to the erotic, too—there must be, otherwise the fantasy would be entirely one-handed—and it's expressed sweetly in our last two tales, "Onyx" by Felice Picano and "Gucci" by Michael V. Smith. In the former, the most highly charged moments come when the hunt is on; the sex is just the chaser. In the latter, the most highly charged moments come after the sex show; it's the yearning not realized that's the most moving.

Do find pleasure in the variety. I did.

Some thanks: to Frédérique and Don and Felice at Cleis Press, book professionals with whom it's a great pleasure to work; to Kirk Read, so much a part of Asa's and my life, though he's missed two deadlines in two years; to friends Justin Chin and Lawrence Schimel, who are never shy about sharing their opinions; and to the former staff of the old A Different Light Bookstore in San Francisco, who over five years of *Best Gay Erotica* guided me through my many old-dog days of computer tricks: Jim Breeden, Caroline Boyden, James Rafferty, and especially Ken White and Tommi Avicolli Mecca.

Introduction:
On to the Sex!
Randy Boyd

If you're reading this introduction to *Best Gay Erotica 2001,* either you like a slow buildup before doing The Bump and Grind, or you're doing what my high school journalism teacher said people usually do with their yearbooks: Go back and read the fine print some days, weeks, months, or even years after previously only gorging on the meat of the book (with yearbooks, that's the photos).

Either way, I'll be quick about it. You didn't buy this book to read this intro. You bought it to read about pulsating cocks dripping with pre-cum; soft, pink buttholes quivering with anticipation; hard, manly pecs glistening with sweat. You picked up this collection to explore the rush of the man who was a stranger on the street seconds before and is now in your living room, your armpits, your ass. Perhaps you can relate to the exhilaration of finally burying your face in the distinctive-smelling crotch of that hot neighbor, coworker, repairman, or gym buddy you thought you'd never have. Or maybe the hottest sex for you is sex with someone you know, care about, and actually love. Whatever your spin, you bought *Best Gay*

Erotica 2001 for the sex, and you opened it the way I would open it, thinking: On with the sex!

Consider this, then, a brief debriefing.

Damn, we gay men have had some good sex. Throughout history and around the globe. In all kinds of places with all types of men in all sorts of situations filled with twists, surprises, and, yes, even eroticism. Because we are sexual beings, because we are men, because we are hunters who don't always know the sexual orientation of the hunted, because the privacy of our own homes isn't always the most convenient or erotic of places…because, because, because of an infinite number of reasons (as varied and vast as we gay individuals are), our sex always has the potential to be hotter than South Beach in July (you blond Argentinian with one of the best, plumpest asses I've ever laid my hands on, if you're having this translated into Spanish, here's licking at you, kid). Hell, sex is so good, it even survived the confusion and chaos of the last twenty years of the 20th century. And it still survives the confusion and chaos of the beginning of the 21st century. Go figure. Sex and cockroaches—that's what will still be around after any Armageddon. So we embrace sex, shove our faces in it, invite it into our orifices, give it long, slow sensuous kisses, hug it, worship it, love it. And write about it. Oh, how we write about it!

Choosing the stories for this collection was both a pleasure and a challenging task that notched up my sexual heat over the period in which I read the submissions. What was I looking for ultimately? What kinds of stories grabbed me by the balls and kept my interest, like the mouth of a well-trained cocksucker on my perfectly shaped, long, and bulbous black dick? First and foremost, stories that stayed with me after reading them, stories that I couldn't just set aside upon completion and move on to the next submission or next task in my day. This usually meant stories that held twists and unexpected turns. Stories that took me places I'd never been before (not many of those around). Ones that provided a fresh take on the familiar. Or stories in which the authors' passion clearly exploded onto the page. Then there were intense stories that took no prisoners, stories in which the writer wasn't afraid to grab a particular fetish by the balls and hold it up for all the world to see. That takes guts æ yet the results can be very erotic, even if the reader doesn't share the author's particular lust. Boldness can be its own reward. So can honesty.

The writers in this collection have been both bold and honest, creating characters who admit to cravings that most gay men walking down the street might think about, but would sooner suppress than admit to (to say nothing of act on). Moreover, the authors of these stories clearly enjoyed their creations. For them, putting their creation on paper wasn't only about getting their nut, as some urban men call it. For these writers, the journey was just as thrilling and important and erotic as arriving at the destination. For a few, the journey was actually better than arriving (and who hasn't been there?).

Good writing takes honesty. Each human being possesses a unique, individual perspective on life and the world. Sure, we share common experiences, but, like a snowflake or fingerprint, no two human perspectives are exactly alike. When a writer writes from the heart—or any other vitally important organ—he writes from his own unique perspective, and the reader is thereby afforded a glimpse into the writer's mind. When the writer truly shoots his wad on the page by baring all or part of his soul, passion is bound to show through; and no matter the subject, a unique take on life and the world evolves and emanates. The familiar is made fresh, and it is then that we the reader see universal truths about ourselves and our world æ and we connect. Like two pairs of eyes locked on each other during orgasm, the results can be powerful.

This book holds powerful jets of energy, sexual and emotional and physical. It barely contains its own body heat. It brings honesty and passion to demonstrating the power of the thing they say humankind thinks about every few seconds. This book presents sex. On to it!

Knowing Johnny
Bob Vickery

The single bulb that lights up the hallway is busted, and I have to negotiate my way to Rico's apartment by trailing my fingers against the wall, counting the doors. In the dark, the smells of the place seem a lot stronger: boiled cabbage, mildew, old piss. Heavy-metal music blasts out from one of the doors I pass, and I get a sickly sweet whiff of crack. Fucking junkies. I can hear loud voices arguing in the apartment across the hallway, then the sound of furniture breaking. Rico's apartment is the next one down. I grope my way to it and knock on the door.

I stand there for a minute, waiting. "Who's there?" a voice finally asks from inside.

"Open up, Rico," I say. "It's me, Al."

I hear the sounds of bolts being drawn back. The door opens an inch, still chained, and Rico's eye peers at me through the crack. He closes the door, undoes the chain, and opens it wide this time. "Get in," he growls. I slip in, and Rico bolts the door behind me. The room is small: an unmade bed, a beat-up dresser, a table by the window. The kid Rico told me about on the phone is sitting at the table, looking scared and trying not to show it. It's quieter in here than in the hall, even with the sounds of traffic coming in from the window. I can faintly hear above our heads the clicking of writergod's keyboard.

I keep my eyes trained on the kid. He's sitting in a shaft of light pouring in from the street, and I take in the shaggy blond hair, the strong jaw, the firm, lean body. "Where'd you find him?" I ask Rico, without turning my head.

"Out on the street, hustling," Rico says. "I convinced him he could do better with a little management." Rico walks into my line of sight. "He tells me he's 18." Of course, writergod has Rico say that to keep the censors happy.

"What's your name," I ask the kid.

"Johnny," he says. There's a slight quaver in his voice.

"Did Rico rough you up?" Rico stirs, but I silence him with a gesture. "Did he force you up here?" And again, writergod is having me ask this for the sake of the fucking censors. If there's coercion, the story won't sell.

Johnny shakes his head. "No," he says. "I wanted to go with him. Rico told me about you. I thought maybe you could help me." His voice is steadier now, firmer. But the wideness of his dark eyes still gives away his fear.

I look at him for a long moment, gauging him. "How good are you at taking orders?"

Johnny licks his lips and swallows. "Real good," he says.

This is the first sex scene of the story. Writergod usually limits it to oral only, saving butt fucking for the end-of-story finale. "Stand up," I say. Johnny climbs to his feet. "I always sample my merchandise first, Johnny," I say. "I want you to come over here and suck my dick. Suck it until I shoot my load."

Johnny's eyes flicker toward Rico, and then back at me again. He shifts his weight to his other foot, but doesn't move.

He seems to be weighing his options. "OK," he finally says. He walks over to me and drops to his knees. His hands are all businesslike as they unbuckle my belt, pull my zipper down, and tug my jeans and boxers down below my knees. I keep my face stony, but my dick gives away my excitement. It springs up and swings heavily in front of Johnny's face. Johnny drinks it in with his eyes. "You got a beautiful dick," he says.

"Just skip the commentary," I reply.

Johnny leans forward and nuzzles his face into my balls. I feel his tongue licking them, rolling them around in his mouth, sucking on them. He slides his tongue up the shaft of my dick, as if it's some kind of Popsicle, and then circles the cockhead with it. I stand with my hands on my hips, looking down at the top of his head. Rico stands behind the boy, watching. His dick juts out of his open fly, and he's stroking it slowly.

Johnny's lips nibble their way down my meaty shaft (all our shafts are "meaty"; writergod won't let us in the story without a crank at least eight inches long, and thick—always thick—topped with "flared heads," or "fleshy knobs," or "heads the size and color of small plums"). When Johnny's mouth finally makes it to the base of my stiff cock, he starts bobbing his head, sucking me off with a measured, easy tempo. The boy knows how to suck cock—I give him that. He wraps one hand around my balls and tugs them gently as his other hand squeezes my left nipple. I close my eyes and let the sensations he's drawing from my body ripple over me.

Rico comes up next to me and yanks his jeans down. He strokes his dick with one hand while his other hand slides under my shirt and tugs at the flesh of my torso. I reach over and cup his balls, feeling their heft, how they spill out onto my palm so nicely. I lean over and we kiss, Rico slipping his tongue deep into my mouth. Rico lets go of his dick and Johnny wraps his hand around it, skinning the foreskin back, revealing the fleshy little fist of Rico's cockhead (another favorite phrase of writergod). He takes my dick out of his mouth, sucks on Rico's for a while, and then comes back to me. I spit in my hand and wrap it around Rico's thick, hard cock, sliding it up and down the shaft. Rico lets out a long sigh, a hair's breadth shy of a groan. He starts pumping his hips, fucking my fist in quick, staccato thrusts. Johnny pries apart my ass cheeks and worms a finger up my bunghole, knuckle by knuckle, never breaking his cocksucking stride. I lose my cool, giving off a long, trailing groan. Johnny pushes against my prostate, and my groan increases in volume. I whip my dick out of his mouth just as the first stream of spunk squirts out, arcing into the air, slamming against Johnny's face. My body spasms as my load continues to pump out, splattering against his cheeks, his closed eyes, his mouth. Rico groans, and I feel his dick pulse in my hand. Johnny turns his face to receive this second spermy shower, and soon Rico's jizz is mingling with mine in sluggish drops that hang from Johnny's chin. Rico bends down and licks Johnny's face clean, dragging his tongue along the contours of the boy's face. The clicking sound of writergod's keyboard rises in volume and then suddenly stops.

We all look up. "Do you think he's done?" Rico finally asks.

I shrug. "With the scene, maybe," I say. "He still has to finish the story."

Johnny climbs to his feet and looks around the room. "Christ, what a dump. I hope we don't have to stay here long."

Rico laughs. "Hell, this is fuckin' swank compared to where I was before." He starts pulling on his clothes. "Writergod had me lying on some teahouse floor with a bunch of guys shooting their loads on me. Then he just left me there, stuck in that stinking piss-hole." He looks around. "I just wish there was a TV here."

I offer a handkerchief to Johnny. "Here," I say. "Rico missed a few drops." Johnny takes it and wipes the last of my load off his face. I pull out a deck of cards from my jacket pocket and sit down at the table. "Poker, anyone?"

There are only two chairs, so Rico has to sit on the edge of the bed. We start with five-card stud. "It's no fun unless you play for money," Johnny grouses.

I shrug. "I don't have any money. Do you?"

Rico grins. "We could always play for sex." We all laugh. As if we don't already get nothing *but* that from each other. Johnny finds matchsticks in the drawer of the dresser, and we divvy them out.

I deal the first hand. "So what have you been up to, Johnny?" I ask, glancing at him. "Any interesting locales?" Johnny and I have worked together more times than I can remember. I've fucked him in locker rooms, in the back seats of cars, in alleys, on secluded beaches, once even on the torch of the Statue of Liberty. Johnny is always "the kid" in writer-god's stories, sometimes going by the name of Billy, sometimes Eddy or Andy—always a name that ends in "y." I look at him across the table, feeling the old frustration. For all the hot sex we've had together, I hardly know the guy. No conversation, no snuggling together under the sheets—just fade to black and then the cycle starts all over again.

"Oh, I was in a great place last story," Johnny said, laughing. "I was a street hustler in Cozumel who hooks up with an American tourist. You know him; it was Cutter."

"Shit," Rico mutters. I glance at him but he keeps his eyes focused on his cards. Cutter's a stock character that writergod uses for his more upscale stories, usually about some married man straying to the other side, or a well-heeled gay yuppie partying in the Keys or P-town. I've only worked with him a couple of times, the last time being when I was rough trade that he picked up in a leather bar on a slumming expedition. Rico and I both think he's got his head up his ass.

"Did you have a good time?" I ask.

"Oh, yeah, it was great fun," Johnny says. I look for sarcasm, but his smile seems sincere. "After writergod wrapped up the fuck scene on the beach, we just hung out there, sunbathing, snorkeling, shell-collecting—the whole tourist thing." Johnny nods at the room around us. "Until I wound up here."

"I'm sorry you're disappointed," I say. I'm aware of how pissy my tone sounds.

Johnny grins. "Who said anything about being disappointed?" He looks across the table at me and winks. My throat tightens.

"Hey, are you guys going to flap your jaws or play cards?" Rico asks. He throws three cards down on the table, and I deal him three more. But the wheels are turning in my head. Writergod usually writes several stories at the same time. I glance at Rico sorting through his cards. Rico's all right, but I wouldn't mind it if writergod suddenly pulled him for another story and left Johnny and me alone.

Johnny drops two cards on the table, and I deal him two more. I keep what I have. Rico starts the betting off with five matchsticks. Johnny throws in his five matchsticks and raises five more. Outside the window, a police siren wails and then trails off into silence. "Which one of your past scenes would you most like to go back to," I ask Johnny, "if you had a choice?"

Johnny grins and shakes his head. "You'll just laugh."

"No, I won't, I promise." I throw in the ten matchsticks and raise another ten.

"It was a college story," Johnny says. "Writergod had me gang-fucked in the UC Berkeley library by the college football team. After he wrapped up the story, he didn't use me for weeks. I got to hang out there all that time, doing nothing but reading." He glances at me. "Have you ever read *Leaves of Grass,* Al? Or any of Robert Frost's poems?"

I don't laugh, like I promised, but I do smile. "When would I read poetry?" I say. "Between blow jobs in a back alley?"

Johnny gives a rueful smile and shrugs. "That's my point. I hardly ever get to spend time in places where I can improve my fuckin' mind."

Rico sees my ten matchsticks and calls. We show our hands. Johnny's got a pair of eights, Rico two pairs, aces and fives. I win with a straight, jack high. I gather up my winnings and deal us all new hands. Rico leans back on the bed and stretches. "I wouldn't mind going back to the story where I was a ranger in Yosemite," he says, picking up his cards and sorting them. "I ended up fucking these backpackers on top of Half Dome." He shakes his head and gives a wistful smile. "It was my one time out in nature. I loved it—all that bitching scenery!" He nods toward Johnny, "I know what you mean, kid. That was an exception. Writergod usually sticks us in some pretty crummy places."

I open my mouth to comment, when I feel my feet begin to tingle. The tingling moves up my legs, my torso. I know only too well what that means. "So long, guys," I barely have time to say. "I'm off to another story."

There's a knock on the door, and then Old Bert sticks his head in. "I got the lad here for you, Captain," he says. "Just like you told me to." He knows better than to give me a wink. The last time he tried such impudence, I had him flogged, but his mouth still curves up into a randy leer. I can hear the rest of the crew off in the distance fighting over the *Magdalena's* spoils.

"Bring him in," I say gruffly. I'm lying on the bed that belonged to the *Magdalena's* former captain. Since we've tossed him overboard with a slit throat, I don't think he'll be needing it anymore.

Old Bert opens the door wider, pushes the *Magdalena's* cabin boy in, and closes the door behind him. The lad stumbles forward and then straightens up to face me. His dark eyes glare at me for an instance, but I can see the fear in them as well. He quickly lowers them. *So Johnny's in this story too,* I think. *Poor Rico, stuck in that room by himself.* The boy stands in the middle of the cabin, his hands at his side, head lowered, waiting.

"Hablas ingles?" I ask him.

He nods, his eyes still trained on the floor.

"Look at me, lad," I say. He raises his eyes again, eyes that are as black and liquid as the sea on a moonless night. My gaze sweeps down his wiry, muscular body and then back to his face again. "What's your name?" I ask.

"Juan Francisco Tomas Santiago, sir," he says. His voice is barely audible.

I laugh. "That's quite a mouthful for such a young lad," I say. "I shall call you 'Johnny'."

There's a moment of silence. I can faintly hear the clicking of writergod's keyboard. I've never been in a period story before; writergod usually confines me to slums and back alleys.

The heat of the tropical sun pours in, as thick as Jamaican molasses, and I feel my head grow light from it. I lie back indolently in the captain's bed, my eyes traveling up Johnny's body: There's a coltish quality to his muscular young frame that makes my dick swell and lengthen. Johnny watches silently, his eyes now never leaving my face.

"Get naked," I say.

The blood rushes to Johnny's face, and he shifts his weight to his other foot. *Writergod should watch that little bit of business he always has Johnny do,* I think—*it's getting repetitious.*

Slowly, hesitantly, he unbuttons his shirt and lets it fall to the floor. His torso is as smooth and dark as polished driftwood, the muscles beautifully chiseled. Johnny slips off his shoes, pulls his breeches down, and steps out of them, kicking them aside. He stands naked at the foot of the bed, his hands at his sides, his cock lying heavily against his thigh. His face is as pure as any angel's, but he's got a devil's dick: red, fleshy, roped with blue veins. In the stifling heat his balls lie as low and heavy as tree-ripened fruit. My throat tightens with excitement. "Turn around," I say.

Johnny slowly turns around. His ass is a very pretty thing, high and firm, the cheeks pale cream against the darkness of his tanned back. My dick stirs in my breeches, swelling to full hardness. Johnny completes his rotation and faces me again, his mouth set in a grim line.

"Well, come over here, lad," I say, giving an exaggerated sigh as I slip off my breeches. "And give me a reason why I shouldn't just slit your throat and toss you overboard."

Johnny stands where he is, head bowed but with his hands curled into fists. The silence in the room is as oppressive as the heat. "Aye, Johnny," I say softly. "Is it coaxing you want instead of threats?" I sit up in the bed. "Please do an old sea dog a favor, lad," I say in exaggerated politeness, "and come join me in my bed."

Johnny looks me in the eye, still saying nothing. His mouth curls up into the faintest smile. He crosses the small room and climbs into bed with me. I wrap my arms around him and kiss him, and he kisses back, lightly at first, then with greater force, slipping his tongue into my mouth. I pull him tightly against me, feeling his hard, young cock thrust up against my belly. I wrap my hand around both our dicks and start stroking them slowly within the circle of my fingers. Johnny reaches down and cups my balls in his hand, squeezing them gently, rolling them around in his palm. I nuzzle my face against the curve of his neck. "Tell me, lad," I whisper in his ear. "Have you ever been buggered before?"

"Yes, sir," Johnny whispers back. "Many times." I don't doubt it. A young lad as handsome as Johnny would be fair game on any ship.

There's a jar of pomade on the table next to the bed. I reach over and scoop out a heavy dollop from it. "Well, maybe I can still teach you a few new tricks," I say, as I work my hand into his asscrack and begin greasing up his bunghole. I slip a finger in, and the muscles of Johnny's ass clamp around it tightly, like a baby sucking on his mother's tit. I push deeper in, and Johnny's body stirs under me. "Do you want more of the same, lad?" I growl.

Johnny nods his head. "If you please, sir," he says.

"Well, since you asked so politely…" I laugh. I grease up my dick with the pomade and hoist Johnny's legs over my shoulders. Johnny takes my dick in his hand and guides it to the pucker of his asshole. I push with my hips, and my dick slides inside him, Johnny thrusting his hips up to meet me. As I start pumping his ass, Johnny meets me stroke for stroke, moving his body in rhythm with mine, squeezing his ass muscles tight with every thrust of my cock.

I laugh from surprise and pleasure. "Aye, Johnny." I say. "Ye're a lusty young buck, I can see that clearly enough. And ye've learned your buggery lessons well." *This is the first story in which I've fucked without condoms,* I think. *Sweet Jesus, it feels good!*

I continue plowing Johnny's ass with long, slow strokes. A groan escapes his lips and I grin fiercely. "That's right, Johnny," I say. "Sing for me. I want to play you like a mandolin." *Where is writergod coming up with this fucking dialogue?* I wonder. I thrust savagely until my dick is full inside him and then churn my hips. Johnny groans, louder. I bend down and kiss him, and he returns my kiss passionately, thrusting his tongue into my mouth. As I skewer Johnny, he reaches up and runs his hands across my body, twisting my nipples hard. He wraps his legs around me and rolls over on top. We're drenched with sweat, and our bodies thrust together and separate with wet, slapping noises. I wrap Johnny in my arms and we roll again, falling off the bed onto the deck below.

I pin Johnny's arms down and plunge my cock deep inside him. Johnny cries out. "Do you want me to stop, lad?" I ask.

"No, sir," Johnny groans.

I thrust again, and again Johnny cries out. I can hear the pirates brawling outside. They're probably drunk by now on the *Magdalena's* cargo of spirits. "Louder, Johnny," I snarl.

"Don't stop, sir!" he cries out.

"That's better," I grunt. I wrap my arms around him and press him tight. My sweaty torso slides and squirms against him, as I pump my dick in and out of his ass. A groan escapes from Johnny's lips. I thrust again, and he groans again, louder. Johnny reaches down and squeezes my balls with his hand. They're pulled up tight, ready to shoot. He presses down hard between them, and my body shudders violently as the first of the orgasm is released. I throw back my head and bellow as my dick gushes my jism deep into his ass. Load after load of it pulses out, and I thrash against Johnny like a man whose throat has just been cut. After what seems like a small eternity, the last of the spasms end, and I collapse on top of him.

I push myself up again. "Climb up on my chest, Johnny," I say. "And splatter my face with your load."

Johnny seems only too happy to oblige. He swings his leg over and straddles me. I look up at him, at the tight muscular body, at Johnny's handsome face, at the hand sliding up and down the thick shaft of his dick. "Aye, there you go, lad," I mutter. "Make your dick squirt for me." I reach up and twist Johnny's left nipple.

I feel Johnny's body shudder, and he raises his face to the ceiling and cries out. A load of jism gushes out from his dick and splatters against my face. Another load follows, and then another. By the time Johnny's done, my face is festooned with the ropy strands of his wad. He bends down and licks it off tenderly, and I kiss him, pulling my body tight against his.

Writergod's keyboard suddenly falls silent. We wait expectantly for it to start up again, finish the story, but nothing happens. I look up at Johnny and we both burst out laughing. "Do you believe that fucking dialogue?" I say. I twist my face into comic fierceness. "Aye, Johnny," I growl. "You're a lusty young buck. How 'bout letting me bugger your ass?"

Johnny laughs again. He climbs off me and helps me to my feet. We hunt for our clothes strewn all around, and pull them back on. I feel as if I'm dressing for a costume ball. I look at Johnny appraisingly as he tucks his shirt into his breeches. "You look really good as a Spanish cabin boy," I say. "It suits you."

Johnny raises his eyebrows. "You're not putting the make on me, are you, Al?"

I have to laugh at that. "Right. Like I don't get enough sex from you as it is." Still, I'm feeling light and playful now that I'm alone with Johnny, between stories. I look around. The cabin is cramped, and a glance out the porthole shows nothing but sea and sky. The deck beneath our feet rolls gently with the movement of the waves. The tropical heat makes the small room feel like a sauna. I jump onto the bed and pat the empty side next to me. "Hop back in," I say to Johnny. "Let's just relax for a while. Maybe talk."

Johnny joins me on the bed, stretching his legs out and placing his hands behind his head. My heart is beating hard, and when I notice this I almost laugh. I've forgotten how many times I've fucked Johnny in how many countless stories, and yet I'm actually feeling nervous. I cautiously wrap my arm around Johnny's shoulders, and he snuggles against me. "This is nice," he says.

"I've been wanting to do this for a long time," I say. "All we do is fuck. We never talk."

Johnny looks up at my face, his eyes amused. "What do you want to talk about, Al?"

I think for a long time. The only subjects I can come up with are back alleys, docks, and quarter booths in the back of porno bookstores. I'm struck by a sudden thought. "Tell me about the poems you read in the UC Berkeley library," I say.

"Do you want to hear one?" Johnny asks, grinning.

"Sure." I nestle back against the pillows, my eyes trained on him.

Johnny pulls himself up to a sitting position and turns to face me. He clears his throat.

> In Xanadu did Kubla Khan
> A stately pleasure dome decree
> Where Alph, the sacred river, ran
> Through caverns measureless to man
> Down to a sunless sea.

Johnny squeezes his eyes in concentration for a second and then looks at me apologetically. "I don't remember much more. Just the last few lines."

> His flashing eyes! His floating hair!
> Weave a circle round him thrice
> And close your eyes in holy dread
> For he on honeydew has fed,
> And drunk the milk of Paradise.

He looks down at me. "Sorry, that's all I know."

I shake my head. "I don't get it." Johnny shrugs but doesn't say anything. "I mean, who would name a river 'Alph'? And who ever heard of hair floating?"

"I don't know," Johnny says, laughing. "I didn't write the damn poem." He lies back down in the bed, burrowing into my arms. "Just let the words create the pictures."

We lie in the bed together, Johnny's body pressed against mine. My arm lightly strokes his shoulder. I can smell the fresh sweat of his body, feel the heat of his skin flow into me. The rocking of the ship lulls me into half-sleep. "This is so nice," I say, half to Johnny, half to myself. Johnny says nothing, just lays his hand on my thigh and squeezes it. I close my eyes.

My feet start to tingle. "Fuck!" I cry out. I look up at the ceiling. "Writergod, you bastard! Can't you give me just a few fucking minutes of peace!" The tingling spreads up my body, and the ship's cabin fades out, along with Johnny.

I got Nash taking point twenty meters in front of the squad, and Myers and Benchly behind us working the radio, keeping the com line open with the base. The others are in different positions, waiting for orders. That leaves me alone, with the kid, Jamison. Earlier reconnaissance reports indicated enemy movement about five clicks north of the base, working its way toward us, but fuck, that was hours ago, and Charley could be anywhere. I look around. We're on elevated ground, with good cover, and I don't anticipate any action for hours; our best bet is to lie low and hope Charley walks straight into our ambush.

I crawl over toward Jamison. "How you doin', son?" I whisper.

Jamison looks back at me, his eyes wide, his mouth set in a tight line. He's a green recruit, just assigned to the squad last week, and this is his first combat action. He still wears the look of someone trying to wake up from a bad dream. "All right, I guess, Sarge," he says.

I put my gun down and squat beside him. "It's a hell of a business, ain't it?"

Jamison grins, and I feel my throat tighten. I've been sporting a hard-on for the kid since he was first assigned to the squad. "What's your name?" I ask. "I mean, what do you go by?"

Jamison looks at me, and a little crackle of energy shoots between us. "Johnny," he says.

I put my hand on his thigh and squeeze. I'm risking court martial, but I'm sick and tired of this fucking war, and after all I may be dogmeat tomorrow. I bend down and plant my mouth on Johnny's. He doesn't hesitate for a moment; it's as if he'd been waiting for me to get the ball rolling. He kisses me back, pushing his tongue down my throat.

Oh, Johnny, I think…. *One of these days, between stories, we'll get that chance just to hang out, to talk, to get to know each other a little. I've got to believe it'll happen.* I look into Johnny's eyes, and for a moment I think he can read my thoughts. He gives a tiny smile and nods, a gesture out of character for the story.

As writergod's keyboard clicks away, I reach down, unzip his fly, and pull out his thick, hard cock.

Foucault's Pendulous...

Ian Philips

I had the dream again. The dream I have every night. And maybe this really *was* the last time. That's what he said: It would be the last. But, God, I hope not. Not after last night.

The dream always begins in utter darkness. Not just the dark of night in some huge city where the buildings blot out the stars. Not just the dark of the earth above this basement in a basement where I always awaken. No, it is the dark that is without light, a dark so dark it is no longer dark. It is the void...

Until, as always, someone lets there be light.

In this case, lights. Two caged light bulbs.

As my eyes wobble into focus, I'm sure I've died and gone to paradise. I'm in the secret VIP playroom of the Mineshaft— a Valhalla to a race of warrior gods who will never walk the face of the earth again. God, just thinking about it now and my dick is as tall and hard as the World Tree.

I guess, before this dream gets any weirder, I should use this moment of clarity to contextualize this story's dreamer, i.e., me.

I'm afraid I can't use my real name in case anyone on my thesis committee reads this. I can't even describe myself. Sorry. I'd never get lucky again at another MLA conference if I did. What I *can* say is that I'm working on my doctorate in comparative literature. And that I rather cleverly used both my BAs in religion and philosophy and all my field research at rest stops throughout the tri-state area of Indiana, Ohio, and Kentucky to write my master's thesis on the queerly coded semiotics within the Odin saga. I know what you're thinking: Norse mythology is pretty out-there for a thesis in English. Still, here I am at Columbia. Here I am in New York.

In my dream, however, I'm in the New York I've always longed to visit. The New York that has almost been eaten away, not by the city's billions of rats, mind you, but by a single mouse. The billionaire mouse that ate Times Square.

In my dream, it will always be 1977.

The bunker smells of beery urine mixed with Crisco mixed with poppers mixed with the thick, snuffed-out-candle smell of spunk. It is one vast crotch, bathed in all these unguents and unwashed for a week and a day, overripe and ready to fall.

I pretend that the enormous rectangle of glistening black leather I'm manacled to is the top sheet from Mr. Benson's bed and I'm his newest slave. I've run away and am waiting for him to find me here. "Please, Sir," I whisper as my asshole gasps and gasps from the removal of the latest fist attached to the latest forearm the size of Popeye's. "I am so unworthy, Sir. Please come and reclaim your property. Don't let that square-jawed, steely-eyed neo-Nazi abduct me and sell me to your age's wicked stereotype of sex-crazed Arab sheiks. I long only to be a white slave to you, Sir."

I stop, swallowing my next words. I sense, somehow, a new presence. I crane my neck up. My head aches from the poppers, which only makes the music—once again they're playing

KC and the Sunshine Band's "I'm Your Boogie Man"—louder and louder. I look toward the only other light in the room besides the one above, highlighting my body. It spotlights the doorway. In it, there stands a tall, thin man in a very odd leather outfit.

He wears a black leather replica of a herringbone-patterned tweed suit and a white leather turtleneck. His eyes are two squares of light. Glasses. On his head, the standard-issue leather bike cap. He takes it off as he enters the room. It seems the gentleman handballer has arrived.

As he moves closer, I realize he's also wearing a black leather toupee. How odd, I think. He doffs the wig, and then the silver-studded black leather scales fall from my eyes.

It's Him! Foucault. *Michel, ma belle.*

He steps to the edge of the sling. My asshole and I shudder. He speaks.

Something is wrong. I know he is speaking French and I know, up until this moment, I have been fluent in French. But he's speaking now and I can't understand a word. I strain to listen as if my ears are plugged thick with wax. I try to crane my neck even further so that I'm closer to his mouth. Alas I hear nothing except the blood gurgling along the veins in my temple. That, and Rod Stewart's "Tonight's the Night."

I must appear bewildered, for he stops and looks into my eyes for the first time, looks over my entire body for the first time. He commences anew, and this time I know I look like a straitjacketed inmate in a cell at Bedlam rather than an academic bound to a sling in the Mineshaft's cellar. For this time when he speaks, words—honest-to-God words—appear, like subtitles, before him.

They spell themselves out across his chest, and I read them. And, as I read them, they break into a smoke of letters that encircles Foucault's head and then trail off, broken, around the room, bumping against the ceiling and into the corners.

I squint my eyes. Despite the ringing bells the poppers have set off in my skull, despite the off-key voices singing along to "Don't Leave Me This Way," I concentrate. I see only the words and, finally, I hear them.

Monsieur Foucault has come tonight to plead with me. *He* is pleading with *me*. It is urgent, he begs, that I stop the endless references to him in every discourse, every journal article, every personal ad, every phone message. It is imperative that I stop the endless troubling of his shade with phallocentric, masturbatory reveries like this one.

I look up at his face. His mouth is a thick line. A vein, like a small garden snake, wriggles beneath the skin of his forehead. His cheeks are red and sunken like the hollow of a brightly painted bowl. I say I am sorry. Truly, I   very sorry.

The ends of his mouth slump. He sighs. He pities me, he says, but tonight it is I who must pity him. I have no idea, he chastens me without even having to wag a finger, what my Foucault-centric obsession is doing to his death. Here he had planned to enjoy several decentered, yet industrious, centuries as a professor in the Academie de l'Elysée. Yes, he reads my eyes now as I've been reading his chest, it is that Elysium, the true Champs Elysées.

Yes, that supposed paradise where he is now haunted by the virilizing dreams of the living. And, like ghosts here, you (he points to me) and your kind shadow me there. The reddening snake on his forehead has begun to dance. I am ruining his death, he shouts.

De Sade, at the mere sight of him and his following flock of boyish ghosts, laughs so hard now that he can no longer enjoy a quiet night of whist and brandy cordials with the marquis and the Borgias (Cesare and Lucrezia). And Bataille and Nietzsche, whenever they pass him on another of their peripatetic conversations, no longer stop to invite him to walk the gardens with them. Even the American, John Preston, he laments, refuses to fuck him because he feels it's demeaning to fist a man whose legend valorizes the desire-driven and genitalized jerk-off fantasies of so many twenty-something post-gay geekoids like me.

Suddenly the anger, the blood, the life drain from his face. I fear he will cry, perhaps even sob. Elton John is singing "Love Lies Bleeding." Instead, he raises himself up to his full height and asks, if he were to pleasure me once, would I swear never to dream of him again?

I nod so vigorously that the leather sheet flaps beneath me and the chains twist as if they were holding up a child spinning in his swing.

He slips an arm from his jacket; hands pull it into the shadows. He removes his glasses; more hands take them. He raises his arms; even more hands gently tug the white leather turtleneck up his torso and across his sharp Gallic chin, cheeks, nose, and over his large cranial dome, as smooth and milky-white as china from Limoges.

I choke when I see the T-shirt he's wearing. It's a classic wife-beater. No sleeves. No collar. A reminder perhaps of his solidarity with the workers of the world. But in the center of his chest is emblazoned a child's drawing of a mustachioed man and the slogan "Hello Nietzsche." I pause and read it again. That's actually when I choke.

It's Nietzsche. It's Nietzsche with a shock of black hair, two black button eyes, a huge mustache that looks as if a black Pekingese crawled in under his nose and died, and, oddest of all, this cartoon Nietzsche is smiling. No, beaming.

My choking finally dies down to several coughs and a sputter when a huge blue and white drum of Crisco on a dolly as red as any hanky in the room is wheeled in and placed just beneath Nietzsche's lips. The hands retreat. Now Foucault himself smiles.

He dips the tips of his fingers into the vat of vegetarian lard as if it were a finger bowl. He dabs the Crisco onto his face with the cold calm of a drag queen preparing to remove her makeup and return to the drab world of strip malls and mini-vans. He grabs a fistful and then another. He lathers it on. In minutes, I no longer recognize my Michel. His head is an egg plastered with white cake frosting.

If he has done this to repulse me, he's failed. No matter what beastly form he assumes, I know what beauty lies below. For below the skin, the thick cartilage and muscle, the hard bone, there it will be: his brain, gray like a rainy April morning over the rue Champs Elysées, with synapses sparking, showering the dark crevices with brilliant colors, more magnificent than any nighttime spectacle of fireworks and lasers above the Arc de Triomphe on Bastille Day.

My swelling dick rolls back and forth on its warm rug of pubic hairs. It is a '30s starlet writhing on a circle of black satin sheets, forever captured in the retina of the camera's eye. We luxuriate in our dreams, my dick and I, until my dick jumps. Now I jump. Warm, sticky hands pull at the lips of my still-gaping hole. I assume they're his hands until another pair pushes at the mouth of my ass, then another pair, and another pair. A final pair shoves itself up inside me like an enormous dildo.

By now, my pelvis should have snapped like a wishbone. It doesn't. My hole, my ass, my cock, my thighs, my belly all grow warmer. Perhaps the Crisco is really a topical anesthetic or, in the evening's earlier flurry of fists, perhaps an epidural was administered that, contrary to all laws of nature, I have forgotten.

I don't know; I don't care. All I feel is the pulsing of my sphincters—two warm rubbery bands holding together the bundle of forearms. Then, slowly, the clasped hands bud within me. A crack. I feel the shift and the wet heat of what I can only imagine to be the Crisco melting out of the blossoming hands.

I want to open my eyes. I want to see him, see all the others. But I can't move; the hands around my asshole, within my asshole, bind me to the sling. I only "see" the melting pad of butter-flavored Crisco that is the vibrating yellow of the light beyond my eyelids.

I am growing sickly dizzy. The theme from *Star Wars* is now being played for the third time. Its chemical equivalent, a smell like an exploding drug lab, punches me in the left and then right nostril. I try to guess how many pairs of hands are swinging the little vial of poppers under my nose. My sinuses rip open and then my brain.

My head is empty; my body is full...

My entrails are falling! I'm shitting all my intestines! I shriek, I think, out loud. Another pair of hands strokes my throbbing forehead and temples. I'm panting. I'm sobbing. I'm empty. The flower has been plucked; the arms have left me.

I gasp. Four, ten, twenty hands push at my hole. Another drug lab explodes in my face. The big ball pushes against whatever is left of my boyish pucker. I want to faint. To scream. To howl.

But I no longer think. I am remembering these words only now as I tell this. At that moment, I have no mind.

Yet, my decentered self knows that these are not hands. Too smooth. They lack the odd-shaped knobs of knuckles or bony points of fingers or the blunt knives of fingernails. I know it is his head. He is crowning within me.

I am breath. I breathe in and swallow more of his hard, warm, stinging skull. I breathe out and hold him in my ass's embrace. I breathe in and my bones break and my skin tears. I breathe out and my blood aches and my nerves weep. I breathe in. I breathe out. I breathe in...

I scream and I scream and I scream. The pride of every great French profile jabs the first, then the second, burning rings of fire that were once my sphincters. The nose, his nose, drags closer and closer to my prostate.

His head stops. I will my body to suck in more. More. More. No luck. But some part of me knows that if I am patient, I will get lucky, more lucky than I have ever been or ever will be.

For Foucault has not finished with me. He presses his face deep into the walls of my rectum, until at last his beautiful big nose pokes into my prostate. He rubs his nose once. Every hair on my body gets hard. He rubs his nose again. I shudder. My spine is a wave of hot gelatin.

He rubs his nose one last time and I sing. An original aria to bring the opera queens in the stalls and troughs and slings several stories above us to their feet. Garbled bits of "La Marseillaise," the "Internationale," Rita Coolidge's "(Your Love Is Lifting Me) Higher and Higher," an improvisational Gregorian chant, and Schiller's "Ode to Joy" from Beethoven's Ninth Symphony.

And deep within, I hear something. No, it is someone. My Michel! He is speaking within me. There is discourse even in our intercourse! I draw in the air around me to sing my aria's final refrain, and then I realize he is singing. *He* is singing with *me*. I swear I hear "…did I ever tell you I'm your hero? I am the subtext beneath your sling."

I bellow triumphantly, my alveoli bursting and my lungs tattering, "I am spread atop the cockhead of God!"

For the encore, there is only one thing left to do: I shoot. But not the usual spunk that looks like several strands of white Sillee-String. No. This time I come words. His words. Some of my favorites of his favorites. I clench and spurt out *panopticon*. My balls throb. Then my whole dick sneezes out *psychologico-medical armature,* and I'm grunting for breath. A final pop: *the desexualization [i.e., the degenitalization] of pleasure.* I pass out.

When I wake, his words are brittle and stuck to the hairs of my chest. I look into the shadows, into the light for him. He's gone…

Until tonight, I pray.

Forgive me, mon seigneur. I did not know how impossible last night's oath would be to keep. Please, Michel, come soon.

I'm sorry, my beloved brain, but now I only love you more.

from Onyx
Felice Picano

As he entered D'Agostino's, Ray had to trace a detour. At the second of the two glass doors leading into the supermarket, a five-foot wooden stepladder had been splayed open. Someone was astride its scaffold, reaching up to the automated device connecting the doors to a ceiling-mounted geared mechanism. Ray couldn't see the fellow's face, only his thick, matte-black curly hair. But the repairman's body—clad in a heavy rugby shirt, knee-length wide-wale corduroy shorts, off-white woolen socks, and clunky, heavily stained ankle-length work boots— was tight and muscular. His buttocks and thighs (exactly at eye level) and his calves (slightly lower) were so well modeled, so evenly tanned, that they implied a kind of perfection through- out. Ray had learned over years of man-watching exactly what might correctly be inferred from a fragment: a hand and wrist held outside a car window, a shoulder blade and neck muscle glimpsed in a department store dressing room just as a V-neck was pulled on. Possessed of who knew what unsuspected brass, Ray whistled sexily and crooned à la Streisand "He-llo, gor- geous!" adding as he passed, "Don't fall!"

The guy looked down, bulky, yellow plastic-lensed goggles framing and partly obscuring his cute, squarish, masculine face. "I won't," he said, sounding amused.

Surprised by his own daring, Ray snatched up a shopping basket and sped into the protective anonymity of the produce aisle. There, he managed to find his grocery list and attempted to concentrate.

Brooklyn Heights was littered with fetching workmen of all ages and races, especially during the day. Ray would race out of his home office in the morning carrying a trash basket he'd failed to put out the night before, only to be greeted by the glowering face of a sanitation worker, a young Botticelli, who menaced, "Next time have it out! Or I'll leave it!" Or he'd be wedging into a parking spot and some Verrochio archangel with rolled-up sleeves and a Marlboro dangling off his lower lip would lean out the window of a pickup Ray had beaten out and yell obscenities, suggesting Ray learn how to drive—sonomabitch! The studly Puerto Rican adolescents who delivered pizza and Chinese at lunchtime wore skin-tight shirts and jeans and flirted brazenly. The African-American son of the newsstand owner on Joralemon Street wore the least amount of clothing legal as he helped out during the summer: iridescent basketball tees and one memorable, shimmering, lilac-hued Speedo lubricious against his bitter-sweet-chocolate skin. The beauty and abundance of the men had been a standing joke between Ray and Jesse since they'd moved there, along with the understanding that these fellows were heterosexual and thus unobtainable. Besides which, even if you *did* fulfill the fantasy and have sex with one, what could you possibly talk about afterward? The latest Sondheim musical? The newest dance-club drug? So Ray concentrated on his food shopping and forgot the young repairman.

The stepladder was still there but vacant when Ray paid for his groceries ten minutes later. He sighed. But right outside the supermarket, he was surprised to see the workman loitering against the back doors of his paint-splattered van, parked not ten feet away in the adjacent alley. He was clearly waiting for Ray, because as soon as he espied him, he turned, opened the doors, and climbed in.

Nervous yet undeniably intrigued, Ray stopped at the van's back door, shifting his grocery bags in case he needed an excuse for his halt. The mechanic was faced away, rifling through storage shelves built into the inner sides of the truck, doing so in a way that more than hinted he was showing off his body. When he glanced at Ray, Ray responded with a smile and what his Mom called a great big Midwestern "Hello."

"Hello, yourself," the workman said. Slight outer-boroughs accent. "You know," he added, "you go around saying things like you said to me in there, you could get into trouble."

Ray shrugged. "I never do that. I just couldn't help myself."

A pause to assess the implied compliment.

"Not that I'm personally offended. But some guys…" The repairman trailed off. He swiveled around, holding powerful-looking snub-nosed pliers in one hand. Ray couldn't help feeling he was flirting, giving Ray front and back views. Uncertain yet emboldened he said, "So, what time do you get off work?" Oldest pickup line in the book.

"Coupla hours. I got one more stop in Caroll Gardens. Why?"

It's now or never, Ray thought. "I live nearby. Thought you might want to stop by for a beer."

The workman lifted the massive goggles off his face and used them to brush back the thick shock of hair. The eyes disclosed were glorious: the palest green, lashes like an old film starlet's, set in high cheekbones. He leaned on one booted foot, which provocatively canted his lower torso forward. "I can get a beer anywhere."

With the revelation of those eyes, Ray's heart had thudded in his chest, a double whammy, given the erection he already had. Say it, he thought, panic-stricken lest he never see those eyes again. "How about I throw in a blow job?" Ray hoped he sounded cool and measured.

No change on the young face—he looked to be about 22, 23. And now Ray noticed that besides his solid physique and electrifying eyes, he also possessed a good complexion, evenly tanned, natural crimson to signify health, no marks or blemishes. "Well," the workman temporized, "I'm not sure when I'll be done here. Or the other place. Gotta be home by..."

Ray dropped the grocery bags and took out his wallet. In it, his card for KlavierStuecke Records. "My address and phone number." Handing over the card, he noted the square-tipped, stubby fingers covered with crosscuts—some old, a few fresh—that took hold of the card. "I live two blocks down, around the corner." Ray was casual as before. "Park in the garageway. No one'll ticket you." He wondered if he was coming on too aggressive, if he seemed too needy.

The repairman glanced at the card. "Like I said, I'm not sure when I'll be done." His voice hadn't fluctuated since they'd begun to speak, so Ray wasn't able to assess what might be at play behind the inexpressive face. But then Ray had also kept his voice to a masculine monotone. The workman didn't return the card, perhaps a good sign. Instead he slid it into one of the pockets in his shorts—a better sign—and turned to look for another tool.

Ray couldn't help feeling a bit dismissed. "Hope you find the time," he said brightly. "Bye!"

Half a block later, stopped at the traffic light at Montague Street, Ray thought, well, I was close, but somehow I screwed it up. His nerve in talking to the guy, never mind trying to pick him up, amazed him. He'd never done anything like that in his life. Certainly not with anyone whose sexuality he wasn't sure of. Hardly even with men he was certain were gay. In fact, Jesse used to tease that if he'd not repeatedly pursued Ray over a period of months, they'd have never slept together, not to mention ended up together.

Nerve. *Chutzpah,* J. K. would call it: J. K. Callaway, Ray's best friend. J. K. had been in New York City more than two decades and used Yiddish words as though he were a member of Temple Beth-El and not an occasional attendee at St. Mary's Roman Catholic Church. Ray decided to call him the minute he got home. J. K. had more *chutzpah* than Bette Midler. He'd be shocked.

As for the young workman, he was sexy, and those eyes, my God, those eyes! He had definitely flirted with Ray, but almost casually, as though he flirted all the time and it meant nothing. Maybe that was true. Someone that cute! He must get hit on ten times a day. All of which suggested that it was unlikely Ray would hear from him. Probably for the best, Ray concluded. Struck as he was, excited as he'd been, he still felt queasy with the idea of touching anyone but Jesse, no matter how much his quite ill and thus celibate lover insisted it would merely be hygienically sound for someone as sex-starved as Ray to do so. Anyway, Ray had plenty to keep him busy that afternoon.

Otto was lying in wait and tested edging past Ray's legs at the office door. Ray's hands were busy, and the little Persian slid inside with a triumphant meow, speeding out of reach under the desk. Ray would pry him out later. He trooped upstairs to put the groceries away, popped a beer, took the rest of the six-pack down to the office's half fridge. He tapped the speed dial that would bring him J. K.'s voice.

Who did not pick up the phone. Who was instead, disgust-ingly, talking to someone else. Ray hit *play* on the answering machine and listened to a message from a college bookstore customer he'd been playing phone-tag with. He phoned that number and got the record department buyer. He'd barely hung up that call—with a substantial order to invoice and pack—when another customer phoned, needing more stock of the Horowitz CD.

He checked the small reserve area and found sufficient copies of all the required items. That meant he need not go to the storage area his little company rented several blocks away in a local warehouse. He counted the CDs into stacks on the big old work table, all the while sparring with Otto, who'd taken a defensive position atop a mass of flattened-out cardboard boxes and who seemed determined to make up for his exile with a vigorous defense of the spot. The phone rang: the second customer, adding another title. Then, since he was on the phone, Ray speed-dialed Jesse's work number and spoke to his lover's secretary, Tasha, who reported that Jesse was at lunch with some colleagues, but that he'd arrived at 11:30 that morning in a good mood. Ray didn't know what that meant. Jesse was always in a good mood, no matter how he felt, no matter how good or terrible the news involved.

He filled and sealed two boxes, then toyed with Otto until the cat extended its claws and hissed. They reconciled and Ray went to the front office computer to input information and generate invoices, bills of lading, and mailing labels. He taped up the orders and set the boxes by the office door for UPS. He sipped at his beer and hit J. K.'s number again.

This time he answered. "This had better be crucial. I'm stepping out the door this very moment."

"It is crucial," Ray assured him.

"Meaning the topic is..." J. K. clarified. "A, sex. B, money. C, me."

"Sex."

"No! You did not have sex!" J. K. protested into the receiver.

"I almost had sex."

"Bor-ring! Almost doesn't count."

"With a very cute repairman. At D'Agostino's," Ray added. "He was fixing the automatic doors when I walked in. He was waiting for me outside and we talked and I offered to do him and gave him my phone number."

There was an intake of breath from the other end of the phone. Then: "Raymond Henriques, I know now why I keep you as my friend. You have completely made my afternoon. You have restored my faith in the sexual appetite of the American working man, not to mention the inexorable action of human bodily fluids. I am sitting down again," J. K. declared. "I am taking off my jacket. I expect to hear every detail. Gloss any item at your peril."

A half-hour of details, it turned out. A great many more than Ray thought were needed. J. K.'s own romantic and sexual life must be pretty sparse for this level of obsession with a single, merely potential, occurrence in Ray's life. But what were friends for? J. K. had come to Ray's aid on more than one occasion, and as for the situation with Jesse's health, J. K. was possibly the most knowledgeable man in New York, had the best instincts in the world, and could be counted on without question. So Ray humored him, even if it meant having to invent details and repeat, "It was a flirtation. Nothing will come of it."

"Nothing will come of it because your hard-up, horny working *mensch* perceived you were...*unserious!*" J. K. replied, his most severe put-down. "Some far less attractive, far less worthy, far less ambivalent queen shall shortly reap the rewards of your *petit* dalliance, believe you me."

Ray did believe J. K. So much so that when he heard a tap on the office door to the street, Ray remained on the phone listening to J. K. go on about his "moral cowardice" while he got up to see who it was, and when he looked out and saw first the paint-splattered van parked across the concrete drive-way, then the curly dark head of the repairman, Ray almost didn't believe it.

"Someone's at the door," he said to J. K. in a hushed voice.

"It's not him, is it? Mr. Sexy Repairman?"

Seeing the fellow moving back toward the van's door, Ray unlocked the door. "UPS," he lied. "Gotta go."

"Call back the second he's gone!" J. K. demanded. "We're not done discussing this encounter or its ramifications."

"Right. Sure," Ray agreed. Then, door finally open, he called, "I was on the phone." Seeing the dark head turn and those amazing eyes, visible through gray sunglass lenses, he added, "You made it! Great! "

"The other job was canceled. I had free time," the repairman said. "Am I parked OK? I'm blocking the sidewalk."

"Anything bigger than a bike will block it. I've got a parking decal you can put in the window that says you're here on business."

Ray left the door open and located the decal, then brought it to the workman peering down Joralemon Street at a police car.

"I can't get another ticket. My boss'll go ballistic."

"Hang this from the mirror in your window. If you get a ticket, I'll pay."

Back inside, the phone rang. Ray hoped it wasn't J. K. It wasn't. It was, however, the second customer he'd spoken to earlier, asking if he could modify his order yet again. Ray said sure and entered the revision directly onto the computer screen, still scrolled to "billing." He'd have to exchange the outer label, reopen and repack the box. Hell!

When he turned around, the office door was closed and the repairman was inside, staring out the window at the street. Ray still couldn't believe he was there.

Ray joined him at the window, just in time to see the police car stop and a heavyset female cop get out, check the van, then get back into the patrol car and move on. "What'd I tell you," Ray said.

The repairman filled the office with his presence, his smell, a complex fragrance Ray couldn't quite figure out, a mixture, he theorized, of machine oil, after-shave, maybe natural musk. Ray wanted to touch the younger man, only inches away, so badly that he was actually trembling.

"I just can't get another ticket," the workman apologized, facing Ray. "Three this year already. It comes out of my pay."

"I understand. No problem."

The visitor looked around at the office with its metal-framed Music Festivals of Europe posters on the walls, the cabinets of CD albums. "This is, what, a German record company? *Blue Danube Waltz?* Ooom-pah-pah bands?"

Ray laughed. "No, keyboard music. Piano, some organ and guitar. Mostly classical stuff. *Klavierstuecke* means keyboard pieces. How about that beer?" Ray turned to the half fridge and the mechanic was there, palms out.

He presented his soiled, square hands, with their stubby fingers and mangled fingernails, skin all cut up. A few of the incisions looked fresh. "I'm all greasy. Better wash up."

"I'll show you the john."

Ray led him out of the office, past the storage area, where Otto stretched and ostentatiously yawned as they passed by, into the master suite. Ray blushed as they entered the large room. He pointed out the lavatory. As the repairman entered, Ray said, "You want Mercurochrome or bandages on those cuts? They look pretty raw. "

"Sure. Alcohol, peroxide, whatever." He ran the tap.

Ray had to graze him to reach the medicine cabinet.

The repairman held his hands over the sink. Ray poured alcohol over them, dabbed them dry with a facecloth, carefully wrapped Band-Aids across the two newest-looking gashes. From this proximity, the repairman was the same height as Ray: eyes level. Less prepossessing now. Even younger. More vulnerable. Ray felt less apprehensive, less unsure. He still didn't know what would happen, but it didn't trouble him. He was simply pleased by the man's presence—so close, so easygoing, so unassuming.

"Now how about that beer?"

Ray thought the fellow looked longingly at the bed as they passed out of the bedroom and back into the office. Or was Ray deceiving himself? The beers were waiting on the desk, and as there was only one chair, they leaned against cabinets, a few feet apart as they snapped open and chugged down the brews.

"So you, what? Work and live here too?"

Ray explained the setup.

"How did you get into this line? It's pretty unusual, right?"

Ray explained that he'd been an A & R man at EMI/Capitol Records. He mentioned popular artists the guy might have heard of. "GiGi Gertz!" The workman was duly impressed. "You don't mind not working with pop stars any more?"

"I had no choice if I wanted to stay in the city. How's that brew? Need another?" During the discussion they'd become more equal in Ray's mind. The power had even shifted in his favor.

"Don't want to drink and drive. Maybe I should be taking off. Gotta get back to the Island. It'll be an hour with the traffic and all."

Ray knew he would have to act immediately, or what J. K. had predicted—him doing all the work and someone else reaping the rewards—would come to pass. He was no longer unsettled by the man's good looks, nor by the thought that what he intended was disloyal to Jesse. His focus had shifted to how to get the young man undressed easily, gracefully, not too aggressively. Ray extended a hand and brushed the front of the guy's shorts, then said in a calm and measured voice,

"I'm not being a very good host, am I? I did promise more than beer."

"Well, yea—hh," the younger man answered. Now he was the one who was nervous, adding, "Look, it's OK if..."

Perversely enough, his uncertainty convinced Ray not to stop what he had started. Ray caressed the repairman's bulge through the corduroy. It wasn't large but it was hard and that seemed to validate anything that might happen. "I think we've got a winner here. Let's go into the bedroom," Ray said in what he hoped was a reassuring yet sultry voice. "It's more comfortable."

Refusing to relinquish his corduroy prize, he towed the young man along the corridor by degrees, gripping his belt to draw him along.

Once across the bedroom doorsill, Ray released the shorts and used both hands to lift the rugby shirt. When the repairman made a gesture of hesitation, Ray reassured him. "Don't be nervous. I'm not going to do anything you don't want me to do. OK?"

The raised shirt disclosed the athletic chest and flat abdomen Ray had imagined. The repairman's torso was by no means huge, thickly muscled, or perfectly "cut," but it was without an inch of fat and hairless but for an inky penumbra circling each nipple, and a tuft rising above and below his navel fading into tanned skin.

"It's not that," the workman said. "It's just that I don't...you know, do this kind of thing."

Ray wasn't listening. He let instinct take over, taking hold of the man's torso and nibbling one nipple, then kneading it between his fingertips as he moved his lips and teeth to the other. Back and forth, once, twice, thrice. When he perceived the repairman would not try to free himself, Ray let go and slowly kissed down the tummy, engrossed in delineating with the tip of his tongue the nearly invisible line of hair evanescing into the reinforced waistband of the promised land of under-wear. Ray paused in his descent only to dally at—circumscribe with the tip of his tongue, teasingly explore—the vortex of belly button. He employed those few seconds of distraction to effortlessly unbuckle the belt, unbutton the shorts-front. The corduroy drifted down, settling gently around densely stockinged ankles. Ray knelt, never for a second ceasing to caress the young man's briefs and, with hands and mouth, never pausing in his stroking of the cotton-enclosed bottom.

Ray was like a child receiving a long awaited present, so temptingly close, he so eager for it, yet willing to restrain him-self from tearing off the wrapping to savor the prospect a few seconds longer. He was conscious of how unconditionally lust had been set free in him as well as by how thoroughly he intended to experience this fellow, and this fellow's sex, when he heard a low moan: basso, guttural. Only with the greatest effort was Ray able to momentarily force his face away from the snowy field of Jockey cotton to glance up and discover from where those sounds emanated, what they were meant to express.

The young workman's head was thrown back. When his face swung into view again, just beyond his flat pectorals with their erect nipples, the voluptuous green eyes appeared smudged, three-quarters shut, his lips a blur. Ray sat back on his knees to relish the sensual victory, then slowly nudged the repairman backward, step succeeding step, all the while taunt-ing him by running his teeth back and forth across the Jockey-covered swelling—until the younger man turned muzzy and stumbling.

At that instant, Ray drew down the underpants, freeing a perfectly shaped penis, which sprung out, shuddering. He also released that specific and individual bouquet he had detected before, intensified tenfold. Essence of Man, they'd called it in the movie *Barbarella*. Ray nudged the guy one more time a bit harder so that he couldn't help but lose his balance. He floundered, then dropped backward, landing athwart the edge of the bed's mattress.

All but deranged by the sight and smell, Ray attacked the longed-for lower torso with face and hands, teeth and lips and tongue, in a barrage of kissing and sucking. Ray consolidated all effort, the entirety of his existence, toward a single end: producing in the sexy workman a thrashing, teeth-clenching, mattress-thumping, unsmotherable, earth-shattering, gut-born roar of orgasm.

When he began to come, the repairman rose off the bed as though intending to levitate, gasping and groaning, before softly subsiding, panting, deflating back onto the bed. Ray at last allowed the fellow's hands to push his face from the still-vibrating body. Sated, relenting, Ray hunched on his heels, surveying the scene, then joined the repairman on the chenille.

The guy attempted to rise, fell back exhausted. "God. I needed that!"

Me too, Ray thought. He had come without touching himself.

Holding the well-muscled arm, he looked at the left hand, the one he had not bandaged. A gold ring on the scarred third finger. "Married," he mumbled.

"Yeah," a little laugh, "but that don't mean I get treated like this at home. And lately," he added more darkly, "I don't get much at all." Then, lest he seem disloyal, he went on, "It's all since the last kid was born. You know, she's had woman illness, that kind of thing."

"You have kids?"

"Two boys and a girl—8, 6, and 2. Want to see their picture?"

"When did you start? When you were 12?"

"You think I'm a kid?" Half-sitting up. "I'll be 31."

"I'd never have guessed it."

"You're, what?" green eyes scrutinizing, "35?"

"Close," Ray said.

"But never married, right?"

"Never married," Ray admitted.

"Which is why you sent me to the ceiling a few minutes ago."

Ray was flattered. Jesse had never complimented him like that. "You liked it?"

"I think I already expressed my appreciation," the repairman laughed, rolled closer to Ray. "Everyone says: for good head, you gotta go gay."

"And now you know which gay to go to," Ray said, feeling esteemed, giddily so. Which was why he was emboldened to add, "Maybe when you're in the area...?" He touched a hot shoulder, "You around a lot, fixing automatic doors?"

"I haven't been. This other guy, older guy, who works there too, he asked for Brooklyn and Manhattan jobs. But he's ticked off a few customers. I could ask for the route...drop by. I couldn't say when, exactly. That OK?"

"I'm here all day. You've got my card. Give a call."

Their faces were inches away from each other. Those eyes!

"You like it, right? Being gay? Doing stuff to guys?"

Ray wasn't sure exactly what he was being asked. "I like doing stuff to you." Then he added. "Why?"

The workman turned away, looked up at the ceiling. "She was my high school sweetheart. We went to the prom in May, graduated in June, got married in September. Everyone thought she was knocked up. But she wasn't. We knew each other since we were, like, in second grade. I hung with her brothers. I like her folks and all. We do things together with her family all the time. The beach. Deep-sea fishing. Barbecues. The whole nine yards."

It came out affectionately, yet rueful. Ray didn't know how to answer. "Sounds comfortable."

"It's comfortable." Again the workman's tone was mixed. "Unlike my friggin' job." He sat up, stretched. "Which can be a bitch. Now I gotta fight traffic all the way back to Massapequa. When instead I could sleep all afternoon. You ever do that—you know, working so close to bed?"

"Not often," Ray admitted. "The phone rings. Orders to be filled."

"The john's that way?" Pointing. Then the repairman was up, winking at Ray as he pulled on his Jockeys, his shorts, and buckled up. All Ray could think was: Look at that body! Look at that face!

He could have stayed in bed and waited and watched the guy come out again, but it might have embarrassed him. So Ray got up and was straightening his clothing when the repairman entered, checking his watch, all business.

"I'm gonna be right in rush-hour traffic."

Ray led him back through the hall to the office and street door. As he stepped out, Ray said, "By the way, you know my name. From the card and all. You are...?"

"Oh, right. Mike. Mike Tedesco." His handshake was butch; one of the Band-Aids flapped off.

"Mike from Massapequa," Ray mused. "See ya around."

"Sure." Hearty. Then, in a different tone, "You know, maybe sometime, you can show me some other stuff. Other gay stuff," he added conspiratorially. "You know what I mean?"

Ray didn't have a clue. "Sure," he said as though he did.

Mike hopped into the van and it dashed into a break in the Joralemon Street traffic, moving so fast that he was gone before Ray remembered the parking decal was still in the truck. Maybe Mike would see it and come back. If not today, then another time.

Ray closed and locked the office, then drifted through the lower floor, stroking the cat, meandering into the bedroom—

so unexpectedly redolent with Mike's fragrance. Jesus, it's strong, Ray thought. I've got to spray in here before Jesse comes home.

He decided he should change the bedcover, too, just in case. Chuck the cat out the door, open the windows, and totally sanitize the place. But just glancing at the bed turned Ray on so much that all he could do was lie back in the midst of that fragrance—Essence of Mike Tedesco—and replay it in his mind. He became aroused again, and ended up masturbating.

The Show Palaces
Marc Almond

where do the lovely lovers of the dark go now, the worshippers in the temple of flesh, the shadow people— now the show palace has closed down, the david, the adonis lounge?

1. 1993

23:00, the show palace, eighth ave., new york

a room shadowy in the muted red light, occasionally a reflection caught in the mirror tiles, a muffled, distorted disco tape and an unintelligible announcement tells us to appreciate carlos or jesus (where else would you find jesus but in a temple?). jesus is sexy. jesus and the gods of flesh. the room is heavy with sex scent and musky dark sweat and scented lube oil. the effect is heady, surreal and serious. four of the five enormous black and latino guys dance lazily and zombie-like in a semi-state of crack trance on the small strewn stage rubbing oil into their lithe bodies and stretching their large semi-erect and oiled penises into forever, like a snake dance in the temple to the great god erotica. occasionally they leave the stage and straddle members of the audience, drawing out dollars from the spectators' pockets with their magical hustler powers—money stuffed into socks and boots for one more minute of close attention. in the dark recesses and deep corners, they linger for longer, straddling and thrusting, larger amounts of money getting more exotic attentions.

24:00, the gaiety theatre, times square, new york

it's the final show of the day, the air is twice as thick with dare, anticipation and sex. fourteen boys of mostly straight origin and toned, white-american apple-pie stock take turns performing and selling their wares to an audience of mostly older gentlemen. against a cheap sparkling curtain of the purest tantalizing glamour, they dance, crouch, spin and flex to classic and current disco and house tunes. beautifully fleshed and marbled, perfect-looking bodies, bruise- and needle-mark-free, thrust- and pose-defining buttocks and pecs, living pages from the athletic model guild. sweet home-boy faces, freckles, eager-puppy eyes, hustler grins, sometimes a tuft or two of hair in all the right places, some-times tear-shaped and teen-like backward baseball caps, white socks and short fuck-me cowboy boots for the tips and added sleaze "erotic erotic put your hands all over my body" moans a familiar diva as eyes meet eyes and dollar touches torso. after removing their few clothes, plain shirt/black jeans, they strut their stuff before leaving the stage for a few moments. one imagines backstage a quick bump of coke, a girlfriend doing her stuff and limp members jolt into brief action. they return stiffly, perky, proud, and erect; some aren't successful in rising to the occasion—nerves, too much coke, too much business, but most meet the demand. they take a bow to the enthusiastic applause, and seats clatter [RL: I think this is awk and it works better w/o it] as gentlemen beat a nasty path to the side-stage lounge to negotiate with the young dancers and a booming, distorted voice bids us to put our hands together for the very talented joey. later, back at the dancer's hotel, maybe the president hotel, off times square, a further performance, more private, maybe a little more awkward, takes place, costs approximately $200—don't suck, get sucked, or only fuck. if it's the last show, maybe come, only maybe. girlfriend? back home in connecticut. "yeah, she knows."

2. 1994

midnight, the savoy, new york

it's friday night and it must be buddha's big-dick contest at the savoy bar, situated by the port authority bus terminal. the bar is stuffed to capacity with banjee boys and their girlfriends, young black and latin hustlers, a couple of transvestites taking a break from sally's hideaway (a sister transvestite bar up the street), dealers, dopers, and strays, village queens out for a dash of low-rent sleaze, and tattooed white boys out for the thrill. buddha, a fat toothless black man with gray curly hair, a diamanté earring and a long gold mandarin's fingernail, is at one end of the bar. he is with a coterie of underage banjee boys to whom he has promised the world, or the half-world that he inhabits after dark. some wear the blue and yellow beads of the latin kings—i have made friends with members of the latin kings' new york gang, so my safety is assured in the bar and on the street out front, which can get quite scary on forty-ninth street and ninth avenue. the gang members stand guard at the door with ever-watchful eyes. the girls, their hair in bangs and plaits, hang dopily around their hustler boyfriends, who ignore them—playing pool, passing joints and snorting coke in the bathroom. their woolen hats pulled down over their ears (giving them a cute goofiness), their teeth encased in gold, their pants hanging off their hips (one leg rolled up), their necks ringed with gold chains. they swagger around the pool table, shoulders slung low, hands curved inward. at 01:30 buddha takes the stage and welcomes the crowd on a microphone with too much reverb.

he berates the transvestites and dares anyone to enter the contest for the $50 prize—the crack dealers wait. there are two contestants tonight, they are waiting in the beer-storage room, being blown by their girlfriends, trying by whatever means to get some life into their flaccid members (suffering from the effects of too much coke). the first to take the stage is a tall, gangly black guy in a woolen hat. he provides a half-hard monster—the crowd yells its approval. buddha produces his ruler and measures the snake-like appendage. "ten inches," shouts buddha and bends to kiss the snake with a gummy mouth. the sheepish contestant, looking a little peaky and sweaty, as his last pipe wore off some hours ago, slopes off into the back room to work up another inch, and so his place is taken by rico, a latin boy with half his teeth missing. he runs out, quickly followed by his girl, before his proud erection flops and it's obvious he is not going to measure up—nevertheless the crowd cheer him on. "nine inches," proclaims buddha.

the crowd surges nearer to the stage in wonderment and awe, as if they have never seen such meat before.

rico runs off, pulling his girlfriend with him to work a little harder. the first contestant, the gangly black guy, runs up again, nearly falling over his own trousers, which are round his ankles. grasping his piece, he has raised another half an inch. it's official. "ten and a half inches," declares buddha, and the crowd is almost at frenzy point. buddha once more gums the guy's extra limb, causing acute humiliation, though of course the contestants can't complain—this is buddha's place and buddha's show, and beside rico needs that pipe.

suddenly there is commotion as the door swings open. a tall mulatto boy with a huge mouth and a shock of curly hair strides in, wearing an overcoat. pushing through the crowd, he makes his way to the little platform. "it's big bird," gasps one of the transvestites.

silence.

"he's gonna win it again," another shouts resignedly, and sure enough, when big bird opens his overcoat he reveals the clear winner by a couple of inches.

"you bitches, i'm the biggest and the prettiest and it tastes good too," drawls the effeminate big bird, and he claims his $50 prize, much to the chagrin of the gangly black guy, who has to make do with second place ($20). he's not disappointed for long though because the village queens are soon in discussion with him about making a donation of their own. the crowd disperses, boys leave with their girls, some with older gentlemen, and down on ninth avenue the crack dealer is waiting. some of the boys will take their elderly friends to the elk hotel round the corner on forty-second street for a short stay.

it is now a year later and buddha is no longer at the savoy. he was fired for letting too many of the latin kings into the bar to do drug deals. some say he's managing a bar downtown. the owners have moved in plastic tables with umbrellas that look truly surreal in the dark, pokey little bar, and have removed the pool table. needless to say, the place is empty. no more big-dick show on a friday night either—never mind, i'm sure they'll soon see sense.

3. 1996

20:00, chi chi la rue's night at the eros, eighth ave., new york

the eros is the only male palace of porn left on eighth avenue, the rest were swallowed up by the great god disney. it's a plucky little cinema, its brave blue neon *eros* sign a beacon to lovers of male erotic dancing and blurred celluloid encounters of male-on-male flesh. the eros sign, in 1950s fashion, promises something camp and kitsch and almost cheesecake. i think of the photos in physique magazines from the 1950s and 1960s—men dressed as gladiators, men spread-eagled on tiger-skin rugs, men with oily quiffs, men with sculpted muscles and fixed dimpled grins with eyes full of fun against glitter backdrops, men in posing pouches with anchor tattoos, biker boys in leopard skin tussling each other like playful puppies in heat, sexy and innocent. the word *eros* in blue neon makes me dream of these things—it makes me dream of bobby kendal in *pink narcissus*—that strange, erotic movie from a lost decade.

dreaming once in this way, i entered through the turnstile into the murky recesses of the eros and was bought to my senses by out-of-focus hardcore images and muffled grunts of pleasure, or pain. the seats, once salacious red velvet, were now dulled, faded and broken, inhabited by silent sheepish figures, some hand in motion, some asleep, all somebody's husband. hands grabbed at me and i realized i was being hustled and propositioned by two or three latin boys in matching briefs and bruises, red and purple, and stained with baby oil. they wanted to take me downstairs to a place probably even darker and murkier, past a broken toilet to a dressing room. they wanted dollars, and far too many dollars, because these weren't the little latin cat-boy extras from a madonna video— these were hustler trash that even the show palace rejected.

one of them checked his watch and said to his friend, "one more dance and then i'm going to the video booths."

(the video booths, if you're wondering, are beneath the show palace, in the basement of a sex shop, a line of male video booths showing pornographic movies, outside the booths, waiting, a line of black and latin hustlers. hustlers circle the customers and the crack dealers circle the hustlers. the monitor dishing out tokens for booths is paid a couple of dollars to turn a blind eye, "keep it moving, guys, get in them booths now," he keeps shouting and the procession keeps shuffling. customer and hustler would disappear into a booth, and five minutes later the hustler would emerge and slope around a corner to buy some coke or crack. this went on all night and all day and got packed around 18: 00 in the evening when business around times square finished.)

the film suddenly stops mid-orgasm, the lights dim and the boys half-heartedly gyrate to some muffled disco music, taking only a small pause before fleecing the audience of any loose change. but that was then. the eros has now had something of a revamp, a coat of paint, a dash of sparkle. the 1950s-style eros sign looks braver and bluer than ever and shouts down decimated eighth avenue, "i'm still here." outside, a sign proclaims "tonight—chi chi la rue." porn director, performer, personality and all-round priestess of porn has brought glamour and tease back to the eros, and as i enter the theater i am dazzled by a mirror ball and blinded by the sequins on chi chi's frock as she paces back and forth, lights exploding christmas all over the stage. burlesque is back as chi chi brandishes porno magazines (featuring her celluloid stud muffins), turns the air blue with cracks, jokes and the cheapest asides of the filthiest tints. she introduces a selection of porno princes to tease us and delight our jaded palates. the stage resembles a pierre et gilles set, with shades of pink and twinkling fairy lights (well, not quite pierre et gilles, but those cheaper imitations who aspire to be them), and it feels good to be sleazy again.

chi chi calls us all naughty boys and slaps us with porno mags and we quake in our seats as this thundering, sequined dynamo storms up and down the aisles. the porno playmates form a fetching tableau while a misplaced attendant, standing self-consciously at the edge of the fraying lurex curtain, eyes us all suspiciously for signs of overexcitement. we dare not be too excited or chi chi will come at us, her boobs like sequined battleships, and slap us over our heads with a shiny, unthumbed copy of *inches*. yes, i can dream of bike boys in togas, posing-pouched centurians, discus-throwing tony curtis lookalikes and sailors on fur rugs and almost...for a moment...almost feel innocent again.

Just Another Night at the World's Greatest Gay Diner

Dimitri Apessos

"I want a chocolate shake with that."

"You do, huh?"

"Yes, please."

"Here you go!"

And with that, Durrell does his ridiculous little Chocolate Shake dance. He always does this when people order chocolate shakes; he positions his arms outward, bent at the elbows as if he's doing the Twist, and shakes his ass around in a belly-dance motion. It's a joke, of course. Durrell's black. Chocolate shake, get it? But, as always, the hapless tourist does *not* get it and sits at the counter, staring, confused.

Durrell sighs.

"I'll get your shake, sir," he concedes, disappointed and defeated.

With that, the hungry tourist turns back to his *USA Today* and Durrell walks over to the ice cream machine, which happens to be positioned right by where you're sitting. In response to his failed joke, you smile widely and shake your head at him in disbelief.

He smiles back, while pouring chocolate ice cream into the shake glass, and leans over to whisper: "I am so over this shit!"

You smile, understanding. Durrell is one of your best friends in New Orleans, and you can always rely on him for a free meal, but in return you have to listen to him bitch about all the ridiculous things drunken tourists say and do all day. You know he's not really bitter about it; after all, drunk heterosexuals and testy homosexuals are the occupational hazards of working in any restaurant on Bourbon Street, let alone the Happy Leprechaun, the only gay diner you have encountered in your many travels throughout gay America. For every sleaze from Jackson, Mississippi, who comes in and tells him how good he would be to him as his "white daddy," and for every straight frat boy who walks in accidentally looking for a burger who gets hostile once he puts two and Cher together to ascertain he is the only heterosexual in the entire restaurant, Durrell has the consolation of making and spending more money than any nineteen-year-old should know what to do with. French Quarter tourists may be obnoxious, but they tip well.

As if reading your thoughts, Durrell puts down the shake glass, uninterested in serving this poor tourist who didn't get his joke, and sits on the counter to talk.

"You should have been here earlier," he relates. "You know that hot blonde stripper from Procession? Claude, or whatever he's calling himself today?"

"The hustler one?" you ask.

"Honey, they're *all* hustlers," he answers. "Anyway, he was here earlier with this big daddy from Florida or some shit, and we was packed, so service was slow, you know? Well, this daddy starts yelling at me that he wants his food, and he can't believe the service is so bad. And the stripper knows me and comes here all the time, so he's, like, whispering to him 'sit down' but this daddy won't listen so he comes up to the counter and starts yelling in my face that he knows the owner and is gonna get me fired and all that."

"Shit, what did you do?"

"I didn't do nuttn', I don't deal with trash like that. But Mike, the cook, gets in the way and yells at him, 'Look, just because you're paying your hustler by the hour, it don't mean you'll get your food any faster! Now sit down and shut up, or get the fuck out!' and this daddy just stands there wit' nuttn' to say but then the stripper gets up and starts yelling at Mike…"

"What was he yelling?"

"Oh, you know: 'Watch what you say. You don't know me!' That kind of shit. As if there's anyone in the Quarter who don't know that he's a hustler."

"Right," you agree.

"Right! So Mike says somethin' like 'I don't need to know you' and the hustler makes to come around the counter and Mike starts hitting him on the head with a frying pan!"

"No shit!"

"No shit! So there I am, twenty minutes after walking in, and I have Mike beating this hustler on the head with a frying pan while the hustler is trying to choke him to death and the daddy is trying to pull them apart, yelling at the hustler, 'Remember, I can't have the cops show up! My wife knows the sheriff!' It was some funny shit!"

You smile.

"I can't believe Mike lost it like that," you say.

"Well, he'd been on for fourteen hours at that point," Durrell explains. "Adam called in sick and Brad couldn't get anyone to fill in, so Mike just stayed on for a double."

Just another night at the Happy Leprechaun, you think to yourself before asking: "So what happened with the hustler and the daddy?"

"Oh, so the daddy pulls out this big wad o' cash and yells at the hustler, 'Stop choking him! I can't have the police come here and see me! Just take this money and stop choking him!' So the daddy gives the hustler this big wad o' cash and runs out of the restaurant and the hustler stops choking Mike, gets his food to go, and leaves."

"You gave him his food after all of that?"

"Why wouldn't I? He got it in Styrofoam; it's not like he was staying here to choke anyone else. And he tipped me, like, twenty bucks!"

Yup, just another night at the Happy Leprechaun.

"So, is Mike fired?" you ask.

"Why would he be fired?"

"Ummm...because he beat a customer on the head with a frying pan, maybe?"

Durrell gives a sneering giggle before saying, "Oh, please. Mike could drop his pants and piss on the grill and they wouldn't fire him. Why, I can think of five or six guys who come in here every day to eat, just so they can hit on him..."

"Wait," you interrupt. "I thought Mike was straight!"

"Exactly!" Durrell responds with a smile. "Well, he calls himself bi, but I don't think he's ever even been with a guy..."

"I am so over everyone in this damn town calling themselves bi," you squeal. "I swear to God they should get with the program!"

"Well," Durrell continues, refusing to acknowledge your interruption, "you know how the queens down here go nuts for straight boys..."

"That's sick," you say, and you mean it. Of all the sleazy things that have bothered you about New Orleans in the three months since you moved from Indiana—and there are many— this is probably the worst. The weekly visitors from Mississippi and Alabama, coming in to stock up over the weekend for a week's worth of sex before going home to their closeted lives; the huge turnover of staff in every bar and restaurant, which allows every manager to treat their employees like dirt; waiting in line for hours to use the bathroom at the clubs because there's always more than one person to a stall: All these things bother you, but you laugh at them anyway. But the obsession that every gay man in New Orleans has with hooking up with "straight boys" reveals so much self-hatred—so much denial—that just thinking about it brings you down.

The phone rings and Durrell answers. It's his on-again/off-again boyfriend, as you can tell immediately by the way his face prepares itself for a long conversation. Balancing the phone between his shoulder and cheek, Durrell reaches into his tip jar and hands you a dollar, motioning with his eyes a plea for you to play something on the jukebox. You find the motion kind of rude and play three songs from the Lulu CD just to punish him. When you come back to your seat at the counter, he is hanging up the phone.

"Bitch," he calls you, as Lulu's version of Bowie's "The Man Who Sold the World" starts to play. "By the way, your roommate was here earlier and he got in a fight, too."

"What about?" you ask, not sure you really want to know.

"There was some guy from Miami here who started yelling at him about his T-shirt. Started calling him a Communist and stuff, and your roommate freaked out and went off on him."

"What T-shirt was he wearing?" you ask, although you know the answer, to see if Durrell knows, too.

"I dunno," he answers. "The red one he always wears with the guy from *Evita*."

You have no time to educate him on the history of Latin American Communism, because the door opens and in stumble—drunk and probably sleepless for more than forty-eight hours—four "ladies" you know well: Bianca, Autumn, Michèle, and Sabrina. Ranging from "drag-for-pay" to "heavy hormone treatment," the four of them have become something of a menace around town, going in and out of bars and restaurants all night—every night—scaring the straight tourists with their bitchy catcalls and loud, androgynous laughter. With them, tonight, they have a boy no older than 20, who seems to enjoy being taken along for a confusing ride.

"Have you heard from Nicole?" Durrell asks you, realizing that within a few seconds all opportunity for serious conversation will be gone.

"We've been playing phone tag," you barely have time to answer before the four "ladies" reach your spot on the counter and, without a break in their loud laughter, kiss you and Durrell hello.

"Hello, girls," Durrell greets them, switching instantaneously from butch to queeny. "Where's Miss Derrick?"

"Oh, girl," Bianca starts, "you wouldn't even believe what Miss Derrick got into! We were at La Ho-Down, when…"

You start to listen to the story when the stumbling boy who is escorting the "ladies" around town sits—or rather lands—on the counter seat next to you and extends a hand in your direction.

"Wassup, dude," he sputters with a huge chemical grin on his face. "I'm Andrew."

You look at him, unsure of what to make of his greeting. From up close you see that he is probably only 18 or 19 years old, visibly rolling his ass off on ecstasy and God-knows-what-else, and incredibly good looking. Underneath his curved baseball cap you see two steely, smiling gray eyes, the focus of a gorgeous, chiseled young face. He is wearing a tank top and baggy jeans and has a perfectly formed upper body — through nature, rather than exercise. Everything about him, from his outfit to his way of speaking, screams "straight boy."

"Hello," you answer, shaking his hand. "I'm Lawrence."

"Wassup," he asks rhetorically as he takes your hand and transforms your handshake into some kind of strange, brotherhood clasp. "You work here?"

"No," you answer. "I bartend across the street. Just getting a snack before I have to be at work in twenty minutes."

"Cool, cool," he nods a little too expressively, revealing just how hard he is rolling at this moment. "Man, this is a crazy town…"

"Yes," you agree. "Where are you from?"

"Michigan," he answers. "I just got in this morning, and I've been drunk since I stepped off the train. My girlfriend's coming down to meet me tomorrow, so I'm getting in as much partying as I can, ya' know?"

"Yeah," you answer, trying to avoid his beautiful, inebriated stare. A less-experienced man would have asked how he—a straight boy from Michigan—ended up escorting a group of trannies and drag queens on his first night in town, but your time here has taught you not to ask such questions. Anyway, you're pretty sure he'll tell you, regardless.

"So, right when I got off the train I asked this kid that was hanging out at the station where I could get some rolls—ya know?—" he starts recounting, meeting your expectations. "He told me I had to hit the gay bars on Bourbon if I wanted to find good shit. I mean, I don't care; I was in the rave scene back home so I got lotsa' gay friends. Are you gay?"

"Ummm," you falter. "No, I just like to get my cock sucked by young boys."

"Right on," he nods, completely missing your joke. "So I'm waiting outside this club, Narnia—you know it? And these dudes here come by, and they were, like, 'Oh, you're so cute!' so they gave me two rolls for free and I've been hanging out with them since."

There's a lot that you find funny about this story, but nothing amuses you quite as much as the fact that he just referred to Bianca, Autumn, Michèle, and Sabrina as dudes. You look over to see if they noticed, but sadly they did not. (They are too busy, still relating to Durrell what happened to Miss Derrick and pretending to ignore the obvious fact that every pair of eyes in the entire restaurant is staring at them.) Dudes, he calls them, despite the fact that they are all in dresses and three of them are wearing fake breasts.

Just another night at the Happy Leprechaun.

"So," you say, to keep this boy talking and to keep the laughs coming. (You don't have to be at work for another fifteen minutes, anyway.) "Are you rolling right now?"

Instead of answering verbally, he leans over, putting his face within two or three inches of yours, so that you can observe his dilated pupils. The proximity makes you nervous and excited. This boy is beautiful. Fucking straight boy! Fucking trannies, bringing him here!

"I see," you respond to his pupils, looking away awkwardly.

Impervious to your discomfort, or perhaps because of it, he puts one toned, tanned arm around your shoulders and whispers in your ear: "So, dude, is this place as fucking gay as it seems?"

"Gayer," you answer.

"Since I've been in town, all I've seen is gay bars and dudes in dresses," he confides in you. "I mean, when I was thinking of New Orleans, I was thinking of chicks showing their tits for beads, ya' know?"

This boy is so far gone that all sarcasm is wasted on him, but it makes you feel better anyway, so you agree: "Yeah, I'm pretty upset about the lack of tits, myself."

"I mean, nothing wrong with gay people!" he interrupts.

"No, of course not!" you say to support him, with mocking jovial tolerance.

Suddenly he leans over even closer and squints, trying to concentrate on your face, from within a haze of ecstasy, as he asks, in all seriousness, as if he just processed your comment from several minutes ago: "So, you get your dick sucked by dudes, huh? What's that like?"

"It's OK," you answer, nodding, and trying to stop yourself from bursting out laughing. You can't wait to tell your roommate about this. "It's not bad, you know?"

"But," he prompts you further, "is it better than a chick?"

"Depends, you know?" you lie, as if you've ever had an interest in receiving oral sex from a girl. Then, in your best Donnie Brasco voice: "Depends on the dude and the chick, ya' know?"

The gravity of this response is too much for straight rolling-boy Andrew. He withdraws his arm from around you, in confusion, takes his baseball cap off, rubs his short brown hair, then puts his hands on the counter and looks at nothing in the distance, emphasizing with: "Wow, dude..."

This joke has gone far enough. You have to be at work in ten minutes, so you excuse yourself and go through the kitchen and the courtyard of the Happy Leprechaun to use the bathroom. (The bar you work at has the nastiest bathrooms in all of the French Quarter, so you always do your business at the Happy Leprechaun before you report for duty.) Your surprise is considerable, when, after taking a long piss, you open the door of the bathroom and find young Andrew standing in the courtyard, a confused look on his face.

You suppose that he, too, has to piss, so you say "Wassup?" and try to squeeze past him. Instead he leans over, right as you pass next to him, and, half-falling over you, tries to kiss you on the mouth. It's a sloppy attempt, even for a straight boy, and you push him away. To put it simply, you can't believe this shit.

Then, right there in the empty courtyard of the Happy Leprechaun, in front of the open bathroom door, Andrew kneels in front of your feet and looks up at you with a gorgeous, mischievous grin. With a svelte, too-experienced-for-a-straight-boy move, he turns his baseball cap around so that the visor faces backward, and starts licking the bulge in your pants. You look around. No one is watching, other than the security camera, but no one ever checks that anyway, so what the heck.

You're already hard, so you push his face away from your crotch for just a second, and undo the button of your pants. With the same grin on his face, Andrew leans back toward you, undoes your zipper, and pulls out your cock. (It is a universal truth that no one ever wears underwear in New Orleans.)

Once again, with style that belies his claims of inexperience, he bends his neck to approach your dick from underneath and gives the shaft two long, playful licks. He pulls back for a second, looks up with an expectant smile, and puckers his parted lips in precisely the width of your cock. Then with one swift motion, he lunges forward and takes your entire shaft in his mouth, moaning with hunger. He pulls back and forth twice, never fully releasing your tip from his mouth, and then slips his mouth off you and slaps your mushroom head against his cheek. As if he's been starving for this exact taste, he takes your cock and manically wipes it over his lips, his nose, and his eyes.

You take his baseball-capped head in your hands and force it back onto your cock. With a girlish squeal, he accedes to your demand and allows you to set the pace. He puts his hands on the back of your thighs and squeezes them with delight as you fuck his face with steadily increasing speed and furor. You bring his head down on your crotch again and again, forcing him to take in every inch of you, as he moans and slobbers with each deep swallow.

You remove yourself from his hungry lips for a second, then you turn your body and his head slightly so that his back and his head touch the tall walls of the courtyard. With him cornered like that, you push your pelvis back and forth on his face, fucking his mouth rhythmically, while he moans in accord with the pace you're setting. You look down at his chiseled cheeks, his beautiful, half-opened eyes, his backward cap, his bronzed body accentuated by the bright-white tank top, and once again you say to yourself: I can't believe this shit is happening. He reaches up and is now hanging onto your exposed butt cheeks, as you rape his supposedly virgin lips, closer to coming with each forceful thrust.

Recognizing the twitches of the muscles on the underside of your cock, he pulls you out of his mouth, looks up at you with begging lust, and whispers: "I want you to come on my face, dude!"

With his left hand he jerks off your shaft while he kisses and sucks on your tip with furious hunger, and you see that he has opened his own fly with his right, and is banging away at his own, large, handsome dick with equal earnestness.

Your tip feels as if it's on fire, your shaft muscles contract with an explosion of joy, and you squirt a heavy load of thick, white jism all over his pretty, straight-boy lips. He moans with delight, and as you look down you see his own cock pop with white foam like a champagne bottle. But your own cum keeps flowing, too, for several seconds, wetting with milky spunk his forehead, those cheeks, his long, boyish eyelashes.

As he kisses and sucks the remaining jizz off your cock with yelps of incredulous lust, you see your slowly drying cum drip from his face and down his long, smooth neck to wet the top of his previously clean tank top, outlining his finely shaped pecs. His moans and kisses are dying down as exhaustion begins to hit him, and you push him away and zip yourself up. You are late for work.

As you straighten your pants and shirt, standing at the exact same spot where you fucked his face, he collapses to the ground with mock-ecstatic fatigue and lets out another girlish giggle. He looks up at you from the dirty courtyard floor with his big eyes full of expectation, all pretense of heterosexuality gone from his recently abused face.

"That was great!" he yawns, childishly stretching his body out on the ground. "Wow, dude!"

Afraid that he is going to ask to see you again, or meet you after work, or, even worse, admit that there is no girlfriend arriving the next day, you walk away without a word. You step into the kitchen, and from there into the dining room of the restaurant, as "To Sir with Love" dies down on the juke-box and Bianca finally concludes her story to Durrell.

"So Miss Derrick, she turns to him and she says: 'No, you *don't* know me, you understand? Cause I'm here incognegro!' Incog*negro!!!* Can you believe that bitch?"

Durrell and the "ladies" burst out in deafening laughter as you pick up your backpack from the counter and wave good-bye to all present. They all wave back, and you hear behind you a customer nervously complain: "Ummm, I'm still waiting for my chocolate milkshake…"

As you close the door and step out onto Bourbon Street, you faintly make out one of the "ladies"—or perhaps Durrell—yelling in response something that sounds a lot like "Eat my ass on a shitty day!" to the poor, thirsty tourist. You look at your watch. You are officially five minutes late for work.

As you cross the street and think of an unnecessary apology, you tell yourself: Yup, just another night at the Happy Leprechaun.

Warm-up

Matt Bernstein Sycamore

It's finally spring, so of course I walk all the way across town to Stuyvesant Park. I swear I've got a hundred pounds of shit in my backpack, not to mention a shopping bag full of file folders and computer disks, but listen, it's warm outside and there's no way I'm gonna miss the park. I get two blocks away and it starts to drizzle but who cares, I get to the entrance and suddenly I'm wired.

I walk right over to this couple in the middle, this guy in a blue warm-up suit or what do they call those stupid things. Jogging suits? Running suits? Whatever—he's with someone else but he's working me hardcore. I walk around but there's no one else I'm in the mood for, so I sit down next to a guy by the entrance who's not bad; I'd suck his dick. I say hi and he looks away, smokes a cigarette. After a few minutes he gets up and leaves. Bitch. I stay seated and the guy in blue walks over and I stare right at him and say hey. He says aren't you cold, because I've only got a T-shirt on, but I'm warm. He walks past me and then back, then looks around and goes across the street to the other side of the park. Does he want me to follow?

I do one more go-around, but there's no one I'm hot for. I pass this older guy who's standing in the shadows, say hello, and he's surprised—probably because no one's said a word to him. People are so damn serious in these places. I cross the street and there's the guy in blue right in the middle of the park getting blown by first one guy and then another. My heart's literally racing, or maybe it's not my heart, but whatever it is means I've got to get over there immediately or I might die.

I sit down right next to the guy in blue, he's got this huge, beautiful dick, and one guy's on his knees sucking it. The third guy is grabbing the other guy's dick. The guy sucking takes a break so I lean over and take that beautiful dick in my mouth, then I get on my knees so that I can get a better angle. The guy who was sucking grabs my dick, but I'm not hard yet, then the guy I'm sucking pushes my head down and his dick thrusts into my throat. It's too big and the force gets me hard and I'm gagging but wanting more and more, he's pushing my head all the way down and it's amazing I'm hard and the other guy's sucking me.

Then I choke and some food comes up, I press up to breathe, and the guy just pushes my head down, oh that amazing feeling of him pressing down, finally I can't take it any more, I push up hard and he releases. I swallow my vomit then go back down on the guy, put his hand on the back of my neck, but then the other guy wants some, I sit up and the fourth guy (what's he been doing?) starts sucking my dick. Then the guy in blue says I'm gonna come and I put my hand on his chest, he comes in the guy's mouth and damn I want that cum so bad.

The other guy gets up and starts spitting out the cum, I wouldn't mind him spitting it into my mouth. Then the guy in blue gets up and I take his place, now my dick's looking large too, he looks back and I look him right in the eyes with heat. The fourth guy's still sucking my dick and the other guy's sitting next to me, I bend over and take his dick in my mouth, he pushes my head all the way down. His dick starts out medium but pretty soon he's huge too and I'm rock-hard in the other guy's mouth though he's sort of hurting me.

I ask the guy whose dick I'm sucking to stand up and put his dick in my mouth. He hesitates, but then he's fucking my face, I pull his hand down to my neck and oh I'm so hard in the other guy's mouth, but I pull his head away so that I don't come. I want the other guy to come in my mouth and I say so, but he already came—probably better that way for me anyway. I pull his head down and we start making out.

The guy who used to be the fourth guy—but now he's the third guy, I guess—he's jerking my dick and I could come but I hold his hand to stop. I pull up my shirt and the third guy rubs my chest—yes—and I'm sucking the other guy's dick. Then he takes out his dick and starts smacking my face, he's grabbing my chest and holding my neck and the other guy's got a finger pumping at the edge of my asshole and his other hand jerking my dick. And I don't even know where I am any more or what I'm doing and then I feel myself coming but I can't even tell if I've come yet, no there I'm coming no I've already come but my orgasm just goes on.

When I open my eyes, there's just me and the guy standing up and he grabs my head to make out but I'm coughing, A dryness in my throat like all this stuff is stuck there. I start laughing, it's spring yes it's spring and then I'm kissing the guy again and pulling up my pants, what's your name, his name's —now I can't remember—and I get up and there are guys wandering all over and good, my bags are still there. I start walking and I'm coughing and laughing, I'm so high from coming, I'm walking down the street with my eyes sometimes rolling back and sometimes I'm just laughing, thinking how amazing sex can be, the insane high, how I need some throat lozenges.

"You Need a Boy"
Doug Harrison

Thursday

Brad and I had sex tonight. Great sex. No whips and chains this time, just good old-fashioned vanilla sex. He didn't feel like being fucked, but that was OK.

Lying next to him got me hard, as usual. I love to run my hands through his long black chest hair and suck on his hard nipples, erect as new pencil erasers. Almost the same color, too. We sixty-nined, him on his back, me hovering over him.

His reputation as the best cocksucker in San Francisco is well deserved. And he's my lover! He comes home to my bed. Well, usually, but that's what open relationships are all about.

I knew from his throaty moans that he was on the edge, so I turned around, buried my head in his crotch, and sucked on his smooth, shaved balls. He gasped, wiggled his cute, hairy ass, and put his legs over my shoulders with his feet under my armpits, pinning me tightly to him while he jerked off.

I pinched his engorged nipples until he came in his lush belly hair, a larger-than-usual thick white load. I lapped most of it up and cleaned the end of his dick with my tongue. I used the rest of his cum for lube as I jerked off, leaning against him, his arms around me, while he reciprocated, torturing my nipples. He coaxed a glorious orgasm from me. I usually don't shoot like he does, and the thin, almost transparent liquid dribbled down my dickhead. We basked in the afterglow for a few moments. And then he announced: "You need a boy!"

I didn't know whether to be perplexed, get angry, or laugh. "What prompts you to come up with something like that at a time like this?" I asked.

"I can't fill all your needs."

"You're doing fine," I said, wondering which of us I was trying to convince.

"You need someone who's more into anal sex than I am. And all those toys of yours—the shackles, the collars, the floggers. You need someone who gets off on all that. I don't want you to be frustrated."

"I can't play with someone that intensely without having a close connection," I said. "Particularly a Daddy-boy connection. I can't love someone besides you."

"You can. I've been thinking about this. Try it."

"You're tired of me pestering you."

"If you want to look at it that way, sure. But I think it will strengthen our relationship."

"Maybe," I said. "But I'm not going to run out and get a boy. They're high maintenance." Brad smiled.

I rolled over on my side. Brad spooned me, and just before falling asleep I felt his dick getting hard between my thighs, as usual.

What would it be like to have my own boy? I wondered dreamily. My very own boy?

Saturday

Today was the first day of the Leather Conference. I met Mark during the morning coffee break. He's articulate, a writer, and an activist. About 5'9", solidly built, with a captivating smile and penetrating dark eyes. I wanted to run my hands through his unruly, dark hair. We looked each other over closely and arranged to have lunch.

We went to a small burger joint. The food was acceptable. The place was crowded with leather folks, both queer and het. Several guys were in full drag: chaps, boots, and jacket. I was conscious of Mark and some other patrons staring at my chest and biceps. Imagine, being a gym bunny at my age. Mark was cruised by young and old alike. We were a quintessential Daddy-boy pair, like it or not.

Eventually I mentioned Brad.

Mark raised his eyebrows while he interlocked his hands and twirled his thumbs in small circles. "So you and Brad have an open relationship?"

"Yeah, we work things out. We can't be all things to each other. He has a girlfriend."

Mark grimaced. "I've never been with a woman. I don't know if I could do it. I'd giggle."

"You'd be surprised at what you're capable of."

We discussed the usual S/M scenes: spanking, bondage, clothespins. He had both a reporter's curiosity and a beginner's interest. He gazed wistfully past me when I mentioned flogging, plus the fact that I was writing a book on the subject.

Sometimes I'm too effusive, and this was only our first lunch date, so I stopped talking and held back momentarily. Just as I was considering the possibility of asking if he would like to be flogged, he said, very slowly, "I'd like it if you'd flog me," followed by, "I've never been flogged, and I'd like to see what it's like."

"I'm flattered," I said. "There's a play party next Saturday, South of Market. You can come as my guest."

"All right," he said, "but promise you won't leave me alone during the party."

"It's a deal." I leaned across the table, took his face in my hands, and kissed him.

Sunday

Mark called tonight. He's nervous about our scene. "I'm scared I won't be able to take it," he said.

"It's not about taking it," I said. "You'll go where you need to go. Trust me."

"I do. But I don't want to disappoint you."

"You can't possibly."

"OK."

Monday

I told Brad I have a date on Saturday. He thinks it's great, even though we usually have dinner together Saturday evening.

I coyly said I was getting a boy, if only for the evening, and he shouldn't ask for something if he wasn't prepared for it to happen. He laughed.

Tuesday

I called Mark and invited him to dinner before the play party on Saturday. He was delighted.

I'm determined he'll have a good flogging experience. It's his initiation, after all, and it's my obligation as a top. It's his reward for what he's brought to the community with his writing and activism. Plus, it could be the beginning of a relationship.

There's a millennia-old tradition of older men mentoring younger men. The Leather Daddy-boy interaction is an obvious contemporary extension. For the first time I'm acutely aware that I could be part of an archetypal tradition. I want to pass on my knowledge, love, and skills.

Thursday

Mark called. His voice was quivering. He's getting more and more agitated about our scene. He talked about his father who died when he was 18, ten years ago. They were very close, and Mark misses him. Mark is mature enough to realize that his search for a Daddy relationship is to balance this emptiness in his soul.

I hope I can be a stable masculine influence for Mark. The question is: Do I want a boy? The answer could be yes. I enjoy our interaction. It's hard not to call him every day. I think of him more and more often, and am looking forward to Saturday. I sit in meetings at work and my mind wanders to our scene, thinking of what toys I'll use, how he will react, what he will look like, and holding him afterward.

Friday

I sent Mark an authoritative, succinct e-mail today:

> Boy,
> Be at my place promptly at 6:30 on Saturday.
> Wear your boots and a white cotton jock.
> Daddy Doug

Saturday

Brad and I slept most of the morning, then went out for a late lunch. I felt some trepidation about my impending date, but didn't discuss it with him. Would Mark and I have a good experience? Also, Brad took fierce pride in being independent, but, in actuality, would he be hurt if I grew close to another man? I hugged him tightly when we got home.

A few minutes before 6:30 the bell rang. Mark stood outside the iron gate, a nervous smile on his face. He wore boots and tight jeans, with his black leather jacket slung over his shoulder. I led him to the foyer.

"Kneel!" I said.

He knelt before me, head bowed. I put a chain collar around his neck and secured it with a lock.

I took his head in my hands and looked into his eyes. "You belong to me for the night."

He wrapped his arms tightly around my thighs and buried his head in my crotch. I was already hard. Very hard. Brad smiled at our tableau from the end of the hall, and gave me a thumbs-up sign.

Mark and I strode to dinner hand in hand. At the restaurant he touched his collar and smiled. "It feels good to wear this."

"I know. I've worn them myself." I was pleased that he was relaxing into a submissive role, even in public.

"Will the party be crowded?"

"Probably. But it won't matter. I'll have you blindfolded, so you can get into your own space."

"I'm in good hands." He put his hand on my thigh, and slowly rubbed back and forth.

"Enough talking," I said. "Let's do it."

I held Mark close on our way to the party house. As we approached the three-story wooden building, we passed the neighboring gospel church. I pointed to a large, neatly lettered sign hanging adjacent to the church's front door. "Everyone Welcome. Something Good Is Going to Happen to You." It was a mere five feet from the party house. We laughed, and entered the house.

I checked us in. We both undressed, putting the bulk of our clothes in plain paper sacks and handing them to the attendant. Mark kept on a white jock and boots, as I had requested. I wore black leather shorts and combat boots. Mark disappeared into the small bathroom with a douche syringe in hand. Does he expect to get fucked tonight? I wondered.

It was my turn to use the bathroom. While pissing, I over-heard Mark introducing himself to one of the crew as a newcomer. "Oh boy, a virgin," was the reply. I hurried from the bathroom.

"Take the toy bag," I told him.

We went downstairs to the dungeon. The large, dimly lit room contained several bondage tables, a small jail cell, a rack, and several whipping stations. The music had just begun, raucous disco with an intimidating beat. "Shit!" I mut-tered. It would be difficult to maintain my own whipping rhythm and impossible to hear nuances in Mark's breathing. The air was warm, almost fetid. Even this early in the evening it smelled like a men's locker room; the carpeting gave up memories of past glories.

The few early arrivals scanned us with curiosity. I was proud to have a good-looking boy in tow.

We stopped before the seven-foot-tall cross. It was X-shaped, constructed from four-inch-wide wooden planks. Four heavy, shiny eyebolts protruded from its extremities. "This is it," I said.

Mark ran his hand over the rough wood and looked at me with a soulful gaze in his puppy eyes. "I've been waiting for this." He hugged me tightly.

I returned the hug. We savored the anticipation. I kissed him lightly on the lips and forehead, thought for a moment, and stepped back.

"Take off your jock," I ordered.

He obeyed. I opened my toy bag, pulled out a black leather jock with metallic studs, and held the pouch over Mark's nose and mouth. He inhaled deeply.

"I've worn this during important scenes," I said. "It's very special. I want you to have it for tonight."

He stepped into it and tightened the waist clasps. I put two matching biceps bands around his upper arms and a matching wristband on his right wrist. I stepped back and looked at him, and said, "You look sexy, leatherboy." Mark beamed, looked at his wristband, and ran his hand languidly over the jock pouch.

I knelt before my bag and removed two large carabiners. Each held a half-dozen whips by their hand straps. I placed the whips in a line to the left of the cross. "Feel free to touch these, to get to know them before we start," I said.

Mark picked up a long, red deerskin flogger. "That one has over fifty tails," I said. "Put these on." I handed him four black leather restraints.

He put them on his wrists and ankles while I finished fussing with my whips. I didn't unpack my four-foot single-tail whip, which looked like a short bullwhip. No sense in frightening him with that.

I tightened the restraints and led him to the cross. I had him stand spread-eagled, and secured his legs and wrists to the cross with short lengths of rope. I put a towel in the crotch of the cross in case he needed to rest his head. He sighed, smiled at me, and said, "Thank you."

I secured his thighs and waist firmly to the cross with flat red and black rope. He turned his head and watched my every move. He obviously had a hard-on.

I walked around the cross, looked into his eyes, and rubbed his crotch with my knee. "If you need anything, like water, or if you have to pee, or if the restraints are bothering you, let me know."

"Safe words?" he asked.

"Don't need them," I said. "I'll read your body language." I kissed him on the lips and put a fleece-lined leather blindfold over his eyes. "Have a great trip, boy."

He shuddered. I strode behind him and ran my hands softly across his shoulders and back, barely touching his skin. He was trembling. I gently massaged his legs and kneaded his shoulders. His breathing relaxed. I took my softest deerskin flogger and held the tails to his nose. He took a deep breath, and when I dragged the tails across his back, his entire body quivered, like a startled doe. His hard-on wilted. Beads of sweat coursed from his armpits, down his side, glistening in the shadows of his ribcage. I resisted the temptation to lick him dry.

Won't get very far tonight, I thought. But that's not what's it's about. We'll have a special time, wherever we go.

I lazily hit him with the flogger, first one shoulder, then the other, barely touching him. He tightened his back and shoulder muscles. "Breathe," I said. "Flow into it." I stood by his side and used my right hand for flogging, while my left hand caressed his back between blows. His skin was warm and yielding to my touch. He eased into his bondage, letting the ropes take his weight.

I moved behind him and the whip took on a life of its own, as I danced about his back, savoring the sight of him from every possible angle. I used one hand, then the other, as I covered his back with blows of slowly increasing intensity. I was floating, and he was becoming more comfortable with the sensations, stretching and arching his back.

I teased him by backing off, decreasing the frequency and lightening the blows, then gradually increasing to a higher peak than before. We played with this oscillating motion, until we reached a point where I was putting as much power as possible behind the whip.

I could hear him crying, despite the loud music. I flogged him until his weeping subsided, then mopped his brow and kissed him. "You're doing well, boy," I whispered.

I unloosened his wrist restraints and wrapped his hands around the cross at waist level. "You'll be more comfortable in this position."

Mark smiled and pursed his lips. I kissed him again.

I grabbed the large, red deerskin flogger and leaned against him, smothering his entire body with mine. I ground my crotch between his asscheeks, and he wiggled his hips. "This is your friend," I murmured as I stood back and dragged the whip sensuously across his shoulders, the tails lying flat. Then I let the tails dangle loosely, their tips lightly tap-tapping his skin as they danced around his back. Mark arched his back, the supple muscles undulating under his smooth white skin.

I began with a quick, light, figure-eight motion that gave the illusion of his back being completely covered by the heavy whip. Mark moaned and ground his crotch into the cross. He probably had a hard-on; I certainly did.

I swung the whip over my head to get more power into the blows. It landed with a resounding thud, and Mark flinched and shook his shoulders. "Come on, boy! You can take it, boy!" I shouted. "Yes, Sir!" he yelled back.

By this time a crowd of eight or ten men had gathered around our play space. A silent Greek chorus. I'm playing to the gallery, I thought. One man, obviously not encumbered with an overabundance of dungeon etiquette, inched his way into our scene to get a better view of Mark's back. I "accidentally" brushed him with the tips of the whip. He backed off.

Mark was sobbing.

"Go for it, boy," I commanded. "You're at the bottom of a filthy river. Swim through the mucky water to the light at the surface. Go for it!" I kept pelting him.

He clenched his fists and shook the cross with his writhing. The loud banging of the cross against the rafters drew a few more onlookers. His sobs turned to growls, and he collapsed into the cross.

I walked over to him and ran my fingers over his back. I blew on the glowing skin, and he melted into the ropes. Then I took a sip of water and squirted it onto his shoulders.

"Oh, Jesus," he mumbled.

In the background, Daddy Jim was working on his third or fourth boy of the evening, cycling through his repertoire of callused hands, paddles, and canes. The boy's shrieks played a strident counterpoint to the cacophonous disco music.

I laughed. "How are you doing, boy?" I asked Mark.

"Good," he sighed.

It was time for the heavy flogger, my old standby. I let Mark sniff it. He moved his head in small arcs, inhaling deeply, drawing in the aroma, trying to capture the essence of the leather. I dragged the tails across his back, letting them slide down to his butt. Then I gently swung the whip so that its tails curled up between his legs, with the tips caressing the front of his jock. He breathed heavily and arched his back. I continued for a few minutes, then knelt behind him, running my tongue over his smooth ass. He stuck his butt out and wiggled provocatively. I gave his bottom a few light slaps while squeezing his hard-on in the confines of his jock.

I stepped back and swung the whip in large arcs, pelting his back with none-too-gentle blows. He yelped, and I put my weight behind the whip. I felt I was stirring thick soup in a pot, churning it to a frenzy. Mark danced on his feet, as much as the bondage would allow.

I reached for the red whip. I used both whips in interlocking figure eights, covering his back with a moiré pattern of red and black as he squirmed and howled. I continued with a trance-inducing steady beat for a long time. Mark finally slumped against the cross, his head leaning on the towel. He was elsewhere. I thought, This is what S/M is about, a spiritual journey.

At last he raised his head. I placed a hand on Mark's shoulder. "I'm proud of you, boy."

"Thank you, Daddy." I put my thumb in his mouth. He sucked it while I used my other hand to flog him with both whips simultaneously. I struck him harder, and he sucked my thumb more wildly. I was getting hard again.

"I want you to take five, boy," I ordered.

"Yes, Sir."

"Count them out."

"Yes, Sir."

I struck. "One, Sir!"

I struck again, harder. "Two, Sir."

I backed up and used only the leather whip. "Aaaah, three, Sir!" he yelled.

I waited till Mark's breathing subsided. "Shit! Four."

"One more," I said.

I hit as hard as I could, almost flinging myself at him.

"Five."

I threw the whip into my case and went to him. "You're beautiful."

"Thank you, Daddy," he sobbed. We stayed frozen together for several minutes, until his crying subsided. I held a towel to his face. "Blow your nose." He did, and I wiped away the snot. I brushed his hair and offered him water. He nodded and took a quick gulp. "You OK?" I asked. "Yes, Daddy," he replied. "Let's keep going."

I shot a glance at two men, both tops, sitting quietly three or four feet away from Mark's head. They had been scrutinizing his face, watching every reaction. One gave me a thumbs-up sign.

I walked behind Mark and ran my fingernails down his back. He groaned and flexed his back muscles. I dug my nails in and pinched his skin. After a few light slaps, I chose a cat-o-nine tails that would produce a sharp, stinging sensation, in opposition to the thudding of the floggers. Its long, braided black handle was like a slightly flexible billy club. I placed it between Mark's asscheeks and worked it back and forth, rubbing his balls from behind. He let out a loud squeal, and arched his back.

I began with a light flick of the wrist, the tails just brushing his back. He moved his shoulders erotically in time with my strokes. I hit harder, backed off, and struck harder again. Mark was with me. We danced a beautiful *pas de deux,* in and out of misty trees. The whip flew from one hand to the other, overhand, backhand, in swirling arcs as his back muscles twitched and undulated. I was in a trance—the whips were an unconscious extension of me.

Welts appeared. I went to figure eights, fiercely striking each shoulder. I had been in Mark's position, and knew this hurt like hell. Mark was crying, his gulping sobs almost becoming screams. He dug his arms into the cross and shook it with his contortions. I had tears in my eyes, as well.

"Just a little while longer," I shouted. "Three, two, one," I counted, as I quickly landed three hard blows. I ran to him, and covered his hot back with my sweaty chest. I timed my gulping breaths to match his sobs. I didn't wait long, however.

This boy had traveled farther than any beginner I had played with. Nonetheless, I didn't think our trip was over.

"Now for the single tail," I whispered in his ear.

I kissed him on the lips. "Stand up straight, and don't arch your back," I told him.

I pulled out the four-foot whip and cracked it a few times. It sounded like gunshots. A half-dozen men hurriedly came to the perimeter of our small circle, probably hoping to see blood drawn during this uncommon scene.

I held the tail a few inches from the end and brushed it along Mark's back with a painting motion. He flicked his back muscles, as if trying to discourage a persistent fly. Then I took aim and made a few practice flicks, drawing closer to him. He flinched each time he felt the air movement from the whip. Finally it landed. "Fuck," he yelped. I gave him a few more of these, and said, "Here it comes." I let him have it. The whip landed full force, and I knew a searing pain would follow. He screamed. A comet-shaped dot appeared on his back. I stood perfectly still, hands hanging in front of me, holding the whip taut, hardly breathing, giving him a few seconds to recover. He tensed and relaxed. I gave him another heavy blow on the other side of his back. We alternated like this for a few minutes, until his back had ten dots on it. I went over to him.

"We're done," I said. "What would you like now?"

He didn't hesitate. "More."

Long red streaks were beginning to appear on Mark's back. I gave him a heavy stroke, just short of cutting the skin. The gallery was undoubtedly disappointed. "One more to even it up," I said. I paused, savoring the sight of this boy who had journeyed so far. Then I struck for the final time. He let out a primordial howl, rising from his gut to an ear-splitting crescendo, gradually decreasing to body-wrenching sobs.

I flung the whip into my case and wrapped my hands around his chest. My torso again melded into his back. I untied the ropes circling his waist and freed his hands and feet. I lowered the spotlight and whispered into his ear, "Hold onto me, and sit down."

We sat at the foot of the cross. "Keep your eyes closed," I directed, and slowly removed his blindfold. I held my hands over his eyes and said, "Slowly open."

He opened his eyes, blinking rapidly.

"Welcome back," I said, kissing the tears on his cheeks. He was trembling, and he smelled like a mixture of fear, transcendence, and relief. I wrapped him in towels and he curled in a fetal position, head in my lap. I caressed his dank hair for several minutes.

"We're going upstairs," I finally said.

"I need to pee real bad," he whimpered. I led him to the bathroom. As we passed through the kitchen, I noticed Brad talking to a small group of men. He grinned at me, nodded, and gave me yet another thumbs-up sign.

Mark and I climbed two flights of stairs to the living room. I wrapped him in a warm blanket, and we lay together, alone on a pile of bearskin rugs.

We lay in silence for a long time, arms and legs inter-twined. Finally, Mark opened his eyes and looked at me. "That was amazing. It was as if you were in my head. Every time I thought I couldn't take any more, you backed off, and then pushed me further. But I was afraid you were going to fuck me at the cross."

I smiled. Mark raised himself on one elbow and ran his fingers leisurely over my chest, from nipple to nipple. I purred and he kissed them. They hardened. He bit them, and my dick hardened. He grabbed my nipple rings and tugged while he ran his tongue along the center of my chest to my abdomen, lingering at my navel. I gasped and giggled. He pulled my shorts and jock down to my knees, his eyes searching mine. I breathed deeply and relaxed. He kissed my cock and took it in his mouth. He licked, slurped, bit, teased. To my surprise, he completely swallowed my long shaft. I began to thrust my hips, and Mark stopped and sat up.

He grabbed a condom and placed in on my dick. Using only his mouth, he completely unrolled it. He squatted over me and stuck his lube-coated index finger up his own butthole. Then he sat on my cock. His supple sphincter muscles grabbed and massaged my shaft as he slowly raised and lowered himself. It felt as if his butthole were giving me a blowjob.

I grabbed his nipples and pinched, none too gently. His long, firm dick twitched up and down. I spit on my hand and rubbed his shaft from base to tip in a slow circular motion, twisting my palm over the head with each stroke. He milked my shaft faster with his talented butthole.

I moaned loudly, raised my shoulders, and arched my back.

"Come in me, Daddy, come in me," he pleaded. "Make me your boy."

"I'm coming!" I screamed. I sat up and grabbed him tightly, biting his neck, thrusting wildly as his ass muscles tightened around my spurting dick.

At the same time, he humped my belly with short, jerky motions, as much as our closeness would allow.

"Come on, boy. Go for it! Squirt on Daddy's belly. Cover me with boy-cum," I shouted. I leaned back on my elbows, and Mark grabbed his dick. A few quick yanks and he erupted as only the young can, gobs and gobs of creamy liquid rising in a crescendo of arcs, landing on my belly, my chest, my chin.

"Oh, God, Daddy," he said. He leaned over me and rubbed his hands over my hairy torso, smoothing his cum into an even layer. He raised himself off my dick and lay beside me.

I put my arms around his shoulders and whispered, "I'd like to leave this collar on you."

Mark breathed deeply, clutched me tightly, and said, "Daddy."

"My boy," I sighed. Brad was right—I did need a boy. To hell with the high maintenance. It would be worth the effort.

For Hire: A Date with John

Sean Meriwether

Shiloh: The Other Size Queen

The door opens and he comes into your apartment. He is very tall and looks like a famous actor, though you can't remember which one. You tell a joke because you're nervous and you've never done this before, at least notwith him. He laughs, a deep rumbling that puts you at ease. He follows you to your bedroom and takes off his boots. His long feet are sculptures of flesh. You feel tiny next to him, but that's what makes him erotic; this is why you requested him. He will posses you, molest you as if you were a teenager. The proportions are correct. He smiles patiently when you attempt to tell him your requirements. He removes his clothes and folds them over the chair next to the bed. You take off your clothes and join him. You lie next to him and run your hands over his long legs. They are soft and warm. He says, What do you want to do? You tell him you want to be bent over his knee and spanked as punishment. He complies. You get hard as his meaty hand slaps your ass. He asks if you want him to fuck you. You do, but you wish he had just done it. He slips on a condom as you bury your face in the pillows, like when you were 15 and your older friends took turns with you. He is gentle, but you want him to be harder. You moan when he speeds up and you bite the sheet beneath your head. You relive the erotic torments of those older boys from your youth and splash the sheets with semen. The tall man behind you grunts and fills his condom. He rolls off your sweaty back. You watch him get dressed and slip the money into the pocket of his jeans. You show him to the door, absorbed in the odor of memory.

Aaron: The Suburban Hustler

The door opens and he comes into your home. This is the third time this month the two of you have gotten together. You joke that you must be supporting him by yourself. He laughs like a boy, with a blush and a dimple. You can't help but like him; he is someone who listens to you, who understands that you love your no-good boyfriend even if he doesn't want to have sex anymore. This boy says men need sex, it is true to their nature. He follows you to the bedroom and you take each other's clothes off. It is like the beginning of a relationship when the first thing you want to do is have sex, then talk. His hands are guided along your body as if he were reading your mind. He kisses you at all the right moments. You don't have to think or worry about anything, just your pleasure and his. It is all so easy and you think, This is how it is supposed to be. He is hung and this time you attempt to take it all. It hurts, but you feel more complete with him inside. Afterward, you lie in his arms, your boy-man, your lover, but the void remains. You want to explain this emptiness inside but you can't find the right words. You cuddle with him instead. He makes you feel like a horny teenager, that your desires are legitimate and should be addressed. You want your boyfriend to understand this, but you know he won't listen.

The boy in your arms understands; he cares about you and wants you to forget your problems. He is very sweet and intelligent and hung, and you can picture the two of you playing house together. You make an appointment for next week and miss him before he even leaves. You stand at the door and wave like a war bride as he drives away.

Bino: The Classic Eros

The door opens and he comes into your apartment. You assume he is of legal age but he looks like a boy, a mature boy. His hair is golden and you run your fingers through his long curls. He looks like a Renaissance painting done in warm oils. You pull him to you and hug him. He has a slight accent and it bewitches you because you can't place it. On impulse you pick him up in your arms and carry him to your bed. He laughs uncertainly. You put him down, strip off his clothes, and admire the androgynous beauty of his tight body. His chest is hard and developed, his ass is compact, each globe the right size for your hands. He falls onto your bed and rolls around, giving an occasional glimpse of his growing erection. His uncut cock makes you think of naked Greeks in the Olympics. He seems very comfortable in your sheets and you want to bind him up and keep him forever. You undress and lie in bed next to him. You roll him onto his stomach and massage his back. You wet your finger and slide it up into him. He moans in appreciation. When you screw him, he groans beneath you. He tells you to fuck him harder, but you are afraid of crushing him into the mattress. Too soon you are beyond worrying as you explode into him. You fall to the side, too exhausted to move. He stands next to the bed and looks like an angel with his tanned skin glowing, his halo of golden hair. He looks stronger than when he came in, more solid. When he leaves, with a handsome tip, you can't help but think you've seen him before and then you remember Donatello's statue of David. You agree that he too should be in a museum—your own.

Iseha: The Video Fantasy

The door opens and he comes into your living room. He is built and as graceful as a dancer. His lean body is carefully sculpted into curves and lines, a perfect specimen of man. You lick your lips and lead him to the couch. His voice is familiar and you remember him from that video you bought. You ask if that's him and he smiles. You compliment him on his capabilities, the way he used his body in particular shots. You have been watching a lot of black and Hispanic boy movies and now you have your fantasy in the room next to you. You ask him to top you, to order you around. He laughs a moment and you think you've said something wrong. Then he strips out of his tight pants and shirt. He wears nothing but a jock. He shoves his crotch into your face and orders you to suck it. He is loud while being pleasured and you worry about the neighbors, but his comments make you so excited you're afraid he'll stop. He tells you to take off your clothes. He puts on a condom and works a long finger up into you before replacing it with something much larger. You think of gang-boy gangbangs as he plows you. He stops. He says he doesn't normally do this, but would you like to have him? He says, How can I be a good top without being a good bottom? You are confused. He lies on his back and stretches his long, lean legs up into the air. You are distracted by what he offers you. You do him for a few minutes, but you don't feel quite right. You ask him to switch places. He finishes the job quickly. When he leaves, you pop in Love for Sale and watch the scene he is in three times. You think, he was just here, and you can't wait to tell your friends. They will be so jealous.

Jonathan: The Tourist Trap

The door opens and he comes into your hotel room. He is a little taller than you expected, but he is attractive in a bookish way. Even though you are horny, you can't get it up. You are nervous that the man at the front desk knows why this boy is here and you double-check the hall to make sure it's empty. He sits down on the bed, his long legs slanting away from his body. You ask him to do a striptease for you. He dances methodically, removing each article of clothing in timed display. He rolls his hips; your eyes scan the mobile mound in his shorts. Finally nude, he approaches and asks if you would like anything special. You tell him you want to suck him, but you mean to say you want to fuck him. He seems to know this, but it will not happen yet, not with forty-five minutes still on the clock. You bury yourself in a trimmed nest of pubic hair as he stands next to you, arms at his sides. Your ministrations wake his cock and it swells between your lips. When both of you are hard, you don't know how to ask him for what you want. You thought he would do whatever you wanted; that was why you invited him over. You think, He must be familiar with the unspoken needs of middle-aged men like yourself. The idea of other men's hands touching his young body excites you and you redouble your efforts to get him up to your level. You'd swear you are doing him better than anyone else who has come before because he tells you so. Maybe he will give you a discount. You finally penetrate him, with fifteen minutes left to the date. You blow your wad in five and it makes you feel sated and guilty. Keeping this secret from your wife makes you desperately hard again and you ask for another hour. He tells you he has another appointment, but can meet again tomorrow. You clear your schedule.

Johnny: The New New Yorker

The door opens and he comes into your foyer. You have to look up to meet his gentle eyes. He is well over six feet tall and thin like a boy should be. His height excites you in a way you did not expect. His voice is gentle and soft and you have to ask him to repeat himself because you keep missing what he says. He has a beautiful smile with even, white teeth. You take his surprisingly small hand and lead him to your bed and lay him across it. He doesn't fit; his long feet dangle over the edge. You remove his shoes and socks. Stripping away his clothes reveals that he wears no underwear, and you sniff the crotch of his jeans without a second thought. You blush. He reminds you of a Walton, innocent in a way that you have not seen in other men you have worked with. As he becomes erect, your attention is drawn to the massive column of flesh that stretches out across his tight stomach. Only a third of it fits in your mouth, but you give it your all. You want it to fill you up, but you are afraid it may break you in half. Take it slow, you tell him, as you lower yourself onto his shaft. Once it breaks the surface you absorb it inch by inch. It never stops. You can feel it in your throat. Your legs spread open as he burrows into you. The pain is exquisite and you see stars swim before your eyes. Then it draws back slowly. You thank god. As the pace increases you are equally full and empty and you can't even beat off because all your attention is on your overstimulated posterior. The boy beneath you flushes red as he pulls out and covers his body in white spurts. He pants as he jerks you off onto his stomach. You shoot across the room. You stare at his massive erection as it subsides and you cannot believe it was ever inside of you. You feel madly proud that you were able to take it. You kiss him tenderly as if you shared something significant and spend the rest of the hour marveling at the enormity the thin boy holds between his legs.

Niko: The New Economy

The door opens and he comes into your apartment. When he speaks he sounds slightly breathless, as if he ran to meet you. It fits in with your fantasy. He is wearing a business suit as requested. You have conquered Wall Street all day at work; now it's time to conquer it at home. You spend every waking moment in the testosterone swirl of the Financial District but are unable to act out your aggression with those co-suited men. Now you can bend down on your knees and bury your face in his wool-blend crotch. You tear open his zipper and pull his dick out and absorb it into your mouth. You picture the two of you doing this on the trading floor and all the other traders stopping to watch. You slip out of your pants and finger yourself. He tells you how good it feels, how hot you are. His sextalk makes you hotter. You bend over the back of your couch and tell him to fuck you with the suit on. He slips on a condom and fucks you with the frantic pace of the Dow. In your mind you are standing on the platform above the trading floor, ringing the closing bell for all it is worth. The men beneath you are naked, sucking and fucking in true bacchanalian fashion. You stop and change positions. On your back you can replace the sweaty face above you with those of the men who work side by side with you. Each one of them screwing you in succession. Oh, yeah, the man says, banging you with the dicks of a hundred men. You blow your wad and it splatters the coat of the man between your legs. You laugh gratefully and toss him a towel to wipe off. That was hot, he says. He tucks his jacket into his bag of toys and leaves you reeling from the ride. God bless the stock market.

Gucci
Michael V. Smith

I'm not saying it bothers me. It's not terrible, and it's not the end of the world, but why women? Yes, I was bored with the usual line-up of jeans and fat cocks parading through the park, the back room, the dungeon party, the police station, or wherever, and I was bored with my movies, bored with my books, bored with the pictures I either conjure up or buy. Bored. I bore myself in bed. Except lately. There are women there, in my mind, undressed, or with their skirts raised, knees wide apart, and my mouth doing things it's never done before. Women are suddenly getting me off. Is it purely the novelty? When I'm tired of pussy will I start fucking dogs?

Tonight, though, Brady and I are at the bar, in the basement, watching a stripper. We like this new guy; he's got tricks we haven't seen before. After that kid with the ornamental gourd some months ago, everyone's been putting a grocery list of products up their butts, from vegetables to canned goods to frozen fish. And lately it's "lubes with tubes" (our favorite being the neon-orange traffic cone two weeks back), but how interesting can that be after the first time? OK, the second or third. Once is a freak show, twice is an experiment. Three times, I say, is pure indulgence. The best you can get out of a crowd on the third strike is a weary "ho-hum."

But this guy—dimples as big in his face as those denting his ass—this guy's got a real talent. He's a showman. For one thing, he can dance; he's got moves I can't stop watching. The slick hair is in and out of his eyes, half-closed in a delirium I prefer to think is more erotic than narcotic. And his thighs, his naked thighs bump the wall behind him as if he were hip-checking the bar. The song is "Upside Down," which I have to admit is campy but not that hot, only I don't care, he's tasty. He's dangerously sweet.

"Who gets the front?" Brady whispers in my ear. He's grinning at me through his freckles. Manly freckles. Brady's got a thick neck, which makes him look more masculine than he is.

"You do," I say.

He chuckles. "I don't know. I'm not sure if he can handle me." He's leaning against my arm. I think I smell the joint in the front pocket of his jacket. "But you're right. We wouldn't want him to see your luggage..." Meaning my foreskin. Brady likes to say I got enough skin to make a set of Gucci luggage. "He might think you're moving in."

"Oh, fuck off," I say and push him away. "You've got no idea what I look like."

He crosses himself. "Thank God."

I don't know where he found it, but the stripper has one of those old bottles of Coke. Glass bottle with the cap still on. Full of pop. He stuffs it inside him, bottom first.

"You're just jealous that I, who is, am, who are, ten years your junior, am also unmutilated," I blather.

Brady's laughing at me. "Got a little bit flustered there, did we?"

I can only point. The boy on stage has successfully buried the Coke bottle completely up his ass, so that only the small round bottle cap is exposed, looking like a tin asshole. I think, Industrial Chastity Belt. No rear entry. Unless you have a bottle opener, which, casually, the stripper materializes from his mouth. Wish granted. I'm telling you, the honey's got a flair for fantasy. He's got magic.

I look around the crowd to see if others are getting him too, if they're noticing what he can do. Brady sees it; he's interested again. The guy to my left, with a belly the exact diameter of the cocktail table in front of him, has a hand in his pocket. He's focused, big-time. It's the guessing game of what will happen next.

Diana Ross sings her second chorus, and the stripper feigns boredom with the music. He shrugs and jumps off the stage. The Coke bottle doesn't budge. Naked, with a weak spotlight following him, he twirls his way to the emergency exit, light flaring off the bottle cap as he spins. He walks out into the street. He's naked, on a downtown sidewalk, with a bottle up his ass, as the bar door closes behind him. We're left alone with the music and the spotlight trained on a red Do Not Exit sign.

I smile at Brady and he returns the grin, which, I'm sure, means he too is wondering if the guy's coming back. And in how many pieces. His attention turns back to the door.

"You know," I say, taking advantage of the surprise element of this moment, "I'm gonna have sex with women."

Still watching the exit, Brady cocks his head. He might not have heard me. He could still be puzzling the fate of the stripper, but something in his demeanor says not. Then the door opens and our five-minutes-of-famer saunters back in — with a cigarette, lit, hanging low off his bottom lip. A couple of men clap. The stripper shakes his magic ass, which has, yes, still got its pop.

"You're just perverted," Brady hisses. When I notice his cheeks are red, burying some of the color from his freckles, I

wonder if he's kidding and flushed from the alcohol, or gen-
uinely pissed off.

"There are lots of bisexual people in the world, Brady."

"But are you bisexual? No, Mick. If you fuck women, it's
just perverted." He does sound angry. Then, as a guy in
overalls approaches the stage and hands our stripper a five-
dollar bill, Brady, thankfully, elbows me and laughs. "Kidding,"
he says.

Before I can respond, the dancer, on a beat, flips—*boom*—
onto his hands. Now the music makes sense. Upside
down—*flip*—you're turning me, you're giving love. The boy is
doing a handstand, triceps straining, ass clenched, and the
neck of the bottle perfectly upright. He's holding the opener
between his teeth, poised in such a way that it's clear to all of
us he's waiting for someone to step out of the crowd and pop
his cap.

Collectively, we pause. In shock, excited at the prospect
before me, I clutch at Brady's arm as he, the bastard, rises
from his chair. He's beating me to it. Whether deliberately or
not, Brady stands beside the boy so that the audience can still
watch as he slips the bottle opener from his teeth. The
dancer's face is growing ruby with the effort, but somehow,
he's still wiggling in time with the music. His hips sway, the
contents of the Coke jiggling at the neck. As Brady lifts his
arm to clutch the glass neck, the bottle rises four inches out of
the dancer's ass, then, like a near-miracle of anatomy, it
shrinks again, disappearing to the cap. He's swallowed the
damn thing. By sheer will, sucked it up again. My jaw drops.
Brady's hand remains where it was, hovering above the boy's
split legs. The man across the way has stopped tugging inside
his pants. We're stunned.

When Brady covers his mouth with his free hand, I know
he's got the giggles, which could be disastrous. *Don't ruin the
show,* I pray. I'm furious with jealousy, but he can't stop now

and spoil the momentum. The bottle slides back up, mechanically, as if it were a scene in a pornographic James Bond flick, and Brady pulls himself together. He's risen to the occasion. As he sets the bottle opener to the cap, I'm wet in my pants. I think I hear metal touching metal. And then there's a slow wet fizz hissing out as the cap drops to the ground and Coke sprays over Brady's face, down the boy's legs, and across the wall. A Coca-Cola ejaculation.

Brady dashes out of the way, lifting his shirt to wipe the spray from his face as he returns to our table. Coke still dapples his ear. "Clean yourself up, will you!" I snap.

"What's that, Mick?" He's all nonchalance.

"I hate you."

"Now don't be mean." He nearly sounds hurt, except that he's turned back to the stage. He's a glutton. Being part of the show isn't enough.

The boy has removed the bottle and righted himself. He's sitting splay-legged on the edge of the stage, holding his drink up to the spotlight like a frisky child in a commercial. I'm sure he's a hustler, though he's got this not-quite-corrupt look, as though he's taken the money but hasn't yet done anything to merit it. I love him. I want to have a body that can do those sorts of dirty tricks. Not that I would. Only think of the confidence I'd have, knowing I could draw anything in and out of my ass without hands.

Snapping his neck back, he tips the bottle above his head and pours. Straight down his throat. We see the Adam's apple bob. He swallows. As he's drinking someone in the back shouts, "I coulda had a V8!" but we aren't listening. We love this. This is real, the kind of real that takes you out of yourself for a while, that makes you special for having witnessed something others won't ever get to see. That's why you can't repeat a show successfully. They're only special once. If the audience knows what's coming next, the moment's killed.

When he drains the bottle, he tosses it to the big guy with the hand trapped in his pocket, and surprisingly, the bugger catches it. Everyone's a showman tonight. I wonder if the glass feels greasy in his palm. I wonder if it smells.

Diana's voice fades into the distance. Show's over. The stripper picks up his clothes as the bartender's voice comes over the crackling speakers. "Give a big hand for the original Coca-Cola kid, Mart-y."

There's a smattering of applause. We know the show was awesome, though nobody claps all that hard. They never do. I, for one, don't want to seem overenthusiastic. The private moment happening in your head between you and the stripper is sacred. A public display of what it meant to you is not cool. Only drunks show pleasure.

I look over to Brady, who's throwing me his best shit-eating grin. "I did good, didn't I?" he asks, waggling his eyebrows.

"You have no idea what that was, do you? You have just participated in the ultimate consumer experience," I say.

"It looked like a sex show to me."

I say the words slowly. "Low-brow. Transgressive. Product. Placement."

He blinks at me as if he has no idea what I'm talking about, then snaps himself lively, saying, "Hey, I got an idea. Can I buy you a Coke? Suddenly, I'm thirsty." He stands.

"You're not really getting a Coke, of all things, are you? You've got a full beer."

"I can't stand it any longer, I've got to ask him." Brady's looking round the room.

"Who? What?"

"Where'd he get that cigarette?" And with a quick pat on my back, he's gone.

Now Brady loves to say he doesn't pay for sex, he's too good at it to need to, but still, I'm a wee bit jealous. What if he does go home with the stripper? It's not unheard of. Strippers have feelings too.

I'm not saying I'm in love with Brady; I'm not. Let me make it clear, I am not in love with Brady. Hell, I dated Tori for years and still can't say what love is, exactly. I've been a mite bit clueless. Two years of living together, and I didn't even know Tori was a woman. Finding out after the fact that your ex-boyfriend is transgendered, your boyfriend was a girlfriend in his own mind —well, it puts a strain on an individual. It's like finding out your husband was a Nazi, or a serial killer, without the bodies. What I'm saying is, it's a shock to the system. Suffice it to say I have yet to absorb the full impact. So, love Brady?, no. But there's a possibility, I'll admit, that something more is going on. With me. It's kind of puzzling on my part, which isn't new. I've got a tired habit of getting curious about friends who are better left as friends.

It's the same for all of us. We get to wondering what he looks like naked, then boom, next time you're both watered to the gills, you're grabbing his dink at the urinal. He usually likes it, or, let's say, shows appreciation, until the next morning when he's sobered up and either you have a big ugly talk about boundaries where he says he needs his space or he cooks you an amazing breakfast and later doesn't return your calls. Which is fine, because you've followed the pattern so often it's what you expect and, by now, it can't hurt you.

Thankfully, that hasn't happened to Brady and me, due to a new approach I've taken regarding friends and relationships: Don't get your hopes up and you won't get involved. So I'm cautiously not in love with Brady, and I'm not curious about him either.

He returns to the table, grinning. "You'll never guess what I just saw."

"His dink."

He turns his chair toward me and leans forward for a complete confession. "More than that," he says excitedly.

"What did you do?"

"Nothing," he says, sounding offended. "I couldn't find him, that's all, so I go to the can to relieve my dingle and here are these two guys talking. And I don't recognize him because he's got his clothes on now."

"You are so shallow."

"No, he's got his back to me, so, you know, there's nothing to recognize. Anyway," he flaps his hands in front of him, giggling and scrunching up his face, "you *won't* believe this," he says, his voice sounding both excited and horrified. "I thought he was just standing there talking, he's with that guy who caught the bottle, they're standing real close at the urinal. Well, when I got closer, I peeked. The stripper was pissing into the Coke bottle. The big guy had the bottle in one hand and a twenty in the other. No big deal, right? Who knows what he wants it for, but I'm a nurse, I see piss in cups all the time. Well, before I can finish up— OK, I haven't even been able to start, I'm too distracted—the big guy hands the twenty to the kid and *takes a sip*."

"Brady!"

"I'm telling you it was gorgeous. I'd have pissed my pants if I hadn't had my dick out already."

"So did they leave together?"

"No. The big guy left but the kid had filled the bottle and had to stop, right, so he's still got more to pee. I guess that Coke goes right through you. He turns to the trough and I'm telling you, I couldn't resist, I had to ask." He pauses for dramatic effect.

"What?"

"Where he got the cigarette."

"Oh. And?"

"He says to me, 'A cop,' and grins."

"No way."

"Well, it's a joke, of course, so I laugh. And then I got one. A line. I look at him and ask, 'Do you want to tell me the truth now, or are you gonna keep it all bottled up inside you?'"

I gasp, "You didn't."

He only laughs, squeaking, as he holds his chest from the effort.

"I can't believe you. You're shameless."

"Oh, you'd do the same thing."

"I wouldn't dare."

"Well, that's why I'm a lot of fun," he says patronizingly, "and you're the ugly-can't-get-a-date-stepsister." I sneer. He continues, "Now listen, I got a real close look at our friend Mart-y, and I've figured out what makes him look more virginal than he is."

"What's that?"

"Makeup. Maybe you could try some to help you with your little problem."

"Very funny."

Brady gets all serious again and says, "I should get his phone number."

"Why?"

"So you can call him and get some Mary Kay tips, dearie." Times like this, I have to remind myself that Brady really cares or he wouldn't say such nasty things. Cruelty is a skill you acquire to protect a soft heart, and when shared with friends, being bitchy is no more than a skin-thickener. We're dogs, play-fighting.

When the stage lights come on again, I'm glad for the distraction. Brady slaps his hands together and rubs them. "Here we go."

"I don't know if I've got it in me for another one," I say. "Not to sound boring."

"But you are, Blanche, you are," he says, quoting *Baby Jane,* which I've never seen. That sort of camp shows your age. I'm about to tell Brady as much when the speakers crackle to life and "I Just Called to Say I Love You" fills the room. The next guy is a blonde, which I like. He has a phone, with a receiver in his hand. You don't need to have someone draw you a diagram to know what's coming. "Oh, no," I say, not hiding my fear.

Brady's got a similar pained expression. "Doesn't look good. There's only one thing to do." He taps the corner of his mouth with his pinkie, a gesture that has somehow come to mean that he's hungry for sex.

"You want to go to the park."

"Well, now that you mention it, I *could* get some fresh air."

"Oh, Brady," I say. I'm not interested in following him there. I like it fast and dirty — just not tonight.

"Now, Mick, I'm not going alone."

I point to my chest. "Tired."

"I've got a doobie," he whispers, leaning over the table, which only draws attention from the weirdoes beside us, "and I only smoke half a doobie and that means I need someone to help make sure I don't smoke the whole doobie and you're my friend so you're going to smoke the other half."

"No."

He leans back, as if shocked. "Don't make me slap you in front of all these nice people," he says, maternally.

That's enough to convince me. "OK, but I'm not staying late." I say this every week, though my intentions are good.

He's already standing, slipping his arms into his jeans jacket. He gulps back a couple more swigs and leaves some behind.

Onstage, the blonde has his balls twisted in the white spiraling phone cord. I sigh inside, dying a little with each tired act. I'm afraid the Coca-Cola kid isn't even enough to save me from a night of unsuccessful masturbating. I'll be re-creating my women-driven fantasies. I can't help but suffer from a twinge of guilt, knowing I don't do girls in real life. Maybe I could beat off thinking of Tori. Middle ground, though we haven't had sex since she's come out as trans. Although her body might not be any different, her technique may have changed. Can I picture that? Does a fantasy life answer to morals, or is my guilt simply fucked up? I'm telling you, sex isn't easy, even in my head.

"Are you with me here?" Brady asks.

We're on the street, moving at a good clip toward the park. There are two bright stars to my right, and the rest of the sky is cloud. I sniff. "Yeah, yeah, I'm thinking."

"Don't strain yourself."

"I'm thinking about my marriage."

"Why, honey, I didn't know you cared," he gushes, wrapping an arm around my shoulder.

That's not funny, and I realize, as fast as Brady popped the cap off that bottle, that he's hurt me. I cover up by saying, "I mean my ex," and slap him on the arm to behave.

"But, you know," he says, "I don't want to be married. I did that." He's more serious now, I can tell, because he has a hand in his pocket digging for matches. Brady's most down-to-earth moments happen while he's smoking a joint. The edge comes back as soon as he splits the last stub of the roach between his fingers and offers you half to eat.

"Not to sound shallow," he says, "but after my ex, Ronnie, died, I started having sex again, and I'll tell ya'," he chuckles, making his voice rise and pitch, "it feels might-y good." He flicks open the lid on his lighter. The butane tickles the hairs in my nose.

"Did you and Ronnie break up before he died?"

"Yeah, the day before," he says dryly.

"No, really, Brady, were you not together when it happened?"

"I was in the can taking a dump," he says. He's so damn hard to pin down, sometimes I could choke him.

His voice gets an apologetic softness to it. "No, we were still living together and everything, though he was bedridden a long time. I just call him my ex 'cuz it's easier than explaining every time what happened. Nobody wants to hear your husband died of AIDS. It puts a real damper on the date."

He passes the joint. "I don't want to do that again. Ronnie was great, mind you, but you can't trust fags. They're always running around and lying, telling you they love you when they don't, and telling you they hate you when they do. There's no figuring them out. I've given up. That's why I have family. Right, my ugly-can't-get-a-date stepsister?"

"Honestly," I say before I can catch myself, "is that how you feel?"

"Honestly?" He makes his head wobble as if he were spinning from the neck up.

"Come on."

"Sure. Sure, that's how I honestly feel."

Strolling into the cruisy part of the park, he offers me a stub of the joint. "Give you a bit of a body-high later." This is the part of our routine where we chew the last bit of paper and pot and make plans for morning brunch. Tonight, everything's dark from the cloud cover. The trees are solid black, like paper cutouts. And the men moving ahead of us, strolling the laneway, are solid masses. There won't be much scrutinizing going on. Brady calls this a "Veronica Dumont night," meaning VD. You can't see what you're getting.

"Well," he says, "time for the meet 'n' greet. It was nice knowing ya'." He extends a hand as if he wants to shake. Not our usual thing.

I clutch my heart. "Are you leaving me for good?" I say, all melodrama.

"You couldn't get so lucky." He squeezes my shoulder, since I haven't taken his hand, and then he's off, into the bushes, leaving me to wander alone. I'm no more in the mood now, even with a buzz coming on, than I was when I started out tonight, but for argument's sake I head for my usual spot, behind the big tree trunk encroaching on the walkway. There's a narrow path into a clearing where it's very dark. The less I can see, the easier it is to fantasize, and the quicker I get off. Job done, "Buddy, can you drive me home?"

I'm there only ten minutes, getting colder, when I decide to warm my hands up by masturbating. I hate the way men jump as if they've been cattle-prodded if you touch them with frozen fingers. My cock, your cock, it's all the same temperature, so I think, What better way to keep 'em toasty? Unfortunately, I have more hands than dick, so my pecker grows colder than my hands warm up. I'm ready to go home, be miserable, and fall asleep when a dark outline pushes through the pine branches. Three feet away from me, I see who it is and whisper, "Gucci," to warn him it's me. I'm shy down here, I don't talk loud enough. He's unbuttoning the fly to his jeans. "Gucci," I say a little louder, but whether he hears me or not, he opens his palm toward me. I step forward, knowing that tomorrow morning will surely hurt, hoping that this time, tonight will be enough.

Gymnasty

Jesse Grant

Real jocks don't watch gymnastics.

But there was something about the pommel horse. It turned me on. I had no idea why. I didn't even know how to use it. In fact, I didn't even know what using it was called. Did you pommel it? Did you ride it? Did you play on it? What?

Not that I'd ever seen a pommel horse up close and in person. My tiny Midwestern farm community high school didn't have a gymnastics team, not even for the girls, so my experience with the accoutrements of the sport was limited to clandestine television viewings of the Olympics and other major competitions.

I remember being left home alone one Saturday afternoon in the summer of my twelfth year. The Olympics were on television, and I tuned in, hoping to watch more of the swimming. My parents and I had been watching the games religiously since the opening ceremonies, and one of the backstrokers had caught my developing eye. Now that no one else was home, I planned to tune inand turn on, and jack off while my shaved, muscled, scantily clad hero raced to glory.

Needless to say, I was profoundly disappointed to learn that the swimming events wouldn't be aired until evening, by which time my parents would have already returned home. I was even more profoundly disappointed to learn that instead of swimming or track or basketball or some other *real* sport, the network would be airing men's gymnastics.

I reached for the remote to click off the set, planning to head down the street and search for a baseball game, when the camera panned a row of gymnasts performing their warm-up exercises. What bodies! What faces! And check out the bulging crotches! I decided to watch, just for a few minutes, telling myself that no one would know and that this was the Olympics so it was OK anyway.

Real jocks don't watch gymnastics.

But I did watch. I watched and watched and watched. And every time they showed a competitor on the pommel horse, I got lightheaded. I don't remember pulling down my pants and jerking off, but I do remember wiping ribbons of sticky white cum off the television screen.

My swimmer god had been replaced by a newer, better fantasy.

Years later, I was in the university's secondary gym, running up and down the bleachers to strengthen a knee still weak from surgery. I was feeling depressed because the rest of the baseball team was in Florida on a six-game road trip against the top squads in the nation, and John Allensworth, my least favorite person, was playing center field—*my* position—while I recuperated. Allensworth wasn't a bad player; he was just an asshole. Not to mention the fact that he was somehow convinced he should be the starter instead of me, even though I was Team Captain and Conference MVP two years running.

I hadn't done a wash in nearly two weeks. I didn't have a road trip to go on, so I didn't see the need...or couldn't work up the energy...or whatever. When I left the dorm I'd grabbed a sweaty jock, a dirty T-shirt, and an old pair of baggy but clean gym shorts and thrown them into my bag. In the locker room, though, I didn't have the heart to put on dirty clothes. Instead, I just pulled the clean shorts over my naked ass and walked out commando-style.

But I digress. The point is, I was depressed. So depressed, in fact, that instead of running stairs in the main gym, which was filling with people, I'd retreated to the empty secondary gym used by the gymnastics team.

At least I *thought* it was empty.

I'd just finished fifty trips up and down the bleachers and was sweating like a glass of iced-tea on a muggy summer day. Each trip up I pictured Allensworth playing center field, hitting lead-off, stealing my glory. His image angered me, and that anger carried me to the top. Each trip down, I coasted and checked out the gymnastics equipment, feeling my cock harden as I did; without a jock on, it had plenty of room to roam.

What the hell, I decided. I walked from the bleachers to the center of the gym. I wanted to try a cartwheel or a flip or something on the floor exercise mat, but I was worried that I'd reinjure my knee. I walked to the rings next, and pictured myself losing my grip and landing awkwardly on my bad leg. I circled the gym, gazing at but not touching the equipment, ending at my destination all along: the pommel horse.

My dick was rock-hard and throbbing, tenting my shorts to the point where even a blind man would have noticed. I didn't care, though, since I was alone in the gym. I walked the length of the pommel horse, running a finger along its leathered edge, stopping at one end. I gripped it on either side and slid my hands back and forth as if I were jacking the biggest man alive—the Jolly Gymnastic Giant. Entranced, I slid a hand into my shorts and used my pre-cum to slowly masturbate. I rested my head on the horse, inhaling its deep scent of leather and powder and gymnast sweat. In an instant, I was on the verge of coming.

I pulled my hand from my shorts and licked my palm and fingers for extra lube and also because I like the taste of my cum and my spit mixed together. A few quick yanks and I'd have my favorite treat to eat. I reached behind with my other hand to plunge it into my shorts and down the crack of my ass so that I could tease my hole while I came.

"Excuse me," said a voice from behind, startling me and simultaneously making me thank my lucky stars that whoever the voice belonged to had spoken before I'd started fingering my ass. As I spun around to face the intruder, I realized that even though he hadn't seen me finger my ass, he'd almost certainly seen me nuzzling and sniffing the pommel horse while stroking myself to a near-explosion. I also realized that even if he'd somehow missed my jerking off, there was no way he wouldn't notice the eight-inch erection pointing directly at his face. "I need to do some work on the rings," he said, "and I was wondering if you would spot me."

I mumbled something unintelligible, like "Ungh."

He pointed to the rings, as if to clarify. "The rings. I was wondering if you could spot me?"

I tried to push my boner to the side so that at least it wouldn't be sticking straight out, but it wouldn't obey. It gets that way—pointing like a mushroom-capped divining rod—when it sees something it wants. And oh my, did it ever want the little fucker standing in front of me. Dirty blond hair cropped close to the skull, deep blue eyes, skin like cream, tight shorts, no shirt, and the perfect gymnast body.

"You just stand behind me and put your hands on my waist and then lift me so I can grab them," he said. "The rings." He pointed to them again.

"Um, sure," I said, regaining a modicum of composure.

He walked to the rings, followed by my dick and then me. He stood under them, facing away from me. "Just put your hands on my hips," he said, "and then lift when I jump."

I put my hands on his hips, positioning them to cop a feel on the way up.

"That's good. But stand a little closer."

Any closer and my tent-pole prick would be poking his delicious little ass.

When I hesitated, he reached behind with both hands, grabbed me, and pulled me closer.

Prick. Poke.

"Yeah," he said. "That's better." He looked back over his shoulder with a grin. "On three, OK?"

"Yeah, on three."

He wriggled his ass against the tip of my hard-on.

I gasped.

He looked over his shoulder again, still smiling.

I'd been wanting to plant my dick in a gymnast's bubble butt for eight years, and here this grinning dollop of honey was practically begging for it.

"One..."

I formulated a plan.

"Two..."

I hooked my thumbs into the elastic of his shorts.

"Three."

He went up. His shorts came down.

He settled into an iron cross position, his body a perfect T, his shorts halfway down his thighs. A jockstrap covered his cock but not his ass. He held the iron cross, the most difficult position in gymnastics, without wavering, despite the fact that I'd depants'd him.

I circled to the front where he could see me. Once there, I flashed my own mischievous grin.

"How do I look?" he asked. Straining to hold the iron cross, the muscles in his arms and shoulders and neck bulged and fought as if each wanted to be the most prominent, the most noticed. The tip of his hard-on poked out from the top of his jock.

"Good," I answered. "Damn good." I pulled his shorts the rest of the way off.

He responded by lifting and spreading his legs. I'd seen a hell of a lot of guys lift and spread, but never with such grace and power. And I'd never seen a hole like this one. So clean. So tight. So perfect. A little cherry waiting to be plucked and fucked. And the fact that his cock was still hidden in his jock—except for the tip, another little cherry—made his tiny ass pucker even sweeter-looking.

I stepped under him. "Lower yourself."

He obliged, stopping at the appropriate spot.

I nuzzled into his crotch, licking and sucking on first one and then the other of his medium-sized, cotton-encased balls. As I did, he lowered his legs and rested them on my shoulders so that he was still hanging from the rings but was partially supported by me. (I couldn't expect him to hold himself up forever, could I?) When he was settled, I worked my way up his cock, tonguing and gently gnawing the fabric of his jock and his bone-hard six-inch shaft, soaking the thin cotton with my spit.

I paused and looked up at my prey. His eyes were glazed over, his pecs were heaving, his abs were so hard and rippled I could have used them as a washboard. (I certainly had enough dirty laundry.)

He looked down after a moment, and when his eyes finally focused I licked the middle finger of my right hand, looking him directly in the eyes, and then, still looking him in the eyes, pushed it into his hole in a very ungentlemanly fashion.

Judging from his "Oh, yeah!" exclamation and the instant bubble of pre-cum that materialized on the cherry red head of his dick, he enjoyed the intrusion.

I smiled, then went back to work, licking and sucking the wide elastic of his jock where his pre-cum had dribbled down. His juice was salty-sweet—not brackish like some guys'—and I savored his flavor, licking, licking, licking my way to the head of his cock. His was a small knob, not as big around as his shaft, bisected directly in the center on the underside. Circumcised. The dick of the Boy Next Door. I tongued his glans, driving my tongue into his piss slit, all the while fingering his slick little fuckhole and teasing his perineum.

I could tell the tension in his nuts was building, by the movement of his thighs wrapped around my face. At first, there were slight contractions of his quadriceps and hamstrings. As I worked his cock and hole longer and harder, though, the contractions intensified. And when I drove a second and then a third finger up his chute, he slammed his legs together, bulging muscles clamping around my head and drowning out all sound except the pumping of blood to the tensile steel of his legs, ass, and cock.

I dropped my mouth back to his now-rock-hard balls, still encased in cotton wet with spit, then he began to chant, "Oh yeah! Oh yeah! Oh yeah!" like a Hindu prayer mantra. And then his ass muscles clamped on my three fingers and he yelled, "I'm coming," announcing it just as the first volley shot up and out of his cockhead like a pop fly, only to plummet downward and land with a fat splat on my cheek. As he continued to shoot, I worked my fingers hard against his straining tunnel, finding his joyspot, which led to a second moonshot that landed on my face very near the first. After that, he burbled over, soaking the mesh of his jock with fresh, sweet cum.

I pulled my fingers from his ass and lowered him to the ground, wondering if he would be one of those collegiate closet cases who's all hot and bothered until he blows a load and suddenly decides he's straight.

He wasn't.

Lying on his back on the landing mat with his legs spread, he said in a voice far too low and husky to be emanating from his boyish mug, "Fuck me, Slugger. Fuck me hard with that big bat of yours."

His use of the words "slugger" and "big bat" led me to wonder if he knew that I played baseball, perhaps even knew my name. With my dick throbbing and dripping, though, I hardly cared.

"Fuck me like a Mark McGwire home run," he said. "Fuck me like a Roger Clemens fastball. Fuck me like—"

"You talk too much."

I dropped to my knees and shoved eight fat inches of man-meat into his mouth and down his throat to shut him up. He took it easier than any cocksucker I'd ever been with, covering his teeth like an expert and creating an exquisite suction the likes of which I'd never experienced. His tongue danced and twirled on the underside of my shaft like Kurt Thomas on the floor exercise, and he toyed expertly with my nuts as they bounced off his baby-smooth chin.

So many guys I'd been with just made a big "O" with their mouth and bobbed up and down, and so many others choked when they tried to deep-throat me. But not my little gymnast. His mouth made love to my cock like no other mouth before or after. He took me to the edge of ecstasy and held me there for long minutes.

As I plowed my groin into his face, I reached behind and played with his nipples, at first just brushing at the nubs, then pinching and pulling. He wriggled underneath me, enjoying the tit torture. The harder I pinched and pulled, the better he sucked me off. Finally, just as I was about to blow, he pushed me away. "I wanna get fucked," he said, echoing his earlier request.

"Yeah?"

"Yeah, baseball stud, I want that big home-run club up my tight little hole. I want you to—"

"Over here," I said, pointing to the pommel horse.

He followed willingly, and I shoved him against the apparatus. He grabbed the raised handles, spread his legs like Bill Buckner fielding a grounder in the World Series, and braced for my attack.

I hadn't been gentle with him at any point so far, and didn't feel the need to start now. I lined up the fat, pre-cum-slicked head of my rod with the rosebud pucker of his ass and pushed in fast and hard. His chute was still lubed from my spit-covered fingers, and I slid in nearly to the hilt, though not without resistance. "You like that?" I asked.

He moaned, in part ecstasy, part pain. I pulled nearly out, enjoying the sensation of his silken ass chute gripping the tender skin of my cock, then plunged forward, banging my low-hanging balls off his tight-to-the-shaft nuts and grinding my tangle of bush into his ass crack. "You like that?" I asked again. But I didn't wait for an answer. Instead, I launched into an all-out fuck, hammering his hole like Sammy Sosa hitting off a tee.

As soon as I had established a rapid pounding pace, I reached around and felt for his cock, still in his sticky-wet jock. He was rock-hard again. Instead of jerking him off, though, I stretched the wide elastic away from his midsection as far as it would reach. And then let go.

Snap!

"Ohhhhh, God!" he yelled as his ass clamped down mightily on my rapidly swelling rod, temporarily stalling my invasion.

But I was not to be deterred. He'd begged to be fucked, and fucked he would be. I slammed forward so quickly he banged his forehead on the pommel horse hard enough to leave a welt.

I regained my rhythm and my hand returned to his cock, this time for gentle stroking to bring him near the edge, to leave him teetering at the brink, to tease him with my fist as he'd teased me with his throat. But when he cried, "Again! Please! Again!" I obliged. I couldn't resist.

Whap!

This time I was ready for his ass clamp, and fucked right through it.

"Yes," he yelled. "Again! Again!" And the sound of his voice—begging, demanding, completely insane with lust—nearly set me off for good.

"One more like that," I said, "and I'm gonna fill your pretty little boy-butt with a great big load of spunk."

"Oh, yeah. Give it to me, Slugger. Give it to me."

I pulled the elastic of his jockstrap away again, this time even further than the previous two pulls. And then a devious, delicious, delightful thought crept into my sex-crazed brain. I lowered the strap ever so slightly, changing the trajectory on which it would snap back to his groin.

Crack! Right on the nuts.

"Uhnnnh!"

And then we both were coming like only two highly conditioned athletes can come. My swollen eight-inch rod shot big bullets of cream up his red-hot tunnel. His six-inch cloth-encased pistol spit rapid raindrops of white onto the mat below. (On the way out, we spotted a droplet a good ten feet from where we'd been standing—and this was his second orgasm.)

When the waves of sensation subsided, we collapsed to the cum-splattered mat, my cock still up his ass. After a moment, he started to giggle.

"What?" I asked.

"I've always wondered what it feels like when a pitcher gives up a home run. And now I know."

"Oh, yeah?" I said. "Well, I've always wondered what using a pommel horse is called. And now I know."

"No, you don't."

"Yes, I do," I said. "It's called fucking."

He laughed so hard that my softening cock slipped out of his ass. No matter. I shoved it back in later that night.

Knot of Roads

D-L Alvarez

1.

The hometown is a knot of roads. Each road knows some popular music, country or R&B, to generate excitement, ease the pain, or any other clichéd excuse to drink and drive and drive and drive: always ending up back where you started, the pit you were born to. I was guilty of seventeen years of hating my fellow townsfolk and their dim routines. They were an insufferable dust, making the air unbreathable. For years I plotted and attempted Houdini routines, tried to escape those labyrinthine knots, their tight, cramped curves, their boomerang hex. The corroded husks of factory work gathering round my ankles. Forever restless, unwilling to accept my class or circumstance, I eventually committed the greater crime of getting blood on my hands in the rush to perform one of the many rehearsals for running away.

The blood belonged to a proverbial passing stranger, a light-skinned black man named Clarence, who promised a sure split in the cradle of his gold-specked Coronado. That didn't pan out. The two of us only got so far before we were arguing like lovers. In less than twenty-four hours there were threats and a roadside scuffle in which we both fought like girls, or worse actually, clawing and desperately searching the vicinity for weapons to add to our attack. I threw a flattened milk carton at him and missed, then hit him in the face and cut his lip with the pull-tab from a pop can I wore as a ring. He pulled up some weeds, roots and all, and lashed at me with it, getting dirt in my eyes. Eventually I ran off down the highway and hitched a ride back home, the twists of road doling out their miserable curse once more. It wasn't until the driver asked if I cut myself that I noticed the blood at all, Clarence's blood, speckling the back of my right hand. I had never injured a man before, save for the roughhousing my brother and I got into. It felt like both a badge and a scarlet letter.

What inspired the violence?

The same mischief that threw passion, an oil slick, in our path.

Before Clarence promised me a ticket, before he ever spoke a word and so, before I knew he had a name—when he was just the perfect stranger—he taught me all about his insides behind the same gas station where I was that week employed.

And once I knew his interior, I was fooled into believing that getting near to a heart was the same as entering one. Some dark tissue, like a fist around liquids, it sent its dull music to my fingertips. Now that I know the truth, that one's heart is not a vault but a throughway, I'll spare the hurt feelings, and get right to what everyone wants to hear: the sex.

It's a cheap seventies blue movie, moving too frequently out of focus. One actor has a grease smudge on his neck just behind his ear, the other is obviously a model looking for extra work. Action is dull and predictable: one position, an unvaried rhythm until the money shot, which is not a money shot, since the actor—a lug—never pulls out.

I was working at this gas station for the same reason sad-faced girls worked in pet stores; I just looked like I belonged there. I didn't know much beyond the basics under the hood, but my acne-scarred face and dumb stare were exactly what you wanted to find through that film of soapy water on your windshield. It was a comfort: the drawl, the good service filtered through a glaze of cheap pot, my wiry frame that one could easily picture in the act of screwing a cousin, male or female, and not even having the sense to clean up after or feel the least ashamed. Anyway, that's what Clarence's eyes told me, even before he took off his glasses.

His eyes told me what I should be, and I followed instructions because, as you've probably figured out by now, there was nothing better to do. I called him Sir, scratched my prick as if it were just some dumb habit my dirty hands got up to of their own accord. He drove away but wouldn't get far; sometimes the knots work in your favor. At closing I saw him pull up to the pumps. He'd gotten a full tank an hour before so I just made it easy on him, stuck my head through the open passenger window, flashed dumb eyes (maybe he knew it was an act, in which case he overestimated me—it was half an act; either way, the ends were all the same), and said, "We're closed now, but if you wanna pull round to the back, I'll have a look at it."

Of course I'm acting smug in hindsight, but the truth is my heart was going a million miles an hour. I was ninety percent sure he was queer, but at the last minute the remaining ten percent started voicing its opinion. What was the worst that could happen? He could whack me over the head with a tire iron and clean out the till, all on my invitation. After all, that would be another reason to come back to a business at closing time.

Doesn't matter, didn't happen. The breeze moved the black silhouettes of trees around. He cleaned out all the fast food wrappers from the back seat.

I washed my hands with a gritty pink soap. If there were any noises, which there must have been—cars on the highway, the two of us breathing—in my mind they all went dead for a long time. Sensation pushed all sound out, or the ability to recognize it as sound. Same difference.

His eyes quivered out a little Morse code as I stood there watching him watch me: "Be dumb as shit, dot, dot, dash…be an unthinking blanket that nearly smothers me…." It wasn't really my style, but maybe for a short time I could pretend enough to keep him worried and happy. I kept silent; words would ruin any illusion. Instead, all the language went into holding my shoulders slack, and furrowing my brow when he finally got up the nerve to touch me: a worried look followed by a half-hearted smile. Eventually all our gestures, his and mine, were pointing to the same thing. It was as if we were both just marionettes, and the puppeteer was somewhere up his ass. He kept accommodating the act: lying back on the vinyl seat, spreading his legs in the door frame, dressing my prick in spit, coaxing me inside…and I just went there; bent over him for a while, the soft fabric on the ceiling of his car brushing my neck, and then suddenly aware that the weight of everything I sensed and thought was radiating from the gut of another human being. There was a dim consciousness, like a camera inside my skull, watching the whole thing take place. But the greater awareness was liberating him of focus, reaching into a colorful darkness. His eyes were rolled back and his breathing was dictated by my thrusts. The cabin of the vehicle held us in a space where otherwise gravity was slipping. We were ourselves tissue in a chamber, mechanisms exchanging energy and oxygen.

I was not alone in this observation. Later he told me that he could feel himself disappear into the rhythm of the fuck, and how the smell of grease, which was all over me, filled his lungs until he believed he'd merged with machine. My tinkering about had transported him, made him automotive (his fantasy was that I was an auto mechanic, and I took care never to burst this illusion).

Once I came (won't try to lasso that moment with words) he wouldn't let me leave him: physically tightened around me and held me inside. We lay there, gravity reclaiming its position beneath us, sounds turned on again—a television at full volume from the house next door, something like a tractor engine in the distance (though we were not near the country)—his breathing and mine synched up into a slow pulse. The stars tilted. Gangs of boys and packs of dogs passed by. Morning slipped around us unnoticed. The day passed and our bodies lay undiscovered. More days passed and spiders covered us in a sticky lace, rats ate our feet, birds made nests in the crooks of our arms. The gas station went out of business and was eventually torn down. An arcade was built in its place that did well for a few years but, when the center of town moved north, it folded. The lot was deserted for a long while, until one day they built another gas station exactly like the one that had been there years before. All this time I was inside him.

I fell asleep in there, woke up in there: another hard-on, another grin on his face—or maybe it was the first. Yes, I think so, because it was the grin that made me really see his whole face, and not just certain features.

A smooth but busy face: the eyes thinking, nostrils flared, then relaxed, you could see his pulse at his temples, brown freckles on a Dijon-mustard skin, a clean, soft skin that looked as if it were pampered with products, perfect teeth, and good haircut. No one who lived here looked like that.

"Take me the hell away from this place."

It wasn't a request, nor a command. I'm not even sure if I put it into so many words, or if the phrase just burned white at the bottom of the screen, translating my actions: Get two

Cokes from the office, sit in the passenger seat of his car, wish that he would hurry up whatever he's doing in the restroom.

2.

On Tuesday nights the basement at the 4-H club is a place where queers gather to listen to some rock and schlock and to desecrate icons. They pin up a sign dusted in glitter, Licky Favors, and serve dollar beers in big plastic cups.

Old super-8 porn on the walls in slow motion, bumps of crystal in the one tiny toilet. Some girls, but guys mostly, go there and recognize good and bad fractions of themselves all over the place. They see themselves a few years ago, or a few years from now, in the eyes of other patrons, in sad and grand gestures, in the doped-up spectacle. It's a hall of mirrors.

Motion goes into a sort of one-point perspective here, starting with something still, say an old beat-up easy chair, and radiating out. Objects closest to the chair (or whatever center you choose) are the slowest, and they pick up speed the farther away you go. The world just outside, which is as far as anyone ever gets, is moving so fast its speed is invisible, and so walking out there is an illusion of walking into stillness.

The light show is the story of a guy—we'll call him Guy—who is trying to get somewhere or do something, but other men keep interrupting him. Guy never complains. He's so easily distracted, he doesn't even seem to notice that he's repeating himself, that he's locked into the routine of trying to break free of his routine. He leaves his job in one scene, but before long is employed again at a similar or the same job. Mindless work selling objects that don't make sense to him, or caressing the architecture in other people's apartments, a giant sack of never-used tools by his side. Some days he stares at you through dirty windows, some days he forgets who he is in the crawl spaces of suburbia, and every day he gets it in his head to leave. Then he tries to fix his broken bike or sticks a thumb out on the highway, but it's no use. All the men who stop to help him are only after one thing.

Sometimes, if you are the object that is still, you can project your self out into the motion of others, the trick being not to cast yourself out too far. Braced into a corner, you can follow the trajectory of lights and enter the story loop at various points. You can meet Guy and be one more predictable but pleasant sequence in his ancient life.

In the blue shade of a circle of trees, Guy points to all the scars on his body and tells you the story behind each of them. In a hotel, you can get up on the bed on all fours, and Guy will point up into you. Fingers of light entering through a slippery portal.

Because he's a creature of habit, every interaction with him will wind up sexual. Because you're a creature of habit, you will always search him out, in spite of the disappointment he leaves you with. Because he is you, he is always absent, even when he is a flashlight inside you.

A car pulled over to the side of the side of the road and the driver asked where I was headed. "Away from this place," I said, knowing he couldn't really go anywhere. His truck was a prop, the landscape projected in motion behind us, while we remained stationary.

Driver: You've got dirt in your hair.
Me: Yeah.
Driver: And there's blood on your hand. Are you hurt?
Me: Nah...I was in a fight.

I said it, figuring we were close enough to city limits to sound a little dangerous. For the next year I worked two jobs, always wearing my pull-tab ring till I noticed the rust was

staining my finger. While I long professed to be against violence, the notion that I was capable of it never occurred to me.
My thoughts of Clarence took on an erotic cloak as I imagined our fight as an entrance to some fraternal arena I had
previously discredited as anti-intellectual. Taste of sweat, beer,
and blood lingering on my gums. The foot's shuffling tattoo
winds a punch, anticipating that smack and the slight give of
flesh over bone—a knuckle cushion—pushing flights of fancy
while pushing a broom: thoughts meant to quicken the passing of time at work.

Passing time was a challenge, as these jobs actually seemed
to collect time that wasn't being used elsewhere. As I swept
the sugary grime from under a vat used to knead sacks full of
flour into dough, the sound of the minute hand scraping its
way from 3:45 a.m. to 3:46 a.m. was a nail on a chalkboard.

Driver: (pulling over) We should clean that up. I have a
first aid kit under your seat, there.

He leaned across me, his hand brushing inside my thigh,
testing to see if I would pull away. "Here it is," he said. But I
was so gone by then, I had no idea what "it" he was referring to,
I'd lost faith in "here," and "is" was just a sort of distraction
we all used to grope about from one limb to another.

The Future of the Future
Marshall Moore

Scott tightened his connection with his port, logged on, and accessed the site. If he had to work from home while the broken bone in his leg knit itself whole, he meant to make the most of his time. He had projects enough to keep him busy for at least three times that long. Travel arrangements to coordinate. A couple of articles to edit. Why not do all this from the comfort of his sofa? Doctor's orders: Walk around as little as possible in the coming week. *The skin is intact but the bone will not be really solid for at least a week. Let the treatment run its course. Don't fuck it up,* barked the cute bald doctor with the nineteen-syllable last name. (Russian? Ukrainian? Scott had no idea.) *It'll take longer to heal if we have to set it again, and you won't be able to move around at all.*

Thank God I wasn't born twenty or thirty years earlier, Scott thought. God forefend I should be forced to spend days in the hospital, then have to limp around on crutches for weeks or months.

The contact points of the port—the new one from Sony, designer-hip, gleamingly silver—worked much like head-phones, only shaped like a curved letter T. Two points at his temples, one at the top of his skull, and one around back where his neck met his head. The entire Internet hadn't gone plugged-in yet, but it was on its way.

His friend (his ex, actually) Tobias, in Belgium, had sent the link via an out-of-the-blue e-mail: *Click here, and when you're done, start looking for thoughtful and clever ways to express your appreciation.* Smut was the obvious—if rarely dis-cussed—realm to benefit from Internet-based virtual reality applications, but there were still relatively few sites in exis-tence. With the Republicans controlling both the White House and Congress ever since the prolonged debacle of the Clinton years had ended in a whimper (the bang having taken place somewhat earlier), the common assumption on the Net was that the FCC simply zapped porn sites that went interactive, Constitution be damned. Nobody outside Fortress Washington could prove it.

Scott had found one the same day the taxi had run over him. No time to explore, not until now.

He hoped it wasn't solely for heterosexuals.

First, in flat-time:

A black screen. The word *Welcome* blinking in tiny red script. A link.

Scott entered.

Two choices: Proceed in traditional Web mode with tradi-tional Web choices (chat, pictures, message boards, personal ads, blah blah blah), or Plug In Now.

Scott clicked on the universal Interact icon, square above circle, connected by arrows on either side. When he clicked, the face briefly turned into that '60s happy face icon he'd always hated, then turned red, the mouth widening for a split-second into a big O of shock or surprise.

Scott was entered.

Seamless, the transition into cyber-reality. The change came with none of the darkness shot through with red, none of the headache, dizziness, or disorientation users experienced when the technology was launched five years ago. No cheesy sound effects, no cerebral fireworks to announce *You Are Here!* And, best of all, no advertisements. The webmasters here knew what the hell they were doing.

Looked just like his apartment...*was* his apartment. Scott looked around, and corrected himself. Looked like, but the resemblance ended there. The site must have done a scan, accessed stress points, and removed them. In real-time, his apartment was not tidy at all. He had books strewn everywhere, dirty dishes on the coffee table, and hadn't dusted in at least a month. This simulacrum had been cleaned, but not so exactingly as to feel sterile. Books were on their shelves. He could see the surface of the coffee table, although there were still things on it, including a couple of candles he knew wouldn't exist when he signed off. The place looked the way it would if he were having someone over and had actually taken time to straighten up a bit. Good, very good.

Someone knocked at the door.

Scott felt a moment of trepidation about rising to cross the room and answer, then remembered these legs had not been broken. He felt amazingly light on his feet, solid, real. No post-op unsteadiness. No rush of blood out of the head from standing up too fast. An idea popped into his mind: He lifted his shirt and took a look at a stomach that had become beautifully flat, defined...pierced. A tiny gold ring glinted in his navel. He caressed the ring, loving the way it felt under his fingertip, already getting aroused. Again, just a few shades better than reality. Scott wasn't overweight—but he certainly was not in shape. A little soft at the sides. Going gently to seed.

What else looks different?

Before he had the chance to look inside his jeans, the knock came again.

"Hang on!"

At the door, through the peephole, a hunk. Practically drooling, Scott opened the door and let the guy in. Not only was the guy a hunk, he was Scott's special kind of hunk: darkly olive-tan skin, possibly Latin or Middle Eastern, maybe some appetizing combination of races. A bit shorter than Scott, 5 foot 9 or so. Wiry, slender, but with defined muscles visible where his arms disappeared under the sleeves of his shirt. A small tattoo visible on the left forearm. Wavy hair down to his shoulders. Beautiful almond eyes.

"Scott, nice to meet you." He extended a hand to shake. "My name is Esteban. I'm your guide."

Scott could only nod, eyes and crotch bulging.

"We should sit down." Esteban indicated the sofa.

Scott continued to nod, his head bobbing up and down like a marionette's. He allowed himself to be led to the sofa. He wanted to ravish this man so desperately his body ached.

"We'll get to that," said Esteban. "Have some wine."

Two glasses materialized on the coffee table. Scott didn't recognize them and didn't care. He couldn't take his eyes off this beautiful man. If this is what the Internet was capable of, why on earth did people ever unplug?

"Because it's not real life," was the reply, followed by a big grin.

Scott sipped his wine and was delighted: He tasted a fairly light Spanish table red, with the zing of a Rioja but not the weight. Refreshing, not heavy. Perfect. He took another swallow, then another, then found he'd emptied the glass.

"It's not real life. We have the capability of making little tweaks to the baseline here and there, then bringing you up to the level where you want to be. But as long as you're here, you have to remember your body has physical needs. You have to eat and drink. You have to use the bathroom; you have to sleep."

"I have to pay the bills, too. Eventually I have to get some work done." Scott finally found his voice.

"There is that, yes." Esteban studied Scott for a second.

Is he really this attractive, or is it all software?

"That's an impossible question to answer. I can tell that you want to cut to the chase. You didn't enter this site to drink red wine, eat Brie on toast, and have intellectually stimulating conversations. In a second I'm going to put my hand on the back of yours, and you'll be left with what will look like a tattoo. That will be your access point. There will be a red circle, an amber circle, and a green circle, with more or less the same functions as a stoplight: exit, pause, and proceed."

With that, he wrapped his hand—warm, strong—around Scott's.

Scott shifted, to make room for his oozing erection. At this rate the pre-cum stain was going to show through his pants in a few seconds. Esteban politely did not comment.

"And now I want to show you what I think you came here to see. Would you like to follow me?"

What an ass he had, roundly perfect in black Armani jeans. *White men don't have butts like this.* The fabric of his shirt shimmered—black silk. The head of a snake seemed to be tattooed on the base of Esteban's neck—*the rest of it must coil down his back,* Scott wondered. How big? Yes, that was the operative question, wasn't it?

Scott felt he'd acquired another inch or two with the transition into cyberspace. He wanted to take his cock out, to brandish it. He wanted to strip off his own clothes and stroke his whole body—pierced navel, newly sensitized nipples already hard under the fabric of this shirt, rock-hard ass... But his dick, what the hell did it look like? He'd always had a fantasy about being pierced down there too, and had to know whether he was sporting more metal, without the messy inconvenience of actually having a ring installed. He was dying of curiosity, turned on to the point of trembling (*already!*), champing at the bit to find out what the lack of constraint by the laws of physics would let him do. For starters, to put it in Esteban's mouth. His ass. And whatever else he could imagine, thereafter. Orifices not yet invented. Positions corporeal bodies could never wrench themselves into. But that would have to wait at least a few more minutes, wouldn't it?

"Yes." Esteban turned around, winked.

He gestured to the front door.

"First I want you to undress. Then close your eyes, Scott, and keep them closed. Promise me you won't open them again until I give you the signal."

Scott nodded. He started to ask if this was safe, but he had seen the tattoos on the back of his hand. If things got weird he could always bail, and besides—he was in the Internet. This was not some kind of kinky real-life scenario, like from an online hookup or a sex club or an ad he had answered in a moment of horny boredom. Was it?

"Some other time, think about how you'd define the term *safe,*" Esteban whispered, as Scott stripped. "It's one of those words like *real*. People tend to use them without being entirely sure of what they mean." He kissed Scott's ear. "You're a sexy son of a bitch and you know it. They're going to love you, where we're going."

"And where is that?"

"If I told you, then you'd know."

"Do I already know?"

"You may. In any case, you're not far from finding out. Follow me," Esteban told him, taking his hand. "Don't worry about crashing into the coffee table or stubbing your toe, by the way. I'm good at making sure things like that don't happen."

Esteban led him outside—the thrill of being seen by neighbors, random passersby—and Scott's buttocks clenched tight when the cooler air outside hit his skin. Down the corridor they walked, to the elevator. Scott's hallway had a certain smell, comprising old wood, old carpets, old but fragrant cooking scents married for years into a comfortable family. Nubbly carpet tickled the soles of Scott's feet. They came to a stop where he knew the elevator landing should be. The scent of baking bread reached Scott's nose: Mrs. Lukovic, in 408, would be fixing a huge spread for her gang of grandchildren. She could conceivably open the door and see him standing here with Esteban, cock at full attention and oozing. She could conceivably have a heart attack, or stroke, or whatever old Croatian ladies have when they open the door and see their neighbor standing naked, aroused to the point of near-death, hand in hand with a gorgeous unidentified Latin boy. She might totally get off on it. Somehow Scott doubted Mrs. Lukovic had gone dry yet. She probably still had her wild moments.

"Don't think about your neighbor," Esteban told him. "Not that one, at least."

Scott's cock was already flagging slightly.

"Think about Cameron, down the hall."

Schwing

Cameron: soccer player slash bike messenger slash skateboard rebel slash club kid? Just out of high school, maybe a year or so, going to one of the junior colleges down the Peninsula somewhere? Kind of a departure from type, Scott acknowledged, even within the broad parameters Esteban pointed out. But the spiky unkempt hair with the cowry shell woven into one strand, the deep green eyes, and the veined forearms all spoke a language Scott's dick understood. *He likes boys,* an inner voice whispered. *He has gone down on a couple of guys he plays soccer with. Once he got fucked by a total stranger standing up in the restroom in an office building in the Financial District—he went in to deliver a message and got picked up because the guy looked at him a certain way. A young lawyer or investment banker, one of those guys, nice suit, little glasses, with that look on his face. Cameron followed him into the men's room, into the stall, and spread his legs. It went right in. He loved it.* Scott could see it—could feel the clench as the ring of muscle expanded as Cameron was entered. He was the cock, the ass, the guy in the next stall who heard them grunt.

"That's better," Esteban said. "Our elevator is here."

They rode to the parking garage in silence. The elevator did not stop to admit other passengers. Scott struggled with the urge to open his eyes.

"I have a car waiting," Esteban told him when their elevator reached the basement parking garage. He guided Scott across cold—cold!—concrete that smelled of oil and exhaust. Dank breezes blew. The garage smelled dark. Scott's scrotum seemed to shrivel. "You'll like it, but of course, you won't see it."

"You're a depraved man, Esteban."

"No, my friend, you are. I am merely a product of your imagination." His tone of voice conveyed a smile. He chuckled. More of a snort. "Or perhaps I'm not a figment, and you're correct—I am a raging pervert, and you should get away while you can. Run for your life." As he said this, he leaned close. The words were hot breath in Scott's ear.

"I'll get far, I'm sure," Scott said sardonically. "Halfway down the block, at least. A naked man running down the street in this part of San Francisco will attract attention. It's not like this is the Castro at Halloween."

"Hold on."

Footsteps; the sound of a door opening. Smell of leather. Esteban's hand on the back of Scott's head, guiding him into the rear of a car. Buttery-smooth leather beneath his ass, at his back...

"This is very *Story of O*," Scott said when Esteban had shut the door and taken a seat next to him. "Who's driving?"

"The driver," Esteban said. "You can open your eyes now. You won't see out the windows, nor through the partition."

"Mmm...The Roissy Academy in Orinda—that's food for thought. Maybe it's out in Livermore or Stockton. That's even more perverse."

Esteban answered with the Latino equivalent of a Mona Lisa smile.

"Help yourself to the bar," he said. "We have enough time for a quick drink."

"Algorithms and tonic, anyone?" Scott asked.

"There's a very good Riesling in the refrigerator, actually. Why not have a glass?"

Scott found the bottle, glasses, poured for himself and Esteban.

The car pulled off the road somewhere, but Scott couldn't tell whether they had arrived at their destination.

"Slight detour," Esteban said, taking a sip.

He moved like a cat and was suddenly straddling Scott, angling his head forward to kiss. When Scott met his lips, he tasted wine; it trickled into his mouth, warmed slightly from Esteban's mouth, cool at the same time. He swallowed the wine as best he could with Esteban's tongue in his mouth.

A burst of annoyance flared: What the hell to do with the glass of wine? Scott couldn't figure out where to put it. No sooner had the thought registered, than the glass vanished from his hand. No shock registered; disappearing wineglasses made perfect sense within the laws governing this site.

Esteban withdrew enough to wink at him, but Scott pulled him close to resume making out. This felt like being a teenager again.

"These clothes have to come off," Scott said, tugging at Esteban's shirt, fingers grazing the navel piercing. Had to lick that. And lower. "You're not getting out of this car with clothing on, buddy…"

Esteban smiled, chuckled slightly, allowed his shirt to be pulled off. He had no chest hair. "You're right: I'm not. Where we're going, to be admitted, we can't have anything on. But we have time."

"Might as well warm ourselves up, right?" Scott breathed into his ear.

Esteban squirmed, nodded, now underneath Scott and not protesting as Scott's fingers fumbled with the top button on his tattered jeans. Finding purchase, he pulled.

No underwear.

Scott's dick said a sudden *Hello* to his chin.

The car glided into traffic again, almost imperceptibly. What kind of machine was this, that it should move so smoothly? Scott caught glimpses of other cars through windows darkened almost to opacity. Either this limousine was traveling at the approximate speed of a Concorde or other cars were sitting absolutely still. Yet he felt no sense of motion, much less of breakneck speed.

"Blower Bentley, specially converted for us," Esteban murmured. "I take all the credit."

"How fast are we going?"

"Who gives a fuck? I want to taste your dick," Esteban replied.

He moved slightly and began sixty-nining with Scott, again in defiance of what Scott had taken to be the laws of anatomy and physics. Sort of a fast-forward through the awkward particulars of finding the right position. Scott found himself in the sweet spot, spread-eagled across the leather bench of the Bentley, his face between Esteban's legs, a perfect cock oozing a trail of clear fluid, inches from his mouth. The sensation of Esteban's lips and mouth around

Scott's cock, surrounding it, licking it, Esteban's hand around the base of the shaft... Scott shut his eyes and blanked out into the moment before coming back to himself long enough to commence returning the favor. Esteban tasted as good as he looked: salty, vaguely sweet, sublime.

There was no Scott in this moment; he lost himself in it.

There was just the focus on the beautiful cock in his mouth, and by extension the man attached to it, as his own dick and balls were thoroughly licked, stroked, sucked.

Neither of them spoke.

Scott stroked the ridge beneath Esteban's scrotum and then licked it.

Esteban writhed and moaned, his mouth around Scott's cock, licking the head.

Salty fluid in Scott's mouth, pre-cum, which Esteban was oozing in generous amounts.

Scott swallowed it, losing his mind with pleasure from the taste: salt, charcoal, skin, some subtle layer of sweetness beneath, like vanilla or cloves.

At one point Esteban stopped long enough to murmur something in Spanish and rest his head against Scott's thigh.

Scott tentatively touched Esteban's anus with a fingertip, stroked, caressed.

Esteban spread his legs a little wider, groaning around Scott's dick again.

Scott spat on his index finger, wet it well, slid it carefully into Esteban.

Esteban's dick spasmed, seemed to grow even larger; Scott took it into his mouth again and continued pushing his finger into Esteban, encountering enough resistance to be sexy but not so much as to know he was causing pain.

The ring of muscle clamped around Scott's finger.

Esteban stopped ministering to Scott's dick and lay his head against his abdomen, moaning, covered with sweat.

"I could fall in love with you," he gasped, his accent thicker now.

Scott thrust his finger in slightly deeper, then moved it out, then back in, fucking him with the finger while sucking him off.

A louder groan from Esteban.

Esteban's mouth around his dick again, working it harder this time, frying Scott's brain again from the impossible hot wet pleasure of it.

There was nothing but this pleasure, the right here, the right now.

Two fingers in Esteban's ass this time...

Esteban doing the same, first a finger, exquisitely searing feeling of being opened, invaded.

Two fingers inside Scott.

First sign of an orgasm beginning to coalesce in the base of Scott's cock, the juncture of scrotum and penis.

Then:

"Don't come, Scott. We're here."

Esteban withdrew his fingers slowly.

Scott wanted to scream.

"We're here. There's more where this came from, trust me."

How Esteban could maintain such presence of mind...

You're inside the Internet, you dildo, Scott reminded himself. *Don't lose sight of that.* He considered for a second. He had to admit it: These guys were good.

He tried to compose himself.

The door opened, revealing the inside of what Scott took to be a warehouse, orange-lit by thousands of candles.

Two men—one white, one black, both shirtless and clad only in boots and tight leather pants—stood side by side next to the car.

"Follow us," the white one said, exchanging a look with his counterpart. "Don't say a word."

Esteban and Scott slipped out of the car. Scott caught a glimpse of the chauffeur—a Nordic ice goddess who could have been Sharon Stone's younger sister, clad in leather and vinyl—shutting the door behind them. She left black streaks of rubber on the concrete floor (curiously warm underfoot) when she sped out of the warehouse.

"This way," said one of the men.

Scott couldn't tell who had spoken, but he followed them through the dim, cavernous space. They walked side by side. Perfect asses, Scott noticed. Roundly muscular. The kind of place where his tongue fantasized about going on an extended working vacation. Esteban took Scott's hand as they entered a corridor lit only by the occasional candle.

"Where are we going?" Scott whispered to Esteban as quietly as possible.

Esteban answered with a finger over his lips. He nodded his head forward and kept walking.

"No talking," said one of the men they were following.

The space where they were led resembled the sanctuary of a medium-sized church. Soaring ceiling held up by intricately carved columns. More candles. Broken stained-glass windows whose colors were impossible to identify in the flickering light of hundreds of candles. It *was* a church, Scott realized with a certain perverse glee. Or it had been.

Pews? No, he noticed when he looked more closely. The pews had been replaced by rows of chairs. At the back of the sanctuary were folding metal chairs; at the front, a couple of rows of overstuffed armchairs. The chairs in back were occupied by young men—boys—who Scott suspected were his own age: twenties, early thirties. Scott saw white men, blacks, Asians, Latinos, a few he took to be Middle Eastern; some darkly handsome specimens were impossible to place just on sight. He saw long hair and short hair, a couple of shaved heads, dreadlocks. One cowry shell glinted in the dim light: Cameron, from down the hall. *Here?* Metal gleamed here and there: earlobes, noses, eyebrows, nipples, a couple of navels. Anything lower was hidden from view, although Scott didn't doubt there were a few pierced cocks in the room, too. One Asian man with a heartbreakingly handsome face had an enormous, intricate tattooed dragon winding its way up his left arm. One black man with caramel skin and buzzed hair appeared to have been painted with henna—all over. A cursive lattice of black lines covered every inch of a wiry bod. He wore a hoop through his left nostril. Scott wanted to lick him. Would the henna turn his tongue black? He'd take the risk.

"Sit here." The white guy who had led them into the room indicated a pair of chairs.

Scott and Esteban sat. The metal of the chair felt warm, as if someone had just stood up.

The black guy and the white guy appeared to be photo negatives of each other, Scott observed: Their features were similar enough that they could have been brothers, skin color notwithstanding. Perhaps they were half-brothers. That thought enticed Scott like the first nibbles of an undertow, not that he'd get to ask.

"We'll begin momentarily," said the black guy at the altar. "Blindfolds!" he called to someone Scott couldn't see.

Six men decked out head to toe in white latex walked down the central aisle tying blindfolds around the naked guys seated in the folding chairs. Dark flowers of fear budded in Scott's belly, and for the first time he seriously considered pushing the red *I'm out of here* tattoo-button on the back of his hand. Nobody put up a fight, interestingly enough, although nobody looked thrilled to have a blindfold tied on, either. Scott couldn't make out their expressions. He didn't get any sense of being in danger, but he was definitely off a cliff and plunging deeper into the unknown.

The sanctuary smelled of incense, flowers, and sex. Scott leaned close to Esteban to breathe in his scent, too, to commit it to memory.

When Scott's turn to be blindfolded came, he offered no resistance.

The wait began.

He heard footsteps, rustlings, movements he couldn't identify. More people entering the sanctuary and taking seats? That sounded right. Matches striking, perhaps more candles being lit? Also plausible. Naked men stirring on folding metal chairs, seat bottoms becoming uncomfortable beneath trim buttocks? Not just plausible but likely.

More footsteps. Someone behind him this time, standing up and walking down the central aisle toward the altar?

Next, from up front, a liquid flesh-on-flesh sound: kissing. Someone was kissing passionately, grunting, drawing breath in the short, sharp inhalations that accompanied being really turned on.

Unh, oh!

Gasps.

The sound of men moving together, sex commencing.

The murmurs (*oh yeah, man, you've got a great dick, let me taste it*) just audible.

Bodies turning this way and that (*turn around let's 69, you're so fucking hot, they'll love that*), trying out position after position.

From the front, the subtle ZZZ of a couple of zippers being opened, one and then another.

A rhythmic sound: somebody up there jacking off at what was happening on the altar?

It became clear to Scott all of a sudden, and he was as turned on as he had ever been. This was the floor show, but they weren't going to be allowed to see what the men (he presumed) seated in the front were looking at. They could only hear it. Getting more turned on with every passing moment.

Every exhibitionist fantasy he'd ever had, brought to life, and then made bigger. He'd never have dreamed this up on his own. Esteban?

Oh Christ, he thought… *I have to have died and gone to hell. Heaven couldn't be this much fun.*

Hands on his shoulders, a whisper in his ear: "Scott, take my hand, I'm going to lead you up front. You've been selected to join them on the altar."

Something dripping down his chest, smell of sweetness—honey?

His legs felt unsteady when he first stood up, but the sensation passed; he strode toward the stage, dick jutting straight out. Scott gloated, feeling eyes on him, his chest, his navel ring glinting by the candlelight he couldn't see but knew was there, his cock, the muscles flexing in his ass and his legs with every step he took. He couldn't see through the blindfold, not even light filtering through the cloth, but he could sense his surroundings well enough. The smells, the stirrings of the men in the audience, the groans and sliding-skin noises of the boys on the dais…

That's right, look at me.

"Take three steps up, then drop to your hands and knees," whispered the voice. Soft lips touched his ear. Sandpaper rasp of razor stubble. Was this the black guy or the white one? Scott couldn't tell and didn't care. He'd have given anything to make a sandwich with the two—and given more than that to be the filling between them, spread like jelly.

Scott did as he was told.

"I'm going to take off your blindfold now, but I want you to keep your eyes shut. Crawl slowly across the floor until you come to Marco and Colin. When you find them, you can open your eyes and join in."

Scott did as he was told.

He'd never realized it was possible to strut while on one's hands and knees. When his buttocks parted as he crawled, he could tell men were looking between them. *Want to know what my asshole looks like? Take a good look.* Scott crawled slowly, taking his time, spreading his legs wider. *Like how my balls move? Wish I were crawling across the bed toward you? Jack off more slowly—stretch it out. Fantasize with your eyes wide open.*

This was like being lost at sea. This was immolation. Scott felt layers of himself eroding, disappearing, leaving something more raw and atavistic: anti-Scott. Non-Scott.

When he touched flesh, he opened his eyes.

Marco and Colin lay entwined, sixty-nining, eyes shut, sheened with sweat. Small groans escaped their mouths when they paused or adjusted position to take a breath or swallow salty saliva.

The one closest to Scott had fair skin and strawberry-blond hair that would have reached his shoulders had he been standing upright. Scott placed a hand on a granite shoulder (ornately tattooed in a tribal pattern). Colin, most likely. The other guy had olive skin and buzzed black hair—safe to assume he was Marco. Muscles everywhere, not bulky, just built.

They paused, parted, opened their eyes (Colin first, then Marco, when Colin stopped moving) to see who had joined them.

"Nice," Colin said, eyeing Scott, approval obvious from the way he shifted, making it clear the fun had only just started.

A Brit? Even better. There was nothing nice about this boy's dick, once Marco's mouth was no longer around it. Colin had to be packing eight inches, uncut; Marco idly slid his foreskin up and down the shaft as he appraised Scott, seductive, smutty, smoldering...

Marco nodded. "Yeah, man. Real nice. You want to put on a show for these guys?"

"That's why I'm here."

"What's your name?" Marco's face could have sent Ricky Martin crying to the nearest plastic surgeon, demanding improvements. His body had not been adorned: no tattoos, no piercings, nothing shaved. Washboard abs. Light dusting of hair across his firelit golden chest. His pecs...these were the standard by which all others were meant to be measured.

"Scott."

"Come here, Scott," Marco said, wrapping an enormous hand around Scott's dick. "You want to taste what I've got?"

Scott nodded.

"Come here, then."

Other hands on Scott, his ass this time, stroking his buttocks, fingertips grazing his anus, returning, their intent obvious... Colin's hands parting his legs as Marco's gigantic hands guided his face south.

Then a tongue tracing its way up Scott's thigh toward his balls, trail of saliva cooling in the air currents their bodies created.

Scott leaned forward to inhale the musk rising off Marco's abdomen, out of his pubic hair. He smelled like man. He also smelled as if he had worked some kind of scented oil into his skin: amber, cinnamon, something Scott couldn't name.

Exquisite cock, the same size as Colin's, more or less, possibly thicker, but circumcised; veins bulged, and Scott licked them, going up and down the length of him.

Marco gasped, lying back to let Scott taste him. Scott pulled back for a second, then darted forward again to catch a thread of pre-cum as it trickled down the shaft of Marco's cock.

Colin's tongue circled Scott's balls.

Scott opened his mouth to gasp, the electric sensation a dizzy shock... Scott swore, his back arching, mouth open wide to keep from biting down on Marco's dick.

Marco took the opportunity to twist just so and plunge his cock deeper into Scott's mouth.

Scott could taste Colin's spit on it, something subtly different from the other flavors there, brighter, almost metallic, silvery.

He took his time, slowly licking his way up and down the cock, relaxing into it to keep from choking as Marco began to move his hips. Wiry hair ground against Scott's lips. He pushed his face into the thatch of hair and inhaled deeply.

Colin's tongue, still circling, licking up and down Scott's own cock, wetting it...

Scott thought fleetingly, *This is the end of me—no, this is the end of the world, and I love it.*

He glanced up quickly to check whether he could see the audience, but some trick of the light prevented him from detecting more than an apricot blur where their faces ought to be. Were they pixeled out, or was it just the placement of the candles? Scott surfaced long enough to imagine them all in sunglasses, wearing black suits with the trousers unzipped, cocks out, towels at the ready.

Maybe they were taking notes on which boys they liked best.

Maybe they were walking around with no shoes on, picking out the ones they wanted to see.

Colin pushed Scott's legs apart a bit farther and commenced to lick his way across Scott's balls, along the hairless ridge beneath them. Scott squirmed and writhed as Colin's tongue continued its journey. He stopped where Scott thought he was going to stop, and he spread his legs to let Colin do what he wanted...

!!, he thought.

The pleasure shot through him like a series of camera flashes. It felt like hot-white light penetrating the spaces between the molecules of his skin.

Colin's tongue probed, tasted, tested.

Scott felt his body tense for a second, then relax as Colin's tongue and lips did their work, opening him up with deft insistence.

Marco shifted, light gleaming dull orange off his abdomen, his dick reddish-mauve, slick with Scott's spit... .

Scott turned and began to suck Colin off, making a triangle on the spongy floor: Colin's mouth in Scott's ass, Marco's cock in Scott's mouth, Colin's cock in Marco's mouth.

Scott dove into this, immersed himself in the rhythm they found, Marco's cock plunging in and out of his mouth as Colin devoured his ass, tongue driving deep, accompanied by a finger now, searing jolts of pleasure ripping through him, as intense in their way as being fucked with gentle precision.

The sparks of an impending orgasm began to gather—at the base of his cock, inside his scrotum, his ass, his prostate.

An interruption: hands on his back and shoulders alerting him that others had joined them on the dais.

Scott opened his eyes, paused, still mindless and writhing as Colin's tongue and fingers did obscene, divine things to his ass.

The black guy with the henna scrollwork up and down his body was kneeling by him, smiling like he had been shown a glimpse of heaven, white teeth in sharp contrast with his dark skin, and next to him was *(oh my God)* Cameron, from down the hall, blissfully nude and tattooed, dick jutting, hard and shameless, a black jaguar tattooed on his thigh *(I didn't know he had that)*, a smutty smile on his face.

"Been looking forward to this," he said.

Colin stopped what he was doing—Scott caught his breath. Colin wiped his mouth on the back of his hand. Marco looked up.

And then they were five:

Cameron, on his belly, parting his legs as Scott plunged into him;

Scott, parting *his* legs as Marco resumed the rim job Colin had started, but more roughly than Colin, who had come at him with something that approached reverence;

The black guy, whose name Scott never got, kneeling ahead of him—Scott took the handsome, gleaming cock in his mouth as he fucked Cameron, who lay moaning under him, more limber than Scott had imagined;

Colin, lying on his side, sucking Marco off, then moving to share the black guy's dick with Scott.

Scott pulled out of Cameron.

Marco took his place, sliding effortlessly in.

Another guy joined them, the Asian with the dragon tattoo: Scott put his face between a pair of rock-hard, hairless buttocks and licked, the anus opening to him like a rose blooming, groans and muttered words in a language Scott couldn't quite make out as he went deeper, savoring the strange sour charcoal skin taste of him.

Where is Esteban, Scott briefly wondered, as he ate.

Someone entered Scott—he had no idea who it was, but he raised his hips to allow him access, exhaling as a large cock impaled him inch by torturous, exquisite inch. Scott felt himself succumbing to the uniquely familiar and alien mixture of peace and terror as he opened up, helpless and filled up at the same time.

He turned around: It was the henna-scrolled black guy, sweat rolling down his face, who was driving into him. He leaned forward and bit Scott's shoulder, licking the back of his neck, arms around Scott's waist as he powered in, forcing incoherent groans out of Scott's mouth, sounds he couldn't control.

Marco crawled behind them and entered the man inside Scott, who drew ragged breaths, eyes shut, teeth sinking into Scott's skin as Marco's cock hit home.

Cameron knelt in front of Scott, offering his dick to suck, and Scott took it greedily in his mouth as deep as it would go, trying to find a rhythm as the man fucking him moved inside him and was moved inside, himself.

He licked salt, more salt... Cameron shot into his mouth, and Scott swallowed as much as he could...

Colin, suddenly underneath him: "Fuck me now, I want to come with you inside me... ."

Scott did, his cock slipping scratchily past the ring of muscle, meeting some resistance before sliding home.

The beautiful henna-scrolled man shouted and came just then, gallons of scalding cum emptying into Scott; in a chain reaction, he came explosively into Colin...

Someone else came in a hot spray across Scott's back...

"Oh *fuck*, that's right, give it to me..."

Gasps all around, profanity, moaning...

"Jesus," Scott grunted as the orgasm continued to rocket through him.

He shuddered as the guy behind him withdrew his cock.

He pulled carefully out of Colin, lay down, head on (he had to check) Marco's chest, and shut his eyes.

"Have a towel?" said a voice.

Esteban, smiling over him.

"A towel would be good."

"Home, then?"

Scott nodded.

And *sideslipped* back to his own sofa.

"Jesus Christ, Esteban, you guys are good." Scott could barely talk. He lay back on his sofa, nude.

His apartment was never this warm in real-time.

Esteban, now clothed and as dapper as before, stood up and bowed slightly. "We do our best," he said, grinning. "And you're a joy to work with. I cannot compliment you highly enough."

"Thanks," Scott said, resisting the urge to blush and add, "aw shucks." Instead, he asked whether the guys he had just cyberfucked were real. And what about the audience? The location?

Esteban chuckled. He crossed his legs and sipped from a glass of wine that hadn't been there an instant before.

"Define *real*," he said. "It's the same thing I said when you asked before. Define *real,* and define *safe.* They are not absolute terms—not inside the Internet, at least."

"Not outside of it, either," Scott remarked. He felt adrift—in over his head.

"Are you really asking whether those men are also plugged in, just like you, and all experiencing the same thing?"

Scott nodded. "I guess I am."

"Some of them are. Some are not."

"Cameron?"

Esteban maintained his Mona Lisa smile. "Classified information," he said. "If I were to tell you he was also plugged in, that would compromise his right to privacy. But if I were to tell you he was something we dreamt up for you, that wouldn't be strictly fair to you."

"I don't follow you one hundred percent, but I suspect this is an argument I won't win. What about the audience? Real people, tuned in because they like to watch?"

"Could be. You have to admit, we have the perfect construct for those fantasies. You knew they were there, but you couldn't see who they were, or how many. Look, Scott, it's been a pleasure, but I'd encourage you to sign off now, eat some dinner, and get some other things done." Esteban looked as if he were weighing whether to say something else. Something in his face softened. "Look," he added. "I like you. Because of what I do, I am able to see very clearly who you are as a person, and you're a good guy. Log off, take care of yourself, and enjoy this—but be careful not to let it overwhelm you. This is powerful technology."

He crossed the room, walking through the coffee table as if it were a hologram, and took a precarious seat on the edge of the sofa next to Scott.

Scott missed a beat. For a second he was too shocked to speak.

When he had recovered enough to get the words out: "Last question, then. You weren't on the stage or altar or floor or whatever it was with me. You must have known I wanted you there. Didn't you feel left out, that you weren't chosen?"

Esteban smiled, then surprised Scott again by leaning down to kiss him. Soft lips, no scritch-scratch of razor stubble. The kiss lasted longer than Scott expected, and he grew hard again by degrees.

After, Esteban asked, "Are you sure that was where you wanted me? And who do you think did the choosing?"

That said, he reached down and pushed the red button tattooed on the back of Scott's hand.

"Come back tomorrow," he whispered, just before fading out like the Cheshire Cat.

Some things never change.

CONNECTION REFUSED, said Scott's monitor when he attempted a return after a long day filled with hours that crept like traffic on the Bay Bridge.

Fifteen minutes later, the same lack of results confounded Scott.

THIS PAGE NOT AVAILABLE, the pop-up thing sometimes said.

At other times, CONNECTION TIMED OUT.

Scott poured himself a glass of Merlot, and stared out the window as fog blew in off the ocean.

The next day, the same thing, the same *nothing...*

Scott turned down a date with a man he had hooked up with a few times prior to breaking his ankle. He got nothing written. When the phone rang, he looked at the Caller ID box to see who wanted to speak to him, but he never answered.

That altar. The Bentley.

The candles.

Esteban.

Maybe he was real. Maybe Esteban lived with a cute *gringito* boyfriend down in Long Beach and worked part-time at Tower Records or Barnes & Noble. Maybe he was in a house in Barcelona or Fukuoka or Cape Town, with no furniture beyond the basics, and lots of billowing white curtains. Maybe he jogged around the Eiffel Tower in the evenings before logging onto the Net to guide people through naked adventures that existed entirely in the realm of the mind.

Maybe he did not exist at all.

Six weeks later, Dr. Lashyonyh pronounced Scott's ankle healed.

"But you have to get off your computer," snapped the doctor. "These problems you are having with your wrists, this pain—it is plain old-fashioned repetitive strain injury. You should know about that by now. It is from typing on the computer too much, and clicking the mouse. There is nothing on the Net you cannot find in real life. Trust me."

"Sure," Scott said, nodding. "I guess I will have to start looking harder."

He put on his sunglasses in the lobby of Dr. L's office and walked out into an overcast San Francisco afternoon. Nothing on the Net he could not find in real life? His wrists did ache constantly these days. And he kept seeing CONNECTION REFUSED behind his eyelids when he tried to sleep at night. Fine. He would look. The question, then, was *where*. He hailed a cab and rode back to his apartment, thinking.

When We Are Very Old

Andrew Ramer

You sleep in my arms, your back pressed to my belly. I can feel the tremor in your body, the dance of your dreaming. Then you are still, your breath coming soft and even. I bend my lips to the side of your neck, in the stillness of our bed, as the first light of morning whispers its song. You wake, and press your body close to me. The heat of your body warms me as no layering of blankets ever can. Like the sun, the fire of my body wakens. I turn your face to meet me. Wet, my tongue seeks out the tongue of you, speaking the language of two bodies that fifty years of talking have turned into one.

I roll on top of you, my beloved. There where you wait, I find you. Soft belly pressed to soft belly, soft breast pressed to soft breast. And we are eye to eye now. Back and forth between our eyes, a dancing bridge is built of ropes flung over the rock walls of a canyon. Across this rope bridge, deer walk, snakes slither, bear pad, squirrels scamper—all of life going back and forth, back and forth between us.

Your hands on my back pull me down to you. Eye to eye, my tongue explores your face. In the wrinkles around your eyes flash rivers, rivers flowing thick with life. Fish swim in these rivers, frogs, turtles, fresh-water dolphins. I am lost in these rivers, my adored one. I am lost in the cry of whales screaming up from the sea of your breath.

I take your face in my hands, and run my fingers through your hair. Each silver hair is a story. I listen to them all. What richness of years are in your stories. Time. Wisdom. Love. Our bodies rock. Slowly. I press into your stories, tree-root of my body pressed to tree-root of your body, skin opening to skin.

We are so old, my beloved. Time itself stops in our embracing. Days, nights, morning—all become still in our bodies. Even the earth is still. Stopped. Only the sigh of you, breath of you, singing into my body-sighs. And birds fly out of your mouth, clouds, lightning, stars. Like a man who has danced all night, I stagger into your eyes, fall all the way down into your body. We are one. Oneness is happening in this bed of dreaming. Oneness only, on fire. Racing. Liquid fire. Screaming the bliss of creation. As your body explodes into opal liquid light. Together, we explode. Into darkness. And from that moment of darkness, the mother of all suns is born again out of our bodies. Floating on a sea of liquid pearls. Brilliant, giving birth to whole new worlds. Thundering. Hearts thundering. You and I again, heart to heart. Together. Containing everything.

Bear Basher
Thomas S. Roche

Marco and Paulie dragged the guy into my office with his hands cuffed behind him and his knees wrapped with duct tape. There was more duct tape across his hairy face. The guy was dressed like a biker—tight, faded blue jeans, leather vest, high boots, Harley-Davidson T-shirt. He wasn't wearing a belt.

The two bruisers tossed the biker on the floor. He lay there, groaning.

"Quit whining!" I snapped, and kicked him in the ribs. "Marco and Paulie didn't work you over half as much as they coulda. What's the story?"

Marco sneered. "We caught us a fag-basher. Caught him in the alley behind the Darkside."

"No fuckin' shit! Right behind *my* fuckin' club?"

"He had Long Tooth Eddie handcuffed to his Harley, and he was laying into him with a belt. Eddie had his pants around his ankles, ass all black and blue. Guy'd even shoved a fuckin' eggplant up Eddie's ass."

"*Eggplant?*" I snarled.

"Yeah, boss. Literally. Guess it was the right shape. It was a small one."

"Even a small eggplant's still pretty fuckin' big to be shoving up someone's ass."

"Well, yeah. Maybe that's why Eddie was blubberin' so bad."

"Damn," I said. "Eddie's Mr. fuckin' Vanilla."

"Goddamn right. He was screamin' something awful. The sonofabitch drew blood."

"Damn," I repeated. "Is Eddie OK?"

"Physically, yeah, but he can't even speak. He's just a gibbering fool. More than usual, I mean. Got him in the back of the car. He's totally disoriented. This guy musta really fucked him up—emotionally, I mean. I mean, more than he was already fucked up. You know how Eddie is."

"You know this sonofabitch's name?"

"Checked his ID. His name's Crosby. A couple of the guys said they've seen him hanging around outside the Darkside. Probably hunting for easy meat."

"Izzat right?" I snarled, going down on one knee and grabbing the guy's hair. I gripped the duct tape and yanked. The guy screamed as the tape came off holding a good quarter of his beard. "It ain't enough that I gotta deal with the zoning motherfuckers and the city council busting my balls, I've gotta put up with fag-bashers like you going after my clientele with a belt, huh? You think the meat at the Darkside's easy for a fag-basher, is that right?"

I forced the guy's face close to mine and snarled at him: "I said, is that right?" I could smell liquor on his breath. The guy was a hell of a looker—hairy and handsome, thirtyish, built like a brick shithouse. No match for Marco and Paulie, though.

"He—he asked for it!" sputtered the biker.

"Fuck that shit!" I snarled, slapping the guy across the face and slamming the duct tape back across his mouth. It didn't hold so well with all that hair on it, but it shut him up just the same. "That's the oldest excuse I ever heard. Didn't nobody tell you the Darkside's under my protection, asshole?"

The guy tried to say something, and I cuffed him.

"That's right—Big Daddy Jackson watches over his flock, prickwad. Next time, check with your fag-bashing friends, ask 'em if it's safe to fuck with the Darkside! Only it's too late for you, motherfucker! We're gonna show you what we do to fag-bashers on my turf! Marco, you got the stuff ready?"

"Ready and waiting," said Marco gleefully, holding up a ball gag and a set of restraints.

"Set him up," I chortled. "This is gonna be a pleasure, boys. We're gonna show this fag-basher what it's like to be a fag. I think that'll greatly increase his social sensitivity…if you know what I mean."

Marco and Paulie started laughing hysterically. I joined them, and the two bruisers hauled Crosby off the floor and dragged him over to the '48 Indian set up in my office.

Goddamn nice to have a vintage bike to work guys over on. Too fuckin' expensive to get parts for a bike like that, so I had the forks welded together, the center-stand bolted to the floor, the front and rear wheels secured by cables, and wooden stocks fastened to the floor on either side of the saddlebags. Hey, I love a good road trip as much as the next biker, but there are plenty more exciting uses for a motorcycle than riding it.

It was too much trouble to get knee-high motorcycle boots off of an unwilling victim, so Marco and Paulie just slapped the guy into the ankle stocks and padlocked them shut. That meant his legs were sticking forward a little, while his belly rested on the back of the bike; his ass stuck out right where I wanted it. Like he was "asking for it," just like the sonofabitch had said Long Tooth Eddie had been doing. I loved to see an ass in that position—just waiting for my dick, or my belt. Only this time we were gonna use the guy's own belt on that ass.

Marco and Paulie pulled Crosby's arms outstretched and cuffed 'em to the bars of the Indian. Just enough space in there for one of us to climb onto the bike and give that guy the cock he needed. But not until we'd had a little fun with him first, and I don't like to disturb the neighbors.

Paulie yanked the tape off Crosby's face and shoved the ball gag into his protesting mouth. He cinched it behind Crosby's head while Marco came at the guy with a buck knife.

Marco made short work of Crosby's blue jeans—Marco loves that part. Soon they hung in tatters from his hairy legs, and it wasn't much trouble to slice away the ribbons and leave the guy's legs fully exposed but for the high boots. Then Marco ripped off the part around his ass and crotch and I caught my breath—this guy was fuckin' built. Massive fuckin' cock, nuts like fuckin' softballs, practically hanging out of his tighty-whities. Marco disposed of those, and I saw Crosby wasn't just big, but uncut too—his foreskin hung down close to the back wheel of the Indian. His balls and the upper half of his dick had the same coarse fur that covered his ass, his legs, his arms. But when Marco had sliced away the T-shirt under Crosby's leather vest, I realized what a fuckin' bruiser he really was— and what a looker. Guy must have worked out religiously—his body rippled with muscle under his dense mat of black hair.

"Fuck, yeah," I grunted, lifting the guy's belt. "This is *really* gonna be a pleasure."

I went to work on the guy's bare, hairy ass while Marco and Paulie shucked their clothes. Most of my attention was centered on my unwilling, well-deserving prisoner as he twisted and fought against his restraints, bent over the back of the Indian. But then, I couldn't resist casting an eye toward Marco and Paulie as they stripped—talk about a lucky man, that's me. Those two dumb apes would die for me, but I don't ever intend to let it come to that—they're much more use to me alive. Marco's a five-foot-eight Spaniard, an ex–Mexican wrestler—he was known as "Maricon Loco" on stage, and took a lot of shit for it. Maybe he's short, but he's got muscles that could crack your head like a casaba melon—I don't care who you are. See him naked and you'd think on first glance, as I did all those years ago, that the sonofabitch was wearing mohair pajamas. The only thing that'd tip you off is this eight-inch-thick piece of meat sticking out hard—and it's practically always hard, I can testify to that—and dripping pre-cum. Naked, Marco strikes one hell of a pose. In fact, the guy looks best when that thick mat of hair is soaked in sweat, the way it gets when I'm fuckin' him real hard up the ass or making him eat Paulie's spunk—and Paulie can shoot, believe me. I've seen that sonofabitch shoot five feet, and I'm not exaggerating. Not only is he the biggest Sicilian I ever laid eyes on—six-foot-four in his socks—but he's gotta be the hairiest muscle-guy that ever worked in this town. Let's not even talk about his fuckin' prick—it's a goddamn Gatling gun, and a high-caliber mother. I'd seen him stick that ten-inch monster into fourteen guys in a row without losing interest, and shoot eight or nine times in an evening, and we're talking in the days before Viagra, *capische*? Like the rest of Paulie, that dick is as hairy as a wombat—Paulie is the only guy I know who walks into the barbershop and unzips his pants. Well, maybe not the *only* guy, but you get the point.

Neither of those Mediterranean brutes seemed to have a problem working for a six-foot-tall black gangster like me—and before you get smart-assed about it, it's not just 'cause I outclass even Paulie by two full inches and a fair bit of girth in the schlong department. Relationships in the criminal under-world just ain't that simple nowadays. Sure, bein' Big Daddy Jackson's musclemen means Paulie and Marco get to take my

Johnson up their holes whenever I'm horny, but it ain't like I don't reciprocate. You're telling me you'd be able to see a six-and-a-half-foot-tall Sicilian with a Louisville Slugger sticking out of his pants and not want to drop to your knees and worship it? Then you're more man than I, *amigo,* but I think you'd change your mind if you saw that hairy, olive-drab dingus in the flesh. Believe you me, I've seen it happen stranger times than this, and as far as I'm concerned, there's no shame whatsoever with losing your cool when Paulie Piccolo hauls out his hard meat.

"You boys ready for a workout?" I snarled, swiping the fag-basher's belt through the air experimentally while he squirmed on the Indian. "I think this hairy fuck is about to learn what it means to be a faggot."

"You got that right," said Marco, standing ready at attention, jacking Paulie off with one hand, the other arm around Paulie's back. Paulie was already half-hard, but Marco was all the way there. Paulie played with Marco's dick absently, getting it ready for the job before it.

"You ready, basher—what was the sonofabitch's name again, Paulie?"

"Crosby," gurgled Paulie, dropping to his knees and gulping Marco's prick down his throat in one easy thrust.

"Hey! Save that for the prisoner," I said, and brought my hand down as hard as I could.

No point in warming Crosby up—I just tore into him like there was no tomorrow. He jerked and spasmed as my belt landed on his hairy ass. His asshole winked at me, closing up every time the shudders of pain went through his hirsute body. I heard him screaming behind that ball gag, and it was like music to my ears. Still, I wasn't getting the kind of complaints out of him I wanted.

I edged up closer to his swaying, squirming ass. "What, this guy's got balls of brass?" I asked.

"Sure seems that way," chuckled Marco.

"Let's find out," I said, and punched him in the nuts.

Yeah, that did the trick. His whole body was wracked with spasms, twisting so hard that the Indian shook like it was gonna come up from its bolts and cables. I knew it would stay put, though; it'd had bigger, tougher motherfuckers than Crosby strapped to it—sometimes two and three at a time, if you can believe that.

I smacked his balls again, hearing the strangled sounds in his throat. Yeah, now my dick was getting hard. Hearing him gulp and squeal was what did it to me. Soon my prick was throbbing against my leather pants—so hard that it felt like it was gonna fuckin' explode if I didn't get it inside this guy's asshole and ream him out the way he deserved. But now wasn't the time—there was a lot of pain this guy was gonna feel before I shot my load up his shitter. So I punched the guy's nuts three or four more times, feeling my prick surge with each muffled cry of agony from behind the ball gag. He even let out a fart when I whacked him just so, bringing a chuckle from my throat.

"Now that's just rude," I snapped. "Marco, I think the fucker needs something up his ass to make sure he don't embarrass himself again."

"With pleasure," said Marco, who was enjoying Paulie's attentions, pumping his hips forward to shove his cock down Paulie's throat. Without needing to be asked, Paulie eased Marco's glistening prick from his mouth and hawked obscenely, depositing a thick glob of mucus and spit on the tip of Marco's sausage. Marco walked over to the motorcycle; I stepped aside to allow him access to the guy's furry, exposed butt.

"Nice," cooed Marco, guiding the gleaming head of his prick to the guy's hole.

Marco took hold of the guy's hips, flashing a grin as he got ready to violate the sonofabitch. Then, with one easy thrust, he buried his schlong in the guy's hole, breaching a previously impassable barrier. Knowing that sent a surge through my cock.

There was a bellow from behind the ball gag, as Marco's hardness violated the sanctity of the fag-basher's sphincter. He choked back a sob, and Marco let him savor the feeling of being ass-fucked for a minute before pulling back and pumping back into the guy. Then the screams really started in earnest.

Paulie was standing watching the whole scene, jacking off his cock. A thick drop of pre-cum oozed from his pisshole and glistened to the floor.

"Paulie," I told him, "I think this fuck is making too much noise. See if you can't shut him up."

"With pleasure, boss," growled Paulie, and, with surprising nimbleness for a horny-ass, cocksure mountain gorilla, he climbed onto the Indian right in front of Crosby's face.

He unbuckled the ball gag and yanked it out of Crosby's mouth. "Wish I could ram this in your pisshole," snarled Paulie, "but I think you'd fuckin' get off on that too much." He tossed the rubber ball, glistening with spit, to the ground. Crosby coughed and sputtered as Marco pumped his asshole.

"*You* got *me* all wrong," choked Crosby, and Paulie grabbed his long hair, yanking his head up.

"No, now you got me all wrong," snapped Paulie. "I didn't take your gag out so's you could flap your gums, motherfucker, I took it out so you could eat my fuckin' cock. And go ahead and bite down, if you think you can hurt me that way—just remember, your dick's gonna be the next one to feel some teeth."

Then he fitted his cockhead between the guy's lips and pried his mouth open with his thumbs. He rammed the guy's head down onto his cock, and my own cock gave a swell as I watched the guy's throat bulging with the thickness of Paulie's organ.

"Fuckin' A," I cried, "the guy's tougher than I thought— didn't even cough or gag when Paulie just fucked his fuckin' throat. Maybe his fuckin' sorority bitch girlfriend owns a big fuckin' strap-on she makes the guy suck."

Paulie and Marco laughed hysterically while they pumped Crosby from both ends. They picked up speed but kept it even, knowing I would be more than disappointed if they came before giving Crosby a proper double-hole reaming. Goddamn it, those two beasts looked good using this mother-fucker—two hairy, muscle-bound tough guys showing a third just how easy it was to reduce someone like him to a squirm-ing pair of fuckholes panting for hard biker cock.

Man, I was getting so fuckin' hard I was gonna shoot my load before much longer if I didn't get a piece of this. I unzipped my leather pants, reached in, and took my big hard cock out, walking around to the side so Crosby could catch sight of me even around Paulie's bulk.

His eyes went wide and a visible shudder of terror went through him. That made my cockhead swell even more.

"Yeah," I said. "You know what's next, motherfucker. You're gonna take this badboy up both of your fuckin' holes. Only question is, which one's first?"

As if in answer, Marco let out a groan and pumped the guy's ass harder, gripping his hips as he pistoned in and out of Crosby's hole. Paulie yanked his dick out and started jacking off, and you wouldn't fuckin' believe the thick streams of jizz that shot onto Crosby's face, soaking that mat of hair on his face and head, dribbling down onto the Indian. I didn't flinch—that bike seat had seen plenty worse in its fifty-plus years in the universe.

I walked out of Crosby's field of vision, going around back to see which end looked good to me. Both of them looked pretty goddamn fine—it would be a bigger challenge deciding where to stick my meat than I'd expected. Marco had finally finished shooting his load. He pulled out of Crosby's asshole, and a thick stream of jizz ran out, coating the wiry hair on his balls.

My jaw dropped.

"Well," I said. "Would you look at that!"

Sticking out of Crosby's hairy crotch and hanging there in midair was the biggest motherfucking hard-on I'd ever seen—next to mine, of course. It was so fucking long that in Crosby's hunched-over position, it was hanging maybe a half-inch from the back wheel of the Indian. I grinned.

"Fag-bashing motherfucker finds out he likes getting it in the keister, after all," I growled. "Boys, this is a night of triumph for fudge-packers everywhere. Marco, get me the keys to the Indian. I got an idea."

Crosby gave a pathetic moan of terror. He tried to find words, but couldn't—half probably because of all the cum in his mouth from Paulie overshooting, half from dealing with the fact that he had a raging hard-on from getting ass-fucked. While Marco fished the keys out of the top drawer of my desk and Paulie climbed off the Indian, stroking his already half-hard spit-and-cum-slicked cock, I stripped off my leather boots, vest, and pants, pulled my shirt off over my head, then put the boots back on.

"Paulie, open up the window, will you? These old bikes burn kind of dirty. And turn on the fan."

Crosby moaned.

"Looks to me like you need to learn to kiss some faggot ass," I snarled, mounting the Indian as if I were going to ride it. "So why don't you show me what you've learned so far?" Sitting on Crosby's head, I kick-started the Indian and put it in first.

Then I leaned forward hard so my ass was right in front of Crosby's cum-dripping face.

Marco saw what I was up to and, chuckling, grabbed Crosby's head. He yanked it back so I could get into position, then pushed it forward so Crosby's face was forced between my hairy black ass-cheeks.

"That big cock nice and close to the back wheel?"

"Half an inch, boss," chuckled Paulie. "No more."

"Perfect," I said, and popped the clutch.

The whole Indian shuddered as the gears caught. I heard the whine of the wheel spinning free in midair, and Crosby shrieked as he felt the breeze so close to his prick.

"You better hope your dick don't get any harder than it is," I shouted over the roar. "Otherwise, you're gonna find yourself minus one foreskin. Of course, all you have to do is get soft," I laughed. "Prove you don't want to lick biker butt as much as you *know* you do. Either that, or get to work with that tongue of yours, kissing my ass, and maybe I'll be nice enough to ease up on the gas a little."

I hit the accelerator, and Crosby shrieked. Then I felt his tongue burrowing into my asshole.

"Oh, yeah," I sighed. "That's right. Nothing I love more than feeling a homophobic fucker tongue my asshole like he knows he was meant to do. Paulie, you hard again?"

"Like a fuckin' rock, boss," said Paulie eagerly. "Any time you say, we'll nail this guy again."

"That's what I love about you, Paulie," I said. "The Italian fuckin' Stallion."

"Watch it, boss! Don't call me a fuckin' Italian."

"Oh yeah," I chuckled. "I always forget. It's the Sicilian Million." I reached back and patted Crosby's eagerly bobbing head as his tongue worked back and forth into my asshole. "That's the number of times Paulie here's shot his load in a nice hairy butthole like yours, Crosby." I clutched, and listened to the back wheel spinning down as the Indian shuddered and vibrated.

"You keep licking me like that, Crosby," I said, "and all you'll get is a reaming. Once that gorilla Paulie climbs on top of you, though, the suspension of this fuckin' bike is going to be taxed to the limit. I think you'll find your dick pressing hard against that back wheel."

"Let's find out," said Paulie, and I heard a muffled groan from my ass, felt a hot exhalation of breath as Crosby took Paulie's organ into his butthole.

"Is that dick pressing against the wheel?"

"Nice and hard," said Paulie with a chuckle. "You pop that clutch, boss, and it's *ciao*, fucker."

"Keep that in mind, Crosby, while you're licking my ass. I like a nice, deep ass-licking. You lose interest, and I just might let my hand ease up on the clutch."

In response, Crosby's tongue dug deeper into my butthole. Damn, that felt good. The guy's beard was rubbing rough and wiry against my ass, and if there was one thing I wished, it was that I could unstrap him and ram his dick up my hole without losing the coherence of the lesson. I would just have to be satisfied with a nice long rim-job.

"Oh yeah," I sighed. "You suck biker asshole just right, Crosby. I bet you always knew you wanted to be a faggot when you grew up."

I pushed back further on the seat of the Indian, careful to hold tight on the clutch—no way was I going to lose this Crosby guy's monster schlong to an accident when I'd just succeeded in converting him to our way of thinking. I started to stroke my cock while he licked my butt, and I heard Paulie groaning as he pumped harder into Crosby's asshole.

"This time, shoot it on his cock and balls, Paulie," I said. "Smear that fuckin' big cock of his with your cum, *capische*?"

This guy really knew how to lick biker ass. Coaxed by his tongue, I was gonna shoot my load all over the instrument panel of the Indian. And I didn't even fucking care anymore— sure, I would have liked to get a piece of that tight hairy ass, but his tongue up my hole felt so good, I wanted to do it right now. I began to jack my cock harder.

Then Marco was on me, his mouth over the head of my cock, his hand jerking himself off as he sucked me. I groaned, feeling his hot mouth engulf me, and then I came, my whole body shuddering as Crosby's tongue worked my spasming hole and Marco took my hot load down his throat. I went crazy, bucking hard on Crosby's face—and that's when I heard his scream, heard the choking grind of gears, and realized that I'd let my clutch hand slip.

"Oh fuck!" I shouted, reaching for the key.

"Goddamn it, boss," said Paulie. "If I hadn't already shot my load and climbed off of this fucker, his goddamn dick would be in the next county."

I switched off the Indian, climbed down, and walked around to look, just to make sure that his dick was still there. It was there, all right—big and thick and so beautiful it made me want to cry, hairy and dripping pre-cum like he couldn't wait to shoot his load all over the motorcycle tire that'd just almost made him a eunuch.

"Yeah," I said. "That's pretty fucking lucky for you, Crosby."

"And lucky for me," I said, eyeing that still-hard, throbbing dick. Eleven inches long if it was a fuckin' centimeter, and thick around as a can of green beans. If I didn't get that thing in my fuckin' asshole sooner or later, I was never going to forgive myself.

Crosby was sobbing, whimpering, still squirming on the bike. That last trick had given him a bad scare. But even he wasn't prepared for what happened next.

I heard screaming outside my office, Sammy Jane shrieking, "I told you, he's not taking any visitors! He's in a meeting!" And then the splintering of wood as the door came bursting in.

"Holy shit," gasped Paulie, scrambling for his revolver in the pile of his clothes. Marco was reaching for his, too, when we all realized it was Long Tooth Eddie sprawled on the floor in the remains of the door.

"Jackson, Jackson," Eddie was sputtering. "You don't understand, you got it all wrong!"

"Eddie," I chuckled. "Don't worry, we took care of the sonofabitch that worked you over."

"No, no, no," sobbed Eddie. "I fuckin' asked for it!"

"Eddie," I said, helping him to his feet and patting him on the back. "Eddie, Eddie, Eddie, that's classic blame-the-victim thinking! I don't want to hear any more of that kind of talk from you, pal. You did not ask for it. A man has a right to go to whatever sleazy fuckin' faggot bar he chooses, especially one run by me, without risking harassment by reactionary elements in society—"

"No! I fuckin' paid him thirty dollars!"

I stared blankly at Long Tooth Eddie.

"Oh, shit," said Paulie.

"I paid him thirty bucks to work me over in the alley," said Eddie. "I've been cruising him for weeks."

"But you're Mr. Vanilla!" I said to Eddie. Eddie was famous for wimping out when a guy even tried to tweak his nipples.

"I guess I wanted to walk on the wild side a little," said Eddie. "And damn, he was fuckin' good. If I'd known leather sex was like this I would have done it years ago. My mind was so fuckin' blown from the way this guy did me, I couldn't talk for an hour. By the time I came to my senses, I was in the back of Paulie's car outside your office. When I finally figured out what happened...well, I figured I'd better come over and make it right."

Crosby spoke for the first time. "You're a little fuckin' late," he rasped, his throat raw from Paulie's thick cock.

"I thought you'd been casing the joint," I said to him weakly.

"Just getting my nerve up," he choked. "I'm a city councilman."

"Holy shit," I said. Lester Crosby. I remembered him from the newspapers.

"I'm not exactly, um, out of the closet."

There was a long silence as I just stared at Crosby, wondering how fucked I was.

"See, now I feel terrible," I said.

I sat down and fumbled for a cigarette in my shirt pocket for a minute before I yanked my chest hair and realized I was naked. Paulie grabbed a pack from my desk and tossed it to me, with a lighter.

"Marco, Paulie," I said. "Let Councilman Crosby up."

They uncuffed his wrists and freed his ankles from the stocks. He slumped to the ground. Paulie grabbed a bottle of Jack and poured the councilman a drink. He slugged back that one, and the next, and the next.

When I'd taken a few good drags, a thought occurred to me. "Oh, damn," I said. "You're not, like, on the Zoning Advisory Board or anything, are you?"

"Matter of fact, yes," growled Crosby, looking at me.

"Councilman...I don't know what to say. It was just a simple misunderstanding."

"Hardly seems 'simple' to me," he said nastily.

"If there's any way I can make it up to you..." I began. The words were already out of my mouth when I realized that Crosby's dick was still hard—as hard as it'd been when Marco was porking the guy's ass. So maybe I'd noticed before, without realizing it, and that's why I'd said it.

"Well," he said, standing up with Eddie's help. "Now that you mention it, there is one thing...."

His hand closed around his big, hard cock. He stroked it a little. A drop of pre-cum oozed out of the pisshole and dribbled to the floor.

"Oh, shit," I said, feeling my asshole clench, remembering the eager tonguing Councilman Crosby had just given it, and the way my butt had hungered for that huge, beautiful municipal cock.

"You're joking," I said.

"Uh-uh," said the councilman, and Marco and Paulie looked at me, their hairy faces a curious mix of fear and excitement.

I looked one more time, briefly, at Crosby's dick—and that's all it fuckin' took. I was already hard, so I just looked at Paulie, at Marco, and nodded once.

The two gorillas came for me, broad grins on their faces. I heard Councilman Crosby laughing as Marco and Paulie dragged me to the Indian.

Heart
Simon Sheppard

I was in my senior year of college, a good-looking kid if I do say so myself, when my American Lit professor invited me to dinner. To discuss Melville, he said.

Only—and you're way ahead of me here, I guess—*Billy Budd* wasn't what was really on his mind.

"I like you," I said, after we'd polished off a bottle of semi-expensive wine and he was staring at me as if I were dessert, "but—no offense—you're old enough to be my father."

"Your grandfather," he said, and kind of smiled.

"Both my grandfathers are dead," I said. I have no idea why I said that.

His smile went away. He laid his hand on my knee. I was what you might call sexually confused back then. I'd had a couple of girlfriends in high school, had screwed the second one. And since I'd gotten to college, I'd fucked around with both girls and, later, guys, but nothing really serious. And now there I was, sitting on my teacher's back porch, the warm Ohio sky overhead, while Professor Starr, gray-haired, balding, and thick around the middle, was working his way up my thigh. I didn't know what to do. It's not that he grossed me out; he was still sort of decent looking, and must have been attractive when he was young. But that had been a long time ago.

His hand reached the edge of my shorts and I started to get a little jittery.

"Listen, Professor Starr…"

"'Hank,'" he said. "Call me 'Hank.'"

I'd been calling him "Hank" all evening.

"Hank, I've gotta take another pee."

"Well, you know where the bathroom is."

As I walked through the house, I noticed a wall full of pictures of him and some woman—his wife maybe, his dead wife most probably. The whole thing was just pathetic. But while I pissed, my hand started working my dick, and I was half-hard before I was through. I don't know, I figured maybe he'd give good head or something. Maybe he wore dentures.

When I got back to the porch, I pulled my chair close to his, put my hands behind my head, and kind of leaned back, shoving my crotch forward. I sighed and closed my eyes, and, as I knew it would, his hand quickly found its way to my dick and started kneading it into shape. I kept my eyes closed. I sighed again. He unzipped my cutoffs and in seconds I felt his wet mouth on my cock; I didn't wear underwear back then.

I opened my eyes. His place was out in the country, with nothing but a big field behind his house, but still…

"Maybe we should go inside," I said.

He took his mouth off me. "You don't mind, then?" he asked.

"Nah," I said. "You can suck me off. If you want to."

In his bedroom there was no sign of the old lady who probably had been his wife.

"Would you do me a favor?" my professor asked. We were both naked by then. His body was hairy and pudgy, and his dick was chubby, too. He'd made it clear that whatever happened, it wouldn't influence the final grade he'd give me for his course. Which I found more than a little disappointing, because I was pulling maybe a C.

"Depends on what the favor is, Professor. I mean, Hank."

"I want you to put your hand inside me."

"You want *what?*" I was, back then, a lot more innocent than I am now.

"Your hand," he said. "Inside me."

What the hell, I figured. Maybe it would help my grade, no matter what he'd said.

He pulled a can of Crisco from under the bed. "I'll tell you just what to do," he said. And he did, instructing me on every move. Just like in the classroom, he was a bit imposing, even though he was lying naked on his back with my fingers in his ass.

When I got my hand in up to the knuckles, I was a little afraid I'd tear something if I went any further.

"What are you waiting for?" the old guy said. "Keep rotating your hand back and forth. Keep pushing. And get your fucking fist inside me."

"Yes, Professor," I said.

When he opened up for me, I was kind of amazed. His hole just stretched right out to swallow up my hand.

"Ohhhh, Jesus, FUCK!" Professor Starr moaned.

He was hot and wet inside, slippery raw meat, alive.

"Close your fingers down into a fist, son. Gently…gently."

I was sweating like a pig, just astonished at what the old guy's body was capable of. I punched my fist slowly in and out like he told me to, staring down at his flesh stretched around my greasy wrist. Weird. And the most amazing thing of all was that my dick was still hard, and it was drooling like a mother-fucker.

Then, following his instructions—ever the apt pupil—I straightened out my hand and began to slide further up into him.

So this, I thought, *is what people feel like from inside. Empty.*

I negotiated the twists and turns of his guts, my forearm sliding into his heat. The old man was clearly somewhere else, his eyes rolling back in his head, his dick just oozing gallons of cum. He was damn near speaking in tongues.

And that's when I felt it, or at least realized I was feeling it. His heartbeat. I could feel his fucking heartbeat on my hand. Man, I felt as if I could just reach around his fucking heart and squeeze. And squeeze. And squeeze. I reached down with my free hand, intending to jack off, but as soon as I touched my cock, I shot off all over the place, wildly. Big spewing strands. And, astonishingly, my cock stayed rock-hard.

"Oh, fuck me with that fucking arm, son," the old guy begged. I thought I saw goddamn tears in his eyes. And then he started pissing all over himself, the piss dribbling over his hairy belly and soaking into the bedsheets.

I didn't wait to be told what to do. I grabbed his stiff cock with my cum-slick hand and jacked him off, his heart beating faster and faster to my touch. Lub-dub, lub-dub, lub-fucking-dub. Since he'd already leaked all that sperm, when he came it was dryish, more as if he were having a spasm than having sex.

And then, at his instruction, I pulled my arm out of him.

I didn't know what to say. "This place is a mess," I said.

"Don't worry about it," he said.

I looked down at my arm, the whitish coating of grease speckled with shit and blood. *Dude, you could have killed him,* I told myself. And that made me feel...oh, I don't know, but whatever it was, it wasn't bad.

We talked about it a few days later, about what we'd done, but I didn't ask too many questions. I didn't want to know. And we never did it again.

I got a B+ in his class. I'd been hoping for an A, but what the hell. Before graduation, he asked me to dinner again. I accepted, but like I said, nothing happened. I knew he wanted it to, I could tell; but I guess I enjoyed having the power to turn him down.

Well, something did happen, actually.

"You want it?" I asked after dinner.

"Yes, please," he said, like a little child. Fucking pathetic.

"Well, you can look but you can't touch," I said. And I sat back at the dinner table and pulled my dick out, spit into my hand, and started jacking off. When he reached down to his own crotch, I said, "Don't," and he didn't. So he watched like a starving old man while I shot my load, catching it up in my hand, then leaning over and waving it under his nose, letting him smell the saltiness before I licked my own hand clean.

I graduated a few days later and left town.

Back in Colorado, I got a Christmas card from him. He must have gotten my address from the alumni office. It was nothing very personal, just a noncommittal, generic card. But inside, above his signature, he'd written, "Call me. Please." And his phone number. I never called. I guess it felt good, in a twisted sort of way, to think of some fat old guy having a hopeless crush on me. Fuck.

And then, on Valentine's Day, another card, this time in a red envelope. But this card was homemade—a photo pasted onto a folded piece of paper. A photo of a heart. A real one. A real human heart.

And inside he'd written, "I don't expect you'll phone, but here's my number again." The dumb fuck.

Then, the next Christmas, another card, though without anything but his signature inside. And another one the next Christmas. And then nothing. That was three years ago. That was all I ever heard from him. Maybe he just gave up. Maybe he's dead. I guess I really don't want to find out. Y'know? Whatever. Lub-dub. Lub-dub. Lub-dub.

AIDS Is Over

Karl von Uhl

AIDS IS OVER, announced the graffiti, from billboards to bus stops. *HIV IS A LIE,* similarly, was stenciled throughout the city.

Jarrod and Marcus stood in line with countless others, waiting to enter FabYooBliss by Chunklet, their favorite weekend club. They went to anything Chunklet and Hunklet produced: Club Wearisome, for which they dressed up; Science Fair by Night, for which they dressed down; (A Rave Called) Chicken Thigh, which sent them both to the racks. C and H had the best d.j.'s, the best music, the best crowd, the best VIP lounges, the best boys, and the best drugs.

Marcus noticed the stenciled graffito on the sidewalk. *HIV IS A LIE.* He poked Jarrod and said, "Is that a new club or something?"

"No. It's, uh, something else," he said.

"Like what?"

Jarrod rolled his eyes. "Um, Marcus…"

"What?"

"It's, like, really hard to get in a party mood if we have to talk about stuff like that."

"So what is it?"

"Just some stupid saying some people are writing every-where." Jarrod was wearing a zebra-striped, Lycra tank top and baggy denim pants. A small hit of E kept him warm in his windbreaker. "Are you stoned yet?" he asked.

"Nah, I'm saving my drugs for later," Marcus answered. He dressed in baggies as well, with a tasteful half-inch of leopard print boxers visible above the belt-line, and an over-sized Big Dogs T-shirt, which he wore for camp. Both young men were clean-shaven, as was the predominant fashion of the young men around them.

The line progressed smoothly and soon they were inside, surrounded by a million floating points of light from a mir-rored ball. The music was loud enough to vibrate their kidneys. They checked their coats with Barnstormella, the World's Fiercest Coatcheck Grrrl, and went to the dance floor.

"If you believe," sang Cher.

I am so pissed, thought Jarrod. This song is way old and they're playing it way too early.

Marcus danced in curious, half-formed moves, alternately intensely lyrical and brusque, curved and peaked, spliced with epicene emotion and affectlessness. He surveyed the crowd, and caught himself feeling awestruck by their general beauty—so casual, serene, and energized.

The crowd whirled around them, believing in life after love, no dancer necessarily partnered, but everyone on the floor appearing to dance with themselves, with each and none other, all partnered to all and none, lifting in one apparent communal beat that thumped neither/or, believing, believing, believing. Jarrod loved this feeling. He didn't always feel it and thought it was a shame when it didn't happen, and on those occasions he more often than not blamed the crowd, or to a lesser extent his drugs. He danced in his customary fashion, making the same move over and over, feeling the beat consume him.

After about thirty pulsating minutes on the dance floor, they took a break in the subbasement VIP lounge to drink some orange juice. The forced air in the lounge was cool and wet, the distinctive San Francisco humidity intact.

"You ever wonder what the words mean? I mean, in songs?" asked Marcus.

"What do you mean?" Jarrod produced a small brown vial of crystal. He up-ended the vial, twisted the cap, put it in his nose, and snorted. He made a face as the white powder stung his sinuses.

Marcus took the vial. "Like that one really old song, 'Don't Leave Me This Way'? It was, like, all 'don't you leave me this way, I can't survive,' blah blah blah. And then all those people, like, die of AIDS." He snorted the powder and tossed his head back. "It's like creepy. How there's this song about leaving. And then people die."

"You think too much, honey," said Jarrod. "Much too much. Now let's go to the restroom and suck some cock."

"Doesn't anyone date anymore?"

"Marcus," said Jarrod, exasperated.

"OK, OK, gimme another toot."

The restroom, as usual at Chunklet and Hunklet's productions, was a festive orgy. If you really had to pee, the best place to do it was outside in the adjacent alley, because as soon as your dick was exposed here, someone started sucking it. And if you had to poop, your best effort was to find someone who could open the girl's restroom, which was kept locked.

Marcus had a big dick, fashionably uncircumcised and lovingly veined, as if sculpted, and a sturdily boned, fair-skinned body. The crystal spun through his senses as he and Jarrod entered the restroom, their simple shirts dangling from the waistbands of their jeans. The black light from the fixtures played seductively on the crowd, making teeth and eyes of formerly whole faces. With a fluorescent felt-tip pen, someone had written above the stalls, *AIDS IS OVER.* Maybe that's Chunklet's next party, thought Marcus.

He saw Jarrod making out with a young tattooed Hispanic boy. Marcus liked watching his friend make out; it made him feel good.

Marcus didn't have to wait long with his dick out. A boy with buzz-cut brown hair and green eyes, shirtless and smooth, walked up to him, and started stroking it. "Great cock," he said.

"Yeah," said Marcus.

"I'm gonna suck you," said the boy. He was maybe 23, a little old, but still very nice looking, perhaps a mixed Polynesian and southern German heritage, or else a touch of Cherokee somewhere. It was hard to tell in this light.

"Yeah? That's good for a start," said Marcus.

The boy licked the cuff of Marcus's foreskin and Marcus growled. "Your cock tastes good," said the boy.

"Yeah," said Marcus, "so suck it."

The boy took Marcus's hardening cock into his mouth, worked his tongue under the lip of the foreskin. He brought his hand up to roll the skin back, inspected Marcus's cock, then took it in his mouth again. He licked in a circular motion.

Marcus leaned back and growled again, feeling a little light-headed. There was an odd tangy and metallic smell in his nose. He inhaled sharply through his nose, and felt something slither down his throat. More crystal, he guessed. The boy's tongue on his cock was making him hot.

He looked over at Jarrod. A slim black guy had joined him and the Hispanic boy. The three were sharing a single kiss, united by tongues, licking each other's mouth, their cocks out, in varying degrees of hardness.

Marcus watched as the black guy knelt and starting sucking their cocks. First one, then the other, alternating his attention. Jarrod reached over and squeezed the Hispanic guy's nipples, and the Hispanic guy tilted his head back. Marcus felt a tongue on his nuts and growled his approval. This boy knows what to do, he thought.

The thundering backbeat reached even here, and resounded through Marcus's head as the kid sucked him. Marcus grabbed his cock and started jacking it, running the foreskin back and forth over his cockhead as the handsome boy licked. The tune was changing, subtly, although Marcus could tell. "I'm blue," sang the voice, shaded by electronic tints. He'd heard this song a few times before, but it made him feel sexy wherever he was. Here, with a handsome boy sucking his cock, tonguing his piss-slit, he felt as if he could live forever in this moment.

"I wanna fuck you," said Marcus.

"Awriiight," said the boy, drawling out the word. He turned around and dropped his pants.

Cool, thought Marcus. The boy's ass was perfect: two smooth round mounds of flesh blending seamlessly into his thighs, no trace of hair, and a hole hungry to be fucked. Marcus pushed his spit-slicked cock into the boy's crack.

The boy shifted his weight twice, and squirmed against Marcus's cock. Marcus felt his cockhead dig right into the boy's cleft, a heat growing more and more intense as his cock was swallowed up. "Yeah," said Marcus. "That's what I like."

The boy continued squirming, his hole enveloping Marcus's cock. He clenched his hole in time to the music. Marcus felt the heat of the mucous-slick walls on his cock, sending a shower of sparks from his balls to his head. Instinctively he started humping, short, small, easy strokes into the boy's ass.

The boy, keeping his knees in a high, wide squat, bent up at the waist and, eyes closed, turned to kiss Marcus. Marcus licked the boy's face, watching Jarrod out of the corner of his eye. Jarrod was sucking face with the Hispanic boy, the black guy nowhere to be found. No, wait, there he was, licking the Hispanic boy's cheesy hightops. Jarrod jacked the Hispanic boy's cock. The Hispanic boy raised his arms for Jarrod, and licked his deltoid as Jarrod licked his armpit. Jarrod raised his face to the Hispanic boy's and kissed him. The Hispanic boy kissed back, running his hands over Jarrod's torso.

Marcus kept an easy rhythm in the boy's ass, taking his time fucking him. He looked down at his spit-soaked cock gliding into the boy's ass, and drooled a little more spit onto it. Then he drooled onto the boy's back and bent forward so that he could smear it on with his torso. He reached forward and grabbed the boy's cock. Like his, it was intact.

"You're uncut like me," said Marcus.

"Yeah," said the handsome boy.

"I really like that."

"Yeah." The boy grunted. "Fuck me some more."

Marcus placed his hands on the boy's shoulders and stroked his cock to the hilt into the boy's ass, then slowly pulled back. Careful to keep the head lodged inside, he waited a moment before pushing back in. When he pushed in, he heard the boy whimper, a high, sighing noise, almost girlish. It turned him on. He stroked his cock out again, waited a moment, then pushed in full length. Again, the boy whimpered and squirmed as he settled his ass against Marcus's groin. Marcus throbbed his cock, embedded in the boy's smooth ass. The boy moaned and bucked.

"That feels really good," said the handsome boy.

"Yeah."

The song wove itself into a longer mix, laced with vocoder and backbeat, still singing something about someone who's blue, a piano cascading around the synthesized backbeat. Marcus had trouble understanding the words, but rode the beat in his head. His hard cock felt as if it were dancing in the handsome boy's ass. Marcus began dancing along with the two rhythms—the insistent thudding backbeat and his own fuck-beat, double-time then half-time, the phase shift teasing more whimpers from the handsome boy before him, riding his hot hard cock first to, then out of, time with the omnipresent music. The crystal in Marcus's body built structures of infinite pleasure, which vibrated with every touch—the handsome boy's hot sloppy hole, the waves of sound from the dance floor, the humidity of sex in the room—and he knew he was high.

He glanced at Jarrod, who was licking the Hispanic boy's tattoos. Jarrod always got off worshipping someone's body, and seeing it, Marcus grinned. The black guy was next to them, sucking a tall white guy's cock. The Hispanic boy loved the attention from Jarrod. Jarrod licked the Hispanic boy's taut belly, jacked his cock, licked his balls, then turned him around and licked gingerly at the boy's buttocks. The Hispanic boy reached back and spread his cheeks for Jarrod. Jarrod placed his tongue right in the center of his crack, and licked the Hispanic boy's hole.

Seeing it, Marcus could feel a tongue on his hole, even though no one was rimming him. It must be the drugs, he thought. He kept fucking the handsome boy, running his hands along the boy's smooth back and sides, verging into dancing with him. His whole being felt centered on his cock in the boy's ass, on the tide of sensation washing over him, on how good each stroke felt, feeling as if he could fuck this boy all night for the sake of fucking him, of making the handsome boy feel good and liked and wanted.

The handsome boy's hole flexed on Marcus's cock, sending piquant shivers into Marcus's balls and belly. "Yeah," he said.

The boy turned his head. "What?" he said.

"I said, 'yeah.' I like it when you do that."

"Yeah. It feels good." The handsome boy turned his head forward again, impaled himself further on Marcus's cock.

Marcus ground his hips in a circular motion against the boy's ass. The boy whimpered each time Marcus hit his sweet spot.

Marcus saw Jarrod about to fuck the Hispanic boy. This'll be cool, he said to himself. He wondered if he could get Jarrod's attention, then gave up and simply hoped Jarrod would see him watching. The Hispanic boy braced himself against the wall, standing almost erect, his hard cock hidden from view. Jarrod grasped his own hard cock in one hand. Using the other to hold the Hispanic boy's cheeks apart, he slid it in. The Hispanic boy flinched, then settled and backed up to Jarrod. Jarrod started fucking him in quick, rhythmic bursts, pistoning then stopping. Jarrod reached up and squeezed the Hispanic boy's nipples, which made him buck hard against Jarrod's groin.

I oughta try that, thought Marcus. He reached forward and brushed his fingers against the handsome boy's nipples. They were small, but erect and very hard. The handsome boy moaned. Marcus was afraid to squeeze them too hard, so let his fingers play fairly lightly on them. The handsome boy shivered and clamped his hole down on Marcus's cock.

"Fuck," said the handsome boy.

"Yeah, fucking you," said Marcus, hardly hearing what the boy said.

"Do you like that, too?"

"What?"

"You like your, um...your..." said the handsome boy.

"Oh, no. It doesn't feel like anything on me," said Marcus, throbbing his cock in the boy's ass.

" 'kay."

Marcus started making long strokes, his balls slapping the boy's ass. His balls felt warm, and he liked the playful impact they provided. The boy jacked on his cock. Marcus timed his strokes with the boy's jacking hand.

"Fuck," said the handsome boy. "Feels like your cock's inside mine."

"Cool," said Marcus, thrusting into the boy's ass. The handsome boy's hole was wildly wet now, slick with mucous and dickspit.

"I want you to fuck me," said the handsome boy.

"Yeah," said Marcus.

"I want you to fuck me forever." He jacked diligently on his cock.

Jarrod and the Hispanic boy were moving as one, like a machine. Marcus watched them, and for a few minutes matched Jarrod's thrusts with his own. He threw his hands into the air and fucked the handsome boy with his entire body, accentuating his thrusts with his back and legs. The handsome boy was thrown off balance once, but Marcus caught him and kept fucking. The boy whimpered and sank against Marcus, panting and moaning.

It was all one beat in Marcus's head, all one hard, heavy, throbbing, thudding beat, all the drugs, all the sex, all the hole, all the cock, all the boys, all the balls, all the sweat, all the heat. It built in Marcus's groin and slithered up his belly, igniting his spine.

"I'm gonna...," he said, unable to finish the sentence.

"Yeah," said the handsome boy.

Marcus plowed his cock into the handsome boy's ass, held the boy's shoulders. He felt dangled on a precipice, the good feeling growing subtly, so slightly, but growing, encouraged by the boy's hot ass, and he knew the slightest push would tip him over. Marcus distinctly felt the cuff of his foreskin flap over his cockhead in the boy's ass and that did it. The rush charged from his butthole to his navel, up his chest, and into his head, and he bucked hard as he shot load after load of jizz into the handsome boy's ass.

The handsome boy pushed back against Marcus's thrusts, jacked his cock, whimpered one more time. By the time Marcus stopped thrusting, the handsome boy presented him with his jizz-covered hand. Marcus hugged the boy, belly to back, kissed his neck. He looked toward Jarrod and the Hispanic boy, who were still fucking and dancing and dancing and fucking, the fluorescent graffiti floating above them.

"I wanna do that with you again some time," said the handsome boy.

"Yeah," said Marcus.

AIDS IS OVER, said the handwringing on the wall, begging the wrong question.

Body Symphony
Barry Webster

Contrary to popular opinion, Tchaikovsky was not an easy lay. I had to work damn hard to get that sucker to show me his boner.

"William, my dear friend," he said, "I think you are a superb fellow, but such things simply cannot be done. Sexual feelings must no longer shake my fragile soul." He looked down.

"Everything is consumed..." his eyes blackened "...by music."

"Music? You mean it's better than cock and balls?"

"Oh, William, you don't understand!" he said, collapsing into a gilded armchair and bringing his hands to his face, which was smooth as marble, the pale clear skin sloping down to his forest-thick beard. This guy was studsville!

"My music is dying!" He banged one hand on the table, the torchère swayed. "It's slipping from my grasp, and I don't know why! It *must* be caused by *physical desire* puling me about and destroying my concentration!"

"Who says your music's gotten lousy? I couldn't hear your last symphony without wanting to put my hand between my legs."

"It's…" He closed his eyes. "*Romeo and Juliet.* Balakirev says it should be ready now. But I'm stuck. Stuck!" Beads of sweat appeared on his forehead. "At the culminating moment where the contrasting subject must resolve into the main theme, the progression goes B-minor dominant, tonic, then…then what?! I can't resolve it. Everything I try sounds *Russian,* when it's an *Italian* story. The problem eats at my brain. I read the play daily for inspiration—some clue, some way to instinctively inhabit the story—but I fail!"

"I'm an Englishman," I said, unbuttoning my fly. "Doesn't that give me an intuitive understanding of Shakespeare?"

He looked at me for a minute. "Maybe it does." He turned and placed his fist against his mouth. "Yes, I think it might."

"As for Italy," I said, peeling off my trousers and removing my collar, "I'm a hairy little fucker; my grandma's from the Veneto, a direct descendant of the fair Veronans."

He turned to me, eyes widening. "God," he cried, "maybe… maybe!" He stared at me, and suddenly his pupils dilated, he tore off his waistcoat, cravat, shirt, and pants, and when he threw me naked on the bed, I cried out, "Oh, Petie, play me like a piano, make my body a symphony, you raunchy horndog."

His prickly beard drove into my stomach as he began to hum and sing the opening of *Romeo and Juliet.* He mimicked the hypnotic chant of the violas, the throaty wail of the cellos, the furtive plink of plucked strings. His vibrating lips skidded over my chest, as sound, hot breath, and saliva exploded onto my skin. His sticky tongue lapped at my nipples; I smelled tobacco, hair oil.

"Yes, Petie, yes."

Then his great chest fell onto mine and the main theme kicked in. Tchaikovsky sang away as the string section propelled the melody skyward. It fell in dizzying drops, spun in ever-widening loops. His hands made a vise and my groin burned inside it.

"Yes, itch me, Ilyich, itch me!"

Above my face, his mouth twisted and puckered, his tongue plucked lips, breath squealed through his nostrils, his hand beat at the bed frame, castanets clattered in his throat, and his entire body shook when he cried out a trumpet blast.

I gasped, my breath racing, the insane thudding of the contrabass, cymbal-crashes like lightning, a deafening hammer-blow as the tuba-roar filled the room.

A thousand pianists' fingers pressed on my every pore.

Then as the strings trembled on F-sharp, I felt him holding, holding me in such suspense, it was agony.

Suddenly he flipped me over and the tempo raced, violins screamed, kettledrums pounded, Tchaikovsky's spit splattered over my back, shoulders, hair. I saw him in the gilt bronze looking glass, eyes blazing, his right hand on my hip, the other whipping furiously in the air, the entire orchestra surging up and up to the cliff-edge of the highest precipice, and then...

He stopped.

"I can't do it," he cried.

"Yes, you can," I screamed.

"No, I can't."

"Yes, you can."

He paused, then thrust forward a final time with his hips, singing out the notes A, F, and D. A D-minor chord! What a surprising transition! Never heard before in the history of music!

We both cried out at the top of our lungs.

Then we fell to the bed and did a dying fugue of moans and signs.

I said, "You fucking know how, you feisty sleazebag."

Tchaikovsky began to bounce up and down, singing, "F, D-minor!" over and over.

He threw a blanket in the air and as it drifted down to cover us, he started kissing me, singing "F D! F, D! F, D!"

I sat in the Moscow Hall at the opening of *Romeo and Juliet*. Violin bows slashed the air, the conductor's body thrashed like a fish on a hook, and as the piece approached its summit—I couldn't help it—my head fell back, my eyeballs rolled up, and I yelled out "F *D!* F, *D!* F, *D!* F, *D!*"

The Hittite Slave

Larry Townsend

Some men, regardless of their status at birth, are literally born to be slaves. This is an emotional condition that has existed through all the ages of mankind, although recently recognized only by some of our more enlightened researchers. In the Bronze Age cultures of ancient Egypt and her contemporary civilizations, when one man could own another, it was generally the status of a one's family that determined his place in this hierarchy of Masters and slaves. Our setting is Palestine, during a time of conflict between the Hittite Empire and the forces of Pharaoh. Our narrator, a young Hittite officer, is about to be assigned by his commanding general as noble hostage to the Egyptians, in an exchange that is intendedsupposed to guarantee adherence to a newly signed treaty.

On the evening before the final day, when a treaty would be signed to bind both sides, Anittas called me to his tent. With a peculiar display of kindness and fatherly solicitude, the general ordered his servant to bring me a bowl of wine. He then spoke at some length about the need to convince the Egyptians of our sincerity and desire for a peaceful solution to both the border and trade disputes. One way to do this, he continued, was to impress the other side with the number of noble personages within our delegation; the higher the ranks of the negotiators, the more certain the Egyptians would be of our concern.

I should have been suspicious, but I was so surprised and flattered by his sudden attention that I simply sat on the a camp stool, nodding at everything he told me. Thus, when he concluded by asserting the need for me to wear golden armor during the final ceremonies the next day, and to be introduced as a young man of princely status, I did not question him. There were several such men in our group, including Anittas, himself, and there certainly should have been no need for me to bolster their ranks. Yet I did not doubt my General's judgment. When he presented me with the costume I was to wear the following morning, I could only smile and stammer in gratitude for the honor he was bestowing upon me. Even his final remark—to the effect of my being a devoted servant of the Eemperor, willing to make any sacrifice in his name—failed to shake my feeling of pride and gratitude.

And so it happened that I stood among the ranks of noble officers, gilded like a sacrificial beast—and just as stupidly, for I had no idea of my fate until the ceremonies concluded with an exchange of hostages. Anittas selected a younger kinsman of his Egyptian counterpart-part, whereas Menna—barely able to stifle his grin of triumph—pointed his finger at me! When the assembly dispersed, I went with the Egyptians, after Anittas made a great show of bidding me farewell. Although I cursed the role into which fate had cast me, I must admit that my first few days with Pharaoh's soldiers were not particularly unpleasant. I was treated well, and was included among the other foreign nobles who attended Menna.

We were traveling southwest, toward Byblos, which was now firmly in Egyptian hands. The Syrian countryside was not greatlyvery different from ours, although it seemed to be a little more heavily populated. This made it possible to stop at night in an inhabited area, instead of camping on the desert sands. Menna, while maintaining a very proper aloofness, was always acted cordially in his manner toward me, inquiring after my well-being several times. Only his eyes betrayed the interest he really truly harbored, and I was fairly certain that once we reached our destination he would make some move to consummate his desires. I was not wholly displeased by this prospect, for I found him intriguing. Nor did this undercurrent go unnoticed by his subordinates, which probably accounted for their courtesy during this initial period of our association.

Thus, in less than a week, I had become reasonably comfortable in my new surroundings, and had begun to anticipate an easier future than I had at first envisioned. It therefore came as a terrible shock when, on the seventh night, I was suddenly awakened by a troop of Egyptian soldiers. I was hauled roughly from my bed and thrown face down on the floor. My hands were bound behind me by several wrappings of leather thongs, and my arms were fastened to my sides with chains. I had been naked beneath my blankets, and was left in this humiliating condition when the soldiers dragged me into the large farmhouse where Menna had been sleeping.

The entire staff of officers was assembled about their viceroy, all dressed in full battle gear, aswhen I was dragged before them and pitched onto my knees in their midst. Before I could speak to question the reason for this outrage, Menna stepped forward and struck my chest with his foot. The force sent me tumbling backward, and I had to struggle to assume a semi-erect posture, leaning on my side.

"As I am sure you already know," he said harshly, speaking my native Nesite with a heavy accent, "the Hittite armies crossed into Syria early this morning. The treaty has been broken, and by right of law your life is forfeit."

My face must have reflected my horror and disbelief, because Menna stopped his tirade and stared at me, his eyes moving slowly down the length of my body, pausing several times at my groin where my genitals lay exposed and unprotected. Without my willing them, tears came to my eyes as I protested my innocence in any conspiracy, and this must have convinced the Egyptian viceroy of my sincerity. He spared my life, but I no longer had the status of a hostage. I was now a slave—his his slave—and he ordered me transported to Byblos while he ledlead his own forces northward.

Still naked and bound in chains, I was placed in a wheeled, wooden cage used to haul livestock, and carried to the viceroy's house on the coast. At that time I spoke only my native Nesite, and therefore had no way to communicate with the men who guarded me. I was completely alone, bitter in my knowledge that Anittas must have planned the entire treachery before ever arranging for me to be the Hittite hostage. Aware of the inevitable results, he had asensured that no actual prince would be sacrificed.

I wondered whether the planning had gone back even further, whether Utmisch had suggested I be used, whether he had told his friend the reason for wishing me placed into Egyptian captivity.

Although I had no way to know it at the time, Anittas's plot was doomed to failure. King Tushratta of the Mittani promptly allied himself with the Egyptians, and between them they drove our Hittite forces back into the mountains. The emperor counterattacked with sufficient power to save Carchemish, however, and eventually a second, more important treaty was signed by Anittas.

But all of this took many months, during which I was lodged in a cell beneath the viceroy's house in Byblos. Menna must have given very detailed orders regarding my treatment, because I was well fed and forced to exercise every day. I was kept in rags, but they were fairly clean. I was required to bathe regularly, and a servant was sent to instruct me in the Egyptian language. Although Menna spoke enough of our tongue to make himself understood, I now began to wonder exactly what plans he had for me upon his return. I was definitely being too well cared for. Nor should there have been any need for me to learn the intricacies of their language if I was to be no more than a caged captive.

Some orders must also have been given regarding any physical abuse of my body, for the several pairs of guards were all careful never to actually lay hands on me in a sexual way. Some of them did display more than a casual interest in my nakedness, however, and as the weeks passed and I learned more of their language, I came to realize that they were making jokes about my unmutilated manhood. All of them had undergone a ritual called "circumcision," which deprived them of their foreskins. They actually seemed proud of their condition, and during exercise periods, or when I was being transported between my cell and the baths, I was sometimes required to watch when they urinated against the wall of the house or in the alley behind it. Having little else to occupy my mind, I quickly gained a reasonable fluency in their language. At about this time Menna had agreed to the establishment of a new treaty, and the exigencies of command had lessened sufficiently to permit his communicating with his household. A messenger arrived from him one day, and immediately afterward I was placed in heavy metal fetters by my guards. I was to be made like them, they told me, and it required several moments' thought before I realized what they meant.

By then it was too late. My struggles were in vain, for the thick circlets of bronze pinioned my wrists together behind my back, and a set of chains restricted the movement of my legs. I was hustled upstairs, where an Egyptian physician awaited me. The soldiers placed me on my back atop a leather-covered couch, and the chains were struck from my ankles. My legs were then repositioned to keep them spread as wide as possible, secured to supports at the base of my couch. A cord was tied about my neck and fastened to the head of the slab, this to prevent my sitting up. In an apparent act of kindness, the senior guardsman ordered my wrists freed from behind me and repositioned at the sides of the couch. It required two men on each arm to accomplish this.

I was terribly frightened, and furious. I did not wish my man-manhood to be altered, and I knew the operation was going to be extremely painful. The physician, a young man whose body had been completely shaved, and who wore only the light-blue kilt and headdress of his profession, dismissed the soldiers and stood at the foot of the table, gazing down at my naked body with the trace of a smile on his features.

"I am going to be kind to you," he said softly. "A youth of your age is easily aroused, and after the operation an erection will be painful for you until the wounds have healed. I would like to spare you as much misery as possible." With that, he placed his lips about my penis, and began to manipulate me in a way that only a Babylonian whore might have been expected to do. I was stunned to silence, but before my anger could drive me to shout at him, the pleasurable sensations made me collapse backward in my bonds. My shaft rose hard and seeking into the warm moisture of his demanding mouth, and I was helpless to do more than groan in ecstasy as his tongue and lips worked upon my flesh.

I climaxed once, and might have grown soft had he not retained his grasp, swallowed my seed, and continued to suck me deeply into him. He kept this up until I had released my sperm a second and a third time, the final discharge being almost painful as my aching testicles gave up their fluids and my sweat-covered body collapsed in near exhaustion. He continued to work upon my unresponding organ until the helpless flaccidity convinced him I was fully drained. Only then did he reluctantly release his hold.

"Now," he said, "it will be much easier for you." He carried a small table to the side of my couch, and from this he took several instruments. I begged him to spare me, but he shook his head. "Your master has commanded it," he said simply. He held a wooden bowl to my lips. "Drink this," he said, "it will ease the pain." Foolishly, in my seething rage, I smacked the vessel aside with a snap of my head and thus was condemned to feel this most terrible agony without any narcotic.

He seized my penis once again. Staring down the length of my gleaming, naked body, I could see him draw the foreskin outward and set several clamps to hold it away from the shaft. This hurt me, and I fought against my bonds. "Lie still," he said sternly. "You will only increase the pain." And so I had no choice but to lie there while the terrible bolts of agony shot through my entire body.

His sharp copper knife was run around the base of my crown; searing waves of pain engulfed me. I screamed at the frightful sensation, growing angrier with the realization of the finality of his actions. I would forever be without this badge of masculine power. I would be a shorn sheep, like the Egyptians whom I now hated with a passion to exceeding anything I had ever felt for Anittas or my treacherous cousin. I could see the blood thatwhich covered his hands, and watched the specks of crimson begin to form a pool about the base of my sex, oozing upward toward my navel.

When he finished, he bound the wound in white linen, having stitched the skin in several places, exactly like a woman sewing a piece of cloth. I cannot describe the fiery pain that now engulfed me. It was worse, by far, than the beating my cousin had given me—worse than anything I had ever imagined. And, more, I knew that my foreskin was forever gone, and within my own mind I was not unlike the castrated catamites who giggled and simpered about my cousin's harem.

I was allowed to remain on the couch until shadows of darkness obscured the windows of the room. Then some guards returned and released my feet. My arms were rebound behind me before they guided me back to my cell, one of them gently holding my genitals to prevent their being buffeted by the motion of my legs. Even this indignity I accepted as a blessed relief from the throbbing misery I had felt when I first stood up.

After this, I lay on my cot, hardly able to rise for several days. The physician came several times to inspect his work, always with a guard at his back to asensure that I did not attack him. But I was too depleted for this, and even when the wound had healed enough to cause me little pain I was still too embarrassed to do more than lie and stare at the ceiling, plotting the revenge I would have on all of them. Except when I needed to urinate, I could not bring myself to so much as touch my mutilated penis. Only once during all this time, in a terrible, frightening nightmare, did I relieve the terrible pressure in my loins. And even this caused me grievous waves of guilt.

Menna returned with his army, and took up residence in his house. I knew this, for I could overhear the guards speaking outside my cell. Because I had entered into a phase of madness, no one came near me except to poke food through the door. Even this was always done by a servant, with at least four guards in attendance. The physician had ordered me freed from my bonds when the wounds on my penis were healed, and after that I had tried to attack anyone who approached. I do not know how much time had passed, but I was now healed to a point where the marks of the surgeon had receded to a narrow red welt that looked as if it would mark my sex forever.

The viceroy had been back for half a cycle of the moon, when he must finally have decided to make use of me regardless of my reported condition. The physician entered my cell, attended by six guards, who quickly pinioned me against my cot. I had gone naked since the day of my operation, covering myself only at night when the cell became chilly. Thus my body was readily available for inspection. With the soldiers holding me down, the physician carefully examined his handiwork while I struggled and shouted at him, calling him every insulting name I had learned in his wretched language. He ignored my violent protests, and when he had satisfied himself regarding my condition, he poured the contents of a small flask into my water bowl. With the help of the guards, he managed to force most of it down my throat.

I had been tossed back on my cot when they left, and within a very short space of time I began to feel a weakening effect from the potion. It was not a sleeping draught, however, —more an elixir to make me calm and docile. I felt a floating sensation, not unlike the effects of drink, except that the aura came with a deep sense of peace. I no longer wished to fight my enemies; rather, I experienced a longing to soar into the warmth of a midday sky, an act of which I considered myself fully capable.

While I was still affected in this manner, the guards came for me, and I was taken to the bath. Here, the viceroy's servants cleansed me thoroughly and dressed me in a linen breechcloth. My wrists were again restrained with the heavy manacles, and I was conducted to Menna's apartments. It had been late morning when the physician forced the drug down my throat; it was now dark outside, and I could feel the effects draining away. My anger was slowly returning, heightened by the knowledge of this additional invasion of my being. Yet deep within me the flickering flame of sanity kept warning me that Menna was the sole key to my survival. But conflicting with this desire to live, was the conviction that if I did survive, and somehow managed to escape—my dominating thought until the day of my circumcision—I could never return to my own people except as a semi-gelded Egyptian.

Menna satwas alone in a large salon, which adjoined his bedchamber via a great, undraped arch. Two guards entered with me, standing to either side, holding my arms while the viceroy approached to take a closer look at me.

"You have been resisting us," he said, after examining my body with hands and eyes. "You have lost some flesh, —not an unbecoming change." He continued to fondle my chest and arms, gently pinching my nipples, allowing his cool, dry palms to press against the hard, taut walls of my abdomen. "Will you continue to resist me?" he asked.

I did not answer him, merely dropped my gaze to the floor and silently endured his explorations. In truth, there was a sensual quality to his touch; nor was Menna an unattractive man. He was naked beneath a light robe, which hung loosely from his shoulders. His arms and that portion of his chest that was visible to me were solid and well formed. He wore no mantle on his head, and this was covered with a dark, short stubble of hair. His hands were long, with thick, strong fingers. Despite my anger and firm resolve to hate him, I could feel my sex responding to his contact.

Abruptly, he seized my breechclothloincloth and stripped it away. "Let us examine the result of my physician's skill," he muttered. The suddenness of his move had caught me completely off guard. My penis curved outward, heavy and half erect, my testicles drawn tightly beneath it to further cause the tumescent length to protrude from my groin. Menna nodded, continuing his examination. He lifted the shaft, fingered the thin red welt, tested the looseness of the remaining skin. In effect, the cutting had not been as severe as it might have been, and when my penis was completely soft there was still a semblance of excess, just enough that the skin could fold over the scar itself, concealing it. All of this seemed to please him, and at length he motioned for the guards to secure me, face out, tointo a three-legged wooden framework bolted to the floor near the entrance to his bedchamber.

My legs were spread wide, and chained to the bottoms of two uprights. A bronze collar was set about my neck, attached to the apex of the tripod, some six or seven hands-breadths above my head. My wrists, of course, were still joined behind my back. At Menna's signal the guards withdrew, leaving us alone.

"I regret the necessity of these restraints," said the viceroy, "but my men inform me that you have become rather vicious. I hope the day will come... —" His voice trailed off as he dropped his robe, standing before me as naked as I, except for the military sandals on his feet. His body had been completely shaved, but the dark shadows on his chest indicated the heavy growth he would normally have displayed. His body was every bit as firm and well defined as I had expected, and his genitals were no less powerful and masculine, despite his lack of foreskin. His own penis was beginning to rise, and when he stepped toward me we touched in that area before any other.

His lips pressed on mine, his arms crushing me against him, while his flooding desire seemed to communicate itself on me. For a moment my head grew light as I responded to both to the viceroy's embrace and to the final vestiges of the drug, until I could not control my emotions. I felt the rush of lust burning in my loins, the power of my own sex responding to the thrusting pressure from him. Slowly, his tongue forced its way between my teeth; one hand slid down my back, past my own manacled arms, to cup the curve of my buttocks. Gradually, he worked his way down the front of my body, his warm lips and tongue touching every part of me, caressing my neck and shoulders, working a long time upon my nipples. He kissed the rigid muscles of my belly, and finally dropped to the groin where he twisted his tongue through the shield of hair, eventually kneeling before me to take my penis deeply into his throat—an act that I was now coming to accept without my previous distaste.

His attentions had left me gasping for breath, making me un-unsteady and wavering so that the weight of my body pulled several times against the collar. Without this to steady me, I might have fallen. The hard pressure about my neck gave the sensation of being hanged, and somehow this was also sensual. Still, the fact of my present captivity, and all that had gone before, continued to anger me—more so as the effects of the drug decreased. The My inability to control the responses of my own body did not blunt the edge of my mounting fury. While my Egyptian captor knelt before me, I struggled to readjust the inner workings of my body. The hardness of my projecting penis made it difficult, but I finally managed to force a spurt of urine to enter him.

I had intended this as an act of defiance, hoping it would insult him and offend his delicate sensitivities. But it was an act of madness, for I only condemned myself. When the first drops touched his tongue, he abruptly stopped his motion. His lips retained their hold for another moment, during which I was able to unleash the pent-up stream of fluid. When this cascaded into him, he pulled back in shocked amazement, after which the urine poured across the front of his body.

His face a mask of fury, the viceroy slowly came to his feet, ignoring my final trickle that caused a sour puddle to gradually expand across the marble floor. He struck me hard across the mouth, using the back of his hand. His rage mounting, he slammed his fists time and again into my belly, knocking the wind from my lungs while he screamed at me in rage. Although I was almost rendered almost insensible in the first moments, I began to better understand the source of his violent anger. He had wanted me from the first day he had seen me, he said, and he had anticipated this moment through the months he had been away. He had ordered my circumcision so that my body might be clean enough to merit his attentions. He had honored me by assigning his own private physician to attend me, and now I had defiled his person. He ranted on, all the while pummeling me with his fists until my only thoughts were concentrated on maintaining enough control of my balance to keep from strangling inon the collar and chain.

I was saved from death, I think, only by the arrival of the guards. These men burst into the room, responding to their master's cries, probably expecting to find that I had somehow freed myself and attacked him. At the sight of the soldiers, Menna regained enough control to order me removed. I was hurriedhustled from the elegant apartments and thrown back into my cell, the manacles being left upon my wrists, and the bronze collar still about my neck. For the rest of the night I lay in a muddle of pain and confusion, really truly afraid for the first time since arriving in Byblos. My arms ached from their restraints, and my whole body seemed a solid mass of agony from the beating Menna had given me. There was a patch of dried blood on my lips, which I managed to lick away, only to start a fresh trickle where my teeth had cut the inside of my mouth. If I tried to lie on my stomach it increased the pain in my chest and abdomen; if I turned onto my back, my arms grew numb. I knew some terrible fate awaited me in the morning.

Shortly after the first rays of sunlight filtered through the single window in the wall high above me, the soldiers came.

They force-marched me out of the main house, using a back corridor I had never seen before. They took me to a large open square, and stood me on a raised dais, with a wooden frame-work rising to half again my height above. My ankles were chained to the base, and my arms were repositioned to leave me spread-eagled in the open air.

There were already aA few townspeople were already on the street, and more began to crowd the area while the sol-diers set my fetters and whipped me with the short flails they all carried as marks of rank. I assumed it was a marketplace, and I was being put on display. But this would be only a part of it. Soon after the soldiers departed, leaving me chained and helpless, naked before the eyes of the current spectators, a group of rag-gedragged youths began to taunt me. They shouted insults first, then one of them picked up a horse turd from the street. He threw this at me, but missed, striking another young man who stood behind me. After that I became the center of a mock battleground, with the muck of the gut-ters being flung from all directions, much of it striking me. As their game progressed, the boys began to take more deliberate aim, attempting to land their clumps of filth against my face or groin. Much of it struck my midsection, already sore from Menna's beating.

Finally, one of them grew bold enough to mount the dais, where he looked more closely at my mutilated organ. Laughing, he called to the others, and there was soon a small crowd of them examining the scar from my operation and making sportfun of me because of it. Then the one who had approached me first—a bigger youth, who seemed to be a leader among them—made a remark about my hairy body, how barbaric I was, and several of them started plucking at the individual hairs. I was stretched so tightly it was impossi-ble to pull away or otherwise defend myself, and I knew that trying to answer would only goad them to further torments.

But these came anyway. The big one took a knife from his belt and started to shave away the hairs on my chest. Another went to work on my legs, while a third began to scrape my loins. I did cry out, for they nicked me constantly and I was terrified that the one working on my groin was going to take more than the hair. To make it worse, I could feel my penis growing larger and more sensitive. While it never actually became hard, I know my sex hung down more fully than normal, swollen and flaccid despite their abuse.

At length, I dared not move because I could feel the callused fingers lifting my penis, and then the testicles, scraping away with the dull-bladed knife. The derision had grown worse, and more youths had joined in the sport until I had so many of them around me that I could not see my body below the nipples. For some reason, they left my beard and the hair on my head; but when they finished, the rest of my body had been completely denuded, and I was covered with myriad, tiny, bleeding cuts. They withdrew from the dais and, after pelting me with a few more clods of offal, they tired of their game and went running off, down one of the alleys....

Five a Day

Jaime Cortez

Artichoke

Artichoke is a flower, closely related to the thistle. If left unharvested, its coarse leaves unfold to reveal a gorgeous violet interior, the delight of bumblebees and a source of honey most superb. This is not evident to the casual viewer, because Artichoke cultivates extreme impassivity. The exterior is all spines and tough fiber armor, which demands a gingerly approach. You must insinuate yourself and coax away layer after layer of toughness. It is laborious at first, with scant rewards: a nibble of flesh here, a glimpse of pale, hidden skin there. At times, you wonder if there will be anything left under all that toughness, and throughout the process, Artichoke remains inscrutable, happy to let you labor on with no promise of success, seemingly indifferent that you've chosen to brave its barbed, bitter defenses. But eventually, you arrive at the heart. This is what it guarded with such green jealousy, this pale, tender heart. Yours to have now, the heart is doubly delicious for being so hard-earned.

Mango

Mango is the school slut and likes that just fine. Mango inhales its own scent and remarks, "I smell good." Turning around to admire its own sweetly rounded gold-and-red behind, Mango declares, "I look good." Noting the subtle indentations where admiring fingers have gently pressed, Mango purrs, "I feel niiiice. And my taste—well, don't even get me started." Mango sleeps in the nude and rarely alone. In the morning, Mango often wakes to find only the scent of the previous night's lover on the pillow, and it is never a problem. Mango takes four hours to watch Sophia Loren movies and frequently freezeframes the video to take notes. More than anything else, Mango likes an oral lover, that is to say a lover who heaps praise upon its head. Details count. The worshipper who notes its seashell ears and exquisitely formed toes earns more points than clumsy devotees who admire obvious attributes. "My eyes are pretty? Thanks for telling me."

Asparagus

Asparagus is not a complicated sort of guy. He was born small and erect and eventually grew tall and erect, but that is the extent of his development. Asparagus is utterly without mystery. He is green and tastes green. There is no skin to peel, no surprising seeds to bite down on, and no distracting shape or color. Most anyone can have Asparagus, as long as they are ready to do it his way. His sexual modus operandi is based on the Patriot missile:

1. Determine your goal.
2. Locate your goal.
3. Pursue it relentlessly.

Asparagus cums in the style of porn stars or World Wrestling Federation champions, with much attendant noise-making, flailing about, and extravagant facial contortions.

Once he has cum, Asparagus never stops to think about your orgasm. He washes off his pecker, slips on his action slacks, straightens his pointed green cap, and walks out with a wink that he fancies is most fetching. "I'll buzz ya', baby!" he calls over his shoulder. Even he doesn't believe that one.

Apple

Apple is the most sensible fuck in town. Apple is modest in appearance and rather brittle in her manner. She puts on perfunctory lipstick in red or green and provides consistency and friction. She is shocked, judgmental, and jealous of the flagrant, dribbling sensuality of Mango and the pornographic directness of Asparagus. Apple's greatest secret is that one thousand harvests ago, apples and roses shared a common ancestor. But a split occurred, with the apples playing down their blossom stage and devoting themselves to their plump, fruit state. In contrast, the roses channeled their energies into prolonging their blossom stage, their perfume and petals becoming ever more decadent, layered, and frivolous. Apple rejects all this, keeping on its pajamas when fucking, and stifling the urge to moan or drip, because of concern about what the Bartletts next door will think. Despite this, Apple eagerly awaits the day when some lover will hold her rounded sides and exclaim, "You know, I don't know why, but there's something about you that reminds me of roses."

Yam

No one ever fantasizes about Yam. It lies modestly under the soil, lamenting its turdy appearance and fantasizing about what life would be like if it only had Cherry's tempting color, Guava's scandalous scent, or Banana's riotous sense of humor. But Yam knows that no one will ever get past its appearance, so it works on inner beautification and masturbates well and often. On Friday nights, it is dateless, lounging about in the soil, its roots tangled all about it, uncombed. It curls up with its diary, a monocle on each of its squinty eyes. It writes arabesque love poems to the more gorgeous fruits, gets travel reports from passing worms, and formulates philosophy with tree roots. All the while it grows in size, wisdom, and richness, awaiting the day of its assumption, when it will be lifted bodily from the soil, cleansed of dust, released from its drab skin, and allowed to impart its nutritive, sun-colored riches with the gorgeous denizens of the bright world above.

Never Trust a Pretty Face
Michael Stamp

Being too eager for the good life is what did me in. From the minute I stepped inside Fletcher Greenfield's Long Island mansion on that gray, rainy morning, I had dollar signs dancing in my head like sugarplum fairies in the dreams of tots tucked into their beds on Christmas Eve. It was greed, pure and simple. That, and the kid. If I'd been thinking straight, I would have respected the No Trespassing sign, but when my dick started to lead, good sense deserted me and I followed along blindly. It's a weakness of mine. I've always been a sucker for a pretty face.

Fletcher Greenfield was a name I knew well. Everybody in New York did. I'd be willing to bet there isn't one building in the whole state that doesn't have pipes running through it that came from Bachman Greenfield Ironworks. I just never expected I'd be doing business with the man himself, and especially not in his posh palace of a home. It's an occupational hazard. Guys in my line of work rarely get invited to tea.

I'm a private dick, and even though FDR keeps telling us prosperity is just around the corner, times are hard and money is tight. Considering how bad the times are, you'd think I'd be scrounging for jobs, but I work steady most of the time.

It's been my experience that no matter how much a guy cries poor, when he thinks his old lady is mattress-dancing with someone else, he always manages to come up with my $10 a day plus expenses so that he can find out for sure. Following restless wives isn't much of a living, but when I see guys standing on street corners selling apples, peeping through hotel windows and taking dirty pictures starts to look real good. So when Fletcher Greenfield called, I came running. At least there wouldn't be any haggling over my fee. He probably spent that much on a good cigar.

The man looking at me from across his desk had to be in his 50s, but he was in fine physical shape, which made him appear much younger, despite the generous strands of gray in his black hair. His small mustache was dark except for a large streak of gray, making him look as if he'd forgotten to wipe his mouth after lunch.

What surprised me even more than his wanting me for the job was what he wanted me to do. I'd expected him to ask me to follow his wife, or maybe his girlfriend. When you've got big bucks, it must be pretty hard to figure out if a dame really loves you, or if she's just calculating your net worth while you're dick-deep in the cooze.

Being rich had to be tough. Given the chance, I knew I could learn to live with it.

But there wasn't any skirt involved. Greenfield wanted me to find some missing designs he thought had been stolen by a less than reputable competitor. Almost all my work's as a peeper, so I couldn't figure out how he'd come to think of me for the job. All he'd say was that I'd been "highly recommended." I couldn't help wondering who'd done me such a big favor, but I didn't want to press Greenfield for information, so I just accepted my good luck. The only problem was, I didn't feel lucky—maybe because I didn't trust the guy. He was a little too polished for my taste. Call me crazy, but there's something about a guy with manicured fingernails that raises my hackles. Still, the money Greenfield was going to pay me was good, too good to pass up. I'd have to peep through a lot of windows to make what Greenfield was offering me, and I wouldn't have to worry about getting my face bashed in by some unfaithful wife's burly boyfriend.

"So, Korrigan," he asked me, "can I consider you on board?"

Even though a little voice inside me was telling me to cut and run, I told the little bastard to shut the fuck up, and told Greenfield, "I'm your man."

"Excellent. I knew we could come to terms." Greenfield used a silver-handled ink-blotter on the check he'd just written, and handed it to me. "This should be enough to get you started."

"It will do nicely," I replied, slipping the check into my pocket. I stood up to leave, but when I offered Greenfield my hand he didn't take it, didn't even stand up.

"You can see yourself out," he said by way of good-bye, and with that I was dismissed. I didn't take offense—it was no less than I'd expected.

I took the stairs two at a time, anxious to be out of the house and back in the fresh air. But when I reached the bottom of the staircase I heard an urgent whisper, and turned around just in time to see him coming down the stairs.

Framed between the staircase pillars, he looked like a Renaissance painting I'd seen in the Guggenheim once: Soft, gentle features, with eyes such a deep blue that I could have drowned in them. That first look was like getting struck by lightning, and my dick had been the lightning rod.

"What can I do for you, kid?" I asked when I got my breath back, but the sudden sound of footsteps on the stairs sent him scampering like a scared rabbit. Just as well. Even if he wasn't jailbait, he sure looked it, and if he hadn't gone I might have been tempted to do something that would have gotten me into trouble.

All during the drive back to the city I couldn't get the kid out of my mind. My dick was so hard that working the clutch in my '37 Dodge coupe was almost painful. If I hadn't thought it would cause an accident, I'd have jerked myself off in the car.

My reaction to the kid wasn't surprising. After all, there hadn't been anyone since Frankie.

Frankie was just another Bowery boy when I met him. No mother, and a father who'd crawled inside a bottle of rotgut and came out only to slap his son around. He was living on the streets, doing whatever he had to do to survive. Our introduction wasn't the usual: He'd tried to pick my pocket. I'd caught him red-handed, but instead of turning him in to the cops, I bought him a bowl of soup and offered him a place to stay for the night. I'd left him on the couch, but I woke up in the middle of the night to find him between my legs with his mouth sliding down my pole like a fireman on his way to a three-alarmer. Frankie never made it back to the couch.

With due respect to F. Scott Fitzgerald, it was this side of paradise, but it hadn't lasted. Frankie had gotten restless, and the lure of easy money had sent him to work as a whore for Blackie McCabe. He'd still come back to my place from time to time and share my bed—on the house, mind you. I should have left well enough alone, but instead I used Frankie to help me on a case, asking him to get information on one of Blackie's regular clients.

Even though six months had passed, I still woke up in a cold sweat from nightmares of seeing his beautiful face with the .38 caliber bullet someone had planted between his eyes. I knew it had been Blackie, but the pimp's alibi had been air-tight, so Frankie's death had just been forgotten by everyone. Everyone but me.

After leaving Greenfield's place on Long Island, I went back to my office and poured myself a well-deserved shot of whiskey while I sorted through the compromising photos I'd taken of the ex–chorus girl wife of a geezer old enough to be her grandfather.

I turned the radio on, and Lamont Cranston was just about to use his power to cloud men's minds when my office door opened and the kid from Greenfield's place came in. A large bruise on his cheek had marred his Renaissance beauty, and his eyes were red and puffy from crying. "Mr. Korrigan?" he asked softly.

"That's me," I answered, shutting off the radio. "That's a nasty bruise, kid. Greenfield do that to you?"

His hand went to his cheek. "How did you know?"

"I'm a detective, remember. Finding out secrets is my business."

He took the chair opposite my desk, but didn't volunteer anything more, so I asked, "What can I do for you, kid?"

"It's David, Mr. Korrigan, David Bachman."

"As in Bachman Greenfield Ironworks?"

The kid nodded. "My father and Fletcher were partners."

"Were?"

"Yes. He's dead."

"I'm sorry."

"Me, too. I miss him."

"So, what were you doing at Greenfield's place?"

"I live there." At my raised eyebrows, he explained, "He's been my guardian since my father died."

"So he controls the purse strings," I surmised.

David nodded again, only this time he kept his eyes down. "He's the executor of my father's estate. I have to live in his house and do whatever he says…" The kid's words trailed off as his bottom lip began to tremble.

"Are you OK?" I asked.

"I'm fine," he said, but he wasn't fine. He looked pale and shaky and about to come apart like the guts of a Swiss watch, but I kept my mouth shut and waited for him to talk. When he did he said, "I'm sorry. I shouldn't have come here. I have to get back before Fletcher realizes I'm gone." The kid got up from the chair and would have fallen flat on his face if I hadn't gotten up from my desk just in time to catch him.

"You're in no shape to go anywhere, kid. Now tell me what this is all about."

David Bachman slumped against me, and the waterworks started. I picked him up in my arms and he buried his face in my neck.

I kept a couch in my office for those long nights when I was too beat to make it back to my furnished room, and I lay the kid down on it. He wouldn't let go of me, and ended up pulling my bulk down on top of his small, compact body. Losing myself in his tear-filled blue eyes, I asked, "Greenfield took you into his bed, didn't he?"

The kid blinked, sending tears cascading down his pale cheeks. "It was what I wanted, but then he became possessive, never wanting me to leave the house. I thought he loved me, but when I told him I was moving out..."

"He threatened to keep your father's money from you."

David nodded. "I told him I didn't care about the money, so he said if I tried to leave he'd have me sent to jail."

"For what?"

"For stealing those designs. They're not really missing, Mr. Korrigan. Fletcher hid them away somewhere. He said if I try to leave him he'll tell the police I stole them."

It didn't make sense. "Then why hire *me*?" I asked.

"He knows the police will be suspicious if he doesn't do anything to get the designs back, so he hired you to find them. He know he'll be safe, because there's no way you can find them."

I didn't like being played for a sucker, but I wasn't so sure I was ready to give up the golden goose on the kid's say-so. "So what do you want from me?" I asked.

"I need to get away from Fletcher, but I can't do it on my own," David whispered, his lips so close I could feel his breath on my face. "Please help me, Mr. Korrigan."

Knowing I wouldn't be sending him into strange waters, I offered the kid the kind of help I needed as much as he did. "I'm your man, kid," I said, covering his mouth with mine. His lips parted and I slid my tongue inside. He tasted of mint and dark chocolate.

My hands worked quickly as I unbuttoned his shirt. His chest was smooth and boyish, and I ran my hands over it, feeling his tiny nipples harden the moment I touched them. I kissed all the way down to his waist, stopping only to unbuckle his belt and unzip his pants so that I could take them off. His silk boxers came off next, revealing a long, slim dick, surprisingly big for a kid his size. I touched my lips to the tip and it saluted like a career soldier.

Sliding my hands under his ass, I cupped his cheeks in my palms as I prepared to swallow him whole. That's when I felt the welts. "Greenfield did this to you?" I asked.

The kid nodded, then turned away, his face flushed. "He likes to play rough. He ties me to the bed and uses his belt on me. It's the only way he can..."

Playing rough might have been the only way Fletcher Greenfield could get it up, but I had no such problem. Just touching the kid already had me so close to shooting I was afraid I wouldn't get my dick out of my pants in time.

Greenfield might have been his first, but David Bachman had been a good student. He took my dick out of my pants like a pro, then he turned over underneath me so that he was face down on the couch. When he pulled his knees up under him and raised his ass, I didn't need an engraved invitation. I spit on my dick and sunk it into his hole. The kid groaned, but he took it all, bucking against me until I was buried deep inside him, my balls slamming against his ass while I fucked him. I shot quickly, pumping my jism into him until I'd been milked dry. It wasn't until the kid asked me who "Frankie" was that I realized I'd screamed out his name when I came.

So I made my pact with the devil and sealed the deal with my seven inches deep inside David Bachman's ass.

It wasn't difficult to pull off the scam. I learned Greenfield's daily routine, his work habits, his comings and goings—all in hopes of finding the designs he'd hidden away. Each week I turned in phony reports of my progress on the case. Not that things weren't progressing on my end. I was fucking David Bachman regularly, and getting paid to do it. The good life didn't seem like such a dream after all. Until I got the wake-up call.

"Artie!"

I was half-asleep. "David?" I said into the phone, still fuzzy. "What's going on?"

"Fletcher found out about us, Artie! He's going crazy! Please come get me before—"

The line went dead. I jumped out of bed and into my clothes. I drove to the Greenfield mansion like a madman, determined to kill Fletcher Greenfield if he'd laid a hand on the kid. But when I got there everything was quiet. The front door was unlocked and I let myself in. I called out, but there was no answer, so I drew my .38 and went upstairs.

There was a light on in Greenfield's study. His chair was turned away from the door. "Where's David?" I demanded. "If you hurt that kid, so help me..."

When Greenfield didn't answer, I went to the desk and spun his chair around so that he would face me. Greenfield's eyes were staring straight at me, but he was long past seeing anyone. There was blood dripping down onto his $100 suit from the .38 caliber hole right between his eyes.

When I got to David's room I found him naked, tied spread-eagle, face down on his bed. A silk tie had been fastened around his mouth to gag him. "Are you all right, kid?" I asked, putting down my gun so that I could untie him. "Greenfield's dead. Thank God whoever did it didn't know he'd left you in here like this."

"He knew very well."

Hearing that voice made my blood run cold.

"Blackie McCabe," I muttered as the dark-suited pimp walked out of the bathroom carrying a leather belt in one hand and a .38 in the other.

"I'm so pleased you remember me, Korrigan." My eyes went to my gun on the bed, but McCabe said, "Don't even think about it." He picked up the gun and put it in his belt.

"Don't hurt the kid," I pleaded.

McCabe shook his head. "You disappoint me, Korrigan. You're such a smart dick, I was sure you'd figure this out right away. Davy likes being hurt." He slapped the belt hard across the kid's ass. David moaned and raised his reddened asscheeks up for more. "It makes him one of my most popular boys. You'd be surprised how much my customers are willing to pay to beat a rich boy's ass."

"A rich boy?" I asked stupidly.

"Very rich. Davy already has his father's estate. He'll get all of Bachman Greenfield Ironworks too, now that his dear guardian is out of the way. We just needed someone to take the fall for Fletcher's murder."

The realization fell on me like a two-ton slab of concrete. "You had the kid recommend me to Greenfield."

"Very good, Korrigan." Blackie nodded his approval. "I knew you were a smart dick. I thought you might be too smart to fall for our little plan, but I knew Davy-boy would be able to convince you. You always did like the pretty ones, didn't you, Korrigan? Like Frankie?"

"You bastard!" I spat, lunging for the .38 in McCabe's hand. He sidestepped me like Fred Astaire, and brought the butt of the gun down on the back of my head. Everything faded to black.

When I woke up, the room was full of blue uniforms and I had McCabe's .38 in my hand. The cops didn't believe me when I told them I'd been framed, especially when they untied the kid and he started talking. David Bachman told them in a small, teary voice how I'd tied him up and forced myself on him, and how I'd shot Greenfield. The kid sounded real convincing, especially with those tears running down his beautiful cheeks.

I'm not in the peeper business anymore. Now I'm getting my three squares a day courtesy of the state. I spend my days making license plates in the Greybar Hotel." And my nights alone in an 8 by 10 cell. I don't mind the solitude; it's given me a lot of time to think.

After lights–out, I spend hours staring up at the ceiling. If I look real hard I can see David Bachman's tear-stained face when he asked for my help. I still can't believe what a sucker I was. A pro like me getting conned by a kid like him....

I've never been one to give advice, but this pearl of wisdom is worth taking: Sex and business don't mix. I'm living proof of where a stiff dick can lead you. The Fletcher Greenfield case taught me one other hard lesson:

You can never trust a pretty face.

Prolonged Exposure
May Cause Dizziness
Sandip Roy

It's 12:25. He never comes in before 12:30, but I just wanted
to be sure. Just in case, you know. The bench is hot on my
bare butt and I wiggle around trying to avoid the nails. The
sauna smells of stale towels and trapped air. Someone left a
newspaper inside even though the sign explicitly says, "No
newspapers." The pages have dried to a crisp. I glance at
them—the sports pages, oh well. I spread my towel on the
bench and sit down and wait. I have been watching him for
days—from behind my book on the Lifecycle. It was very hard
to concentrate on the book while he pounded away on one of
those running machines next to me in his little butt-hugging
blue satin shorts that showed off those sleek brown thighs.
Once, after he had finished running, he pulled up his blue-
ribbed tank top to wipe his forehead and I almost dropped my
book as I was treated to a glimpse of his flat brown belly and I
saw his belly button was pierced. I could even see the thin line
of hair running from his belly button down into those satin
shorts that looked as if they would just glide off him.

The other day I almost got him. Just as I was about to finish my shower, he came in. He glanced at me and then hung his towel on a hook and came to the stall right opposite mine. He turned on the water and jumped back with a start as the icy-cold spray hit him. He stood away from the stream of water, fiddling with the controls, while I feasted on his body. The slopes of his chest, the taut belly, and the sudden fullness of his butt. His uncut dick. The neatly trimmed patch of pubic hair. Just above the hairline I could see a little tattoo. A dragon perhaps. Maybe that was his Chinese Zodiac sign. I could suddenly see myself between his thighs, my tongue flicking across that little dragon and around his sweet tight balls. And I wanted to see his throat tighten with pleasure as my tongue swirled around his balls and his dick swelled in anticipation of my mouth. And the water from the shower would be cascading down his back and chest and blinding me as I looked up. I could feel my dick stirring. I glanced over at him. He was looking at me in the shower. I turned around to face him and soaped myself in what I hoped was a languorous gesture. I took my time—pumping that liquid dispenser for all it was worth. I hated that evil-smelling pink liquid soap the gym provided. But I lathered myself with it for his pleasure. I ran my hands over my butt and let the water wash away the ringlets of foam, only to do it all over again. I filled my hands with soap and vigorously rubbed myself between the thighs, playing with my dick as I did so. I glanced over and saw his dick had lengthened. It was not hard but it definitely hung a little heavier. He glanced at me and then his gaze shyly darted away.

I turned off the shower and briskly rubbed my hair dry. Then I wrapped the towel carelessly around my waist, letting it slip down just a little, and walked over to the sauna. Just before I went in, I paused theatrically and glanced back. He looked away quickly, but he had been looking. After a while he followed me in. I casually touched myself, slung the towel around my neck, and smiled at him.

He adjusted his towel and sat down nervously, looking straight at the door. He was so heartbreakingly beautiful. The dark brown skin was still beaded with water from his shower. His black hair, glistening and tousled, and those full, perfect lips. Bee-stung, a friend of mine would call them. I preferred to think of them as ripe fruit, a plum perhaps, just waiting to be bitten gently. He had a plain gold chain around his neck. And that chest—firm and defined and naturally smooth, with the perkiest nipples you ever saw. I could just imagine my lips on those nipples, teasing them. I wondered how our bodies would look on each other—my brownness on his. My hairy legs entwined against his smooth, muscular ones. I smiled at him, trying to will him to drop the towel. He glanced at me. I smiled encouragingly. Did a flicker of a smile cross his face? It was hard to tell. His right hand casually brushed his left nipple. Then he leaned back and spread his legs a little more. A little more and the towel would slip off by itself. I wondered if I should say something. Something sexy and funny. A come-on line with a touch of flirtatiousness.

That was when the white guy came in. A thirtyish guy with blue eyes and bulging, gym-nurtured pecs. And the biggest dick I had ever seen. He was always parading around the locker room with a half-hard-on. He had shaved off all his pubic hair so that it looked like a big naked fleshy hosepipe dangling between his thighs. He usually did not even notice me. But that was OK. I much preferred this other boy with the nutmeg skin and slim, tight figure. And average-sized dick.

The white guy put his towel down and parked himself between us. We shrank into our corners and fell to examining our toes. I gave the white guy the "why don't you leave us alone!" look. But he just glanced at us, leaned back, spread his legs, and started to stroke himself. I wondered what he would do if someone walked in. He wouldn't be able to hide that thing under his little white towel. Maybe he'd make a quick tent with the sports page. I gave my lover boy the "let's-ignore-this-monstrous-exhibition-and-do-our-boys-of-color-bonding" look. I wondered if it was polite to walk across this blatantly aroused man and make out with my man. It seemed kind of rude—and I just wasn't brought up to be like that. I stretched and walked to the door, ostensibly to look at the clock. Then I said to no one in particular, "Damn, it's hot in here," and stepped outside and got myself a drink of water from the cooler. Now I felt I could go and sit next to my guy instead of returning to my old spot. It wouldn't look so obvious. I opened the door and went back in and stopped short. He had moved closer to the white guy and was feeling his dick. I stopped, unsure of what to do. The object of my affection did not even glance at me. Forgetting all our telepathic messages in the shower, he started blowing the white guy with great gusto. His towel fell off his waist and puddled around his bare feet. I stood there, stranded, my towel in hand. I looked at his head bobbing up and down. At his smooth brown butt. His hand was pulling at his own dick as he sucked. I watched his dick grow hard. Then he put both hands on the white guy's waist as he tried to get that monster dick inside his mouth. The white guy stood up so that he could fuck his mouth better. He put his hands on my lover boy's head and slammed his cock into his mouth. The white guy closed his eyes and said in a throaty, bad-porn-star voice, "Yeah, baby, suck that big cock." That was so cheesy. I felt bad for my lover boy. He deserved better. But he just made a muffled choking noise and tried to open his mouth wider. I should have left right then. If I had, the white guy wouldn't have had the chance to open his eyes, look at me, and say, "Would you mind watching the door?"

But that was then. Today it will be different. My friends would say I'm pathetic. But I am willing to give him another chance. As one person of color to another. Also, I have checked—monster dick is not in today. And I'm horny. And determined. Afterward I will explain to him about racism in the gay community and why we boys of color must stick together.

I glance at the clock. 12:35—I start reading about college basketball. It's not very interesting but it's all I have. I glance around impatiently, get up, stretch, and walk up and down the sauna room before going back to my spot and sitting down.

12:45—the sauna is getting really hot. I rub the sweat across my chest. I casually arrange my towel over my lap and sit back and try to think sexy thoughts. Just to be ready.

12:47—my throat is parched. I should have brought some water. I walk toward the door and peer out. An old man in sagging blue trunks is taking a shower. He carefully wrings his trunks out. I can hear another shower going but cannot see who is in it.

12:52—I guess I could hop into the shower and come back. But what if he poked his head in right then and, seeing no one, left? But I am not sure how much longer I can last in here. After all, the sign outside does warn that prolonged exposure may cause dizziness.

12:55—getting hungry now. The old man comes in with his wet swimming trunks. I glare at him, trying to will him to leave. He stretches and hangs his wet swimming trunks over the coals to dry. I want to point out the sign that expressly forbids such activity but restrain myself. He sits down, coughing, and cracks his knuckles.

1:02—I am thinking about this Thai restaurant nearby that serves the best tom ka gai. And iced tea with sweet condensed milk—rich, tasty brown.

1:05—I am thinking basil and lemongrass and iced tea refills. My stomach grumbles. The old man coughs and picks his trunks up and leaves. Images of chicken pieces floating in lemony coconut-milk broth are clouding my vision.

1:10—I am starting to get dizzy from hunger and thirst. I try to will my dick to remain alert and playful but it is undoubtedly wilting. I am almost about to go when the door opens. I freeze. It is he. He pokes his head in. And seems startled to see me. I uncross my legs and look him in the eyes. He hangs his towel over the coals and hesitates. Then he quickly steps back out, shutting the door behind him. I wait, thinking maybe he was taking a quick shower before coming back. I wipe my brow and take a deep breath to try and calm my heart rate down.

1:15—he comes back, in his jeans and T-shirt, and picks up his towel. This time he does not look at me as he briskly walks out of the sauna. Now I feel like I can't even leave the sauna till he is gone from the gym. I don't want him to have the satisfaction of knowing I was waiting for him and him alone. I watch him outside, drying his hair.

I close my eyes and think of Thai food. I think of combination lunch Number 5. I wonder whether I'll get it with tofu, chicken, beef, or pork. Tofu would probably be healthiest. Fuck that. I am getting pork. And maybe some of that creamy coconut ice cream for dessert. And definitely fried rice instead of steamed rice.

He's still in the lobby when I leave. He's standing there, gym bag slung over his shoulder, talking to a blond man doing crunches. But I don't care. I walk past with my head held high. I smile. I can almost taste Combination Number 5.

Woof. Yea. Uhuh. Yea, that's it. Uhuh. Yeaaa.

Eddie Moreno

I'd like to believe that it's more than just sex, my life's work, but really—it's just sex. Yup.

What I wanted was to be a singer, songwriter, musician—a voice for generations, putting words and music to the twists and turns in the roller-coaster ride of our entwined, individual lives. I dreamed of performing my best-loved, most heartfelt numbers in front of screaming, beaming crowds, every single one of us moved and teary as my song reveals itself, as if fresh, brand-newly-born, never been sung beforefresh and simple. I wanted to make of our deepest dilemmas bracelets of rhyme and rhythm, riffs, jingles revealing profoundest happiest tears, songs of joy flying out of my melancholy wisdom, while I breathe and sparkle, pushing my life out into the life around me: sweet smart song, so fine, I'm a bird, I'm Joni Mitchell, I'm the first singer or a brand-new baby just googling breath.

But instead I'm a Gay Porn Star. What will *I* leave for future generations? What do *I* create with my movements, my breath? Does my personal expression, like that of the songwriter, speak to each of us in our twisted sweet lives, of love and laughter, grunts of happiness—yeah fuck my ass!, the not-so-tender power piston, my male flesh naked warm wet with sweat, rosy, sweet slap of skin on skin…representing what? in our daily lives?—love, death, and separation, happiness, your dad's green eyes, revelation, childhood joy, epiphany? I'd like to believe that it's more than just sex, my life's work, but really—it's just sex. Yup.

My movement, the sounds I make, coyote howling, proud show-pony rearing my hoofs in black boots steel-toes, throwing my head back and chucking out a smile, or fanning out a frown, the scrape of my toothy scowl, black hair lost in shadow. Pubes? Or head-hair? My boots stay on for sex but I feel like a boy, these movements, the sweat under the heavy lights burning my balls, all feels like the same kid stuff, the same movement in my parents' house, in the front yard, barreling into the rock garden my first time on a bike alone, and sliding into home, through the cactus garden, getting plowed by the barrel cactus we'd tended, jumping up, my yeow arching out like my back on the set under the lights showing off my proud faggot ass; or I'm a kid running into the house ripping my clothes off screaming *yeow, my bike* my boy-song says yolanda *I fell in the cactus, helppp* and she picks out the pricks, touches those sore spots, my sister makes me feel right, times like this we touch closer than usual, she laughs, we laugh, it's like my movie it's like my film my work speaks eloquently, my glowing butt rises over the cactus patch in my Texas childhood garden home, my distant sister holds my hand. My film work speaks to the both of us.

Only she'll never see it. Or maybe she will—she'll watch me open my asshole around a burly man's hands and think of the moments we shared in our lives, Grandma's blankie, driving across the Mojave, how we were so close and separated by miles of water, a Lake Mead of blue misunderstanding swimming up around us, she'll open up a tear, let it fall gently upon our childhood days like cum splattering on my steel-toe boots in the film and in my daily life, she knows my boots mean as much to me as stretched canvas to the painter, her own red Safeway uniform to her and her job her daily life and our sweet connection, I push back and open up, she understands it—this is the closest we've ever been, and she sees it, she'll lick her lips, I'll lick mine. She's watching my first video, she understands my song.

And here comes the chorus—everyone loves the chorus. I reckon it sums up a lot about my mates and peers and colleagues, my family. It rings out loud and resoundingly during the International Mister Leather Conference in the lobby of the Congress Hotel, I hear it on the street, read it online, and of course it totally reigns supreme in the audio-sensational world of Gay Porn overdubs. It goes like this:

Woof!

Yea. Uhuh. Yea, that's it. Uhuh. Yeaaa.

My men and I meet like guys always do: on the dance floor, bumping in the street, getting real steamy in the sauna, pawing each other with our eyes, talking 'bout the tatts we're getting soon, wings on, and soon we're tattooed twins, inseparable, our names always spoken together, together—head to head, face on, hand-in-hand, real sweet, all of a sudden just like that, then just like that, just like the boys mating dirty on our VCRs, like me mating for life in front of the video camera until the scene ends, we spooge ourselves and each other, then fade out. During that real good together time when it's inseparably sweet, we're great mates and best mates all in one, curling up at night, hairy man-spoon pressing tongues together, sweating double on the tool, tongues tied.

Woof!

Yea. Uhuh. Yea, that's it. Uhuh. Yeaaa.

When our scenes end, in our lives, with the men we find ourselves marrying, it's not as clean an edit as I've expressed in my porn creations, but still it fades out, just like that. All of a sudden I find myself in bed with Pete in the morning and the sheets appear untouched, unruffled, still crisp, I'm sitting on the edge of the crisp-sheet Montreal bed in January and I ask him to walk on the new snow with me down cruisy Visitacion to Sainte Catherine but our scene was done and over—just then we'd come clean apart, tongues fallen flat, great mates and best mates gone, clean apart on that snow-warmed bed, tongue-tied now, at a loss for words, no more the man-spoon, we fade out, onto the street, clean apart, alone, the new year's snowflakes balancing on edge one atop the other. Tongues fall flat—what do you say when there's no more lapping on your best-boy's hairy features? In the porn world that I create for ourselves and our boy children, it's smart and light, on the set it's like that, my vision is like that—the way we men separate, autumn leaves on the wind, at sheer velocity we peel apart cleanly: I slap my bottom's hairy ass, and it's over! Easy, just like that—a real beauty thing balancing snow falls in sheet flakes we peel apart completely and smile, our pounding and pumping, our pistoning power-pole positioning was musky, sweet and vacant, real fucking hot. In my hot and vacant man-musky creative filmwork endeavors, I think my rhythmic repetitive thrusting movements speak to everyone, to young and old—whether alone or in the company of friends and lovers, or distant and intimate family. For students and for teachers alike, feeling an urge to go somewhere new, I plow his hole from as many sides as possible, hoeing and plowing, raking and ramrodding to please the farm-boy's best places, on his hands and tough-boy knees. Who can deny that these visually stimulating gay films capture the best moments in men's relationships with men?—the spooging and the pumping and the coming apart cleanly, the speaking in tongues:

Woof!

Yea. Uhuh. Yea, that's it. Uhuh. Yeaaa.

As a boy I liked the snow, keeping us from our school daze, but now I prefer the heat to winter's freeze-dried, stacked-up cold. So I tripped on down under, Oz. One day, at Pete's place, we screwed the videocam onto a tripod in the corner, and worked ourselves up good and troppo between two sexy palms and underneath the languid summer-sway of a back-and-forth fern, swaying and rooting, chests drenched, humping and wet, we slurped away an entire equatorial day, dipping into sweat-puddles and churning out cum-volcanoes for the videocam as if this were our only chance at creation, the living end. On that tape of my life—me a brown Texan kid smiling for the camera and both of us riding mountains and rising waves—I can actually watch him lay himself down inside me, his stinking passion-flower sweat inking across my summer skin like a Polynesian tattoo, his satyr's cock throwing ropes of seed across my fool head.

I traveled some with Pete, though the tour we took together generally took us nowhere in particular. I reckon traveling absolutely broadens the horizons. I've lived in London, loved in Miami, but I figure the sun sweats out its days in São Paulo, Sydney, or Paris for one great reason alone—so that I can savor whatever big-hung man may cross my path on any given traveling, traveling day. I know Mum would approve, if she could only see the sloppy smile rip-snorting across my face as I chew on the piss-stunk underwear of the booted cop who's stopped me for nothing but butt in Prague. Sounds like porn, huh? It's truth; it's just my life. This cold and turreted medieval town built on two sides of a river turns slowly in its stone graces, the sun setting too early, the old cold rising steadily, steadily, rising up from the river's eddy, the cobblestone's coal-black whorls. Mum would absolutely blow a fuse to see me so pleased with my dog's life, big bone in my teeth, grrrr, blow a nut to see me on my knees in front of the stinking Czech pig.

So, though some might object to my objectified life, still, still, I'm meat for hire. It's all sex, my time well spent, yup. Yesterday, down in L.A., I worked with a redheaded muscle butt from Calgary's prime Canadian prairies, big-boy's muscle butt. There wasn't enough sex to be had on the set, so we continued, like guys do, in the toilet at the Burbank Airport—our plane waiting on the tarmac. I plowed his sweet prairie-dog hole till he shot a creamy load all over his backpack there on the floor—kids and their dads coming and going while we rooted quiet and sexy in our somewhat private stall. Then the blond Canadian kid got on his knees real quick, facing me, and begged for my load, running his rough rural hands over his chest and saying, "Yea, come on, right here, cum on me, yeaaaaa," pounding his palms on the valley of the pecs, the Canadian Rockies rising high and mighty, please, he said with his cowboy eyes, beating his chest, please, cum on, so I blew for the blue-eyed pig, and we boarded our plane and flew home. Woof.

Is that all there is? Yea, uhuh, yea, that's it, I reckon. I reckon I rise and fall like the cum-waves, mom and dad's brown-eyed smiley-boy looking up at the moon, my faggot ass arching out like august stars above my Texas childhood home, my cock swinging out like a beam you could hang a house from, raise the boys on, heavy as the setting sun, dribbling sweet on the prairie's lips like a cream cherry you could suck the darkest dreams right out of.

Woof!

Yea, Uhuh. Yea, that's it. Uhuh. Yeaaa.

About the Authors

MARC ALMOND is an internationally acclaimed singer/ songwriter/performer. He burst into prominence in the early 1980s with Dave Ball with the first successful British electro-duo, Soft Cell. They mixed disco and northern soul with lyrics of melancholy stories of low-life characters, bedsit life, and city survival, and thus set the blueprint for groups such as The Pet Shop Boys, Blur, Pulp, and Suede. Marc has continued to produce groundbreaking and successful albums, the most recent of which, *Velvet Nights,* was released in March 1999. The pieces making up "The Show Palaces" are selections from *beautiful twisted night...,* a collection of twenty years of his poetry, prose, and song lyrics.

D-L ALVAREZ is an American-born artist/writer who lives in Berlin. His visual work is held in various collections, including those of the San Francisco Museum of Modern Art and the Whitney Museum of American Art. Most recently his writing appeared in the anthologies *Virgins, Guerrillas, and Locas* and *Tricks and Treats.* His contribution here, "Knot of Roads," is drawn from a collection of short stories set in a fictionalized version of the author's hometown of Stockton, California.

DIMITRI APESSOS is bicoastal, if you count the Mississippi as a coast. At the time of publication he was trying to move permanently from New York to New Orleans and was working on his first novel. God only knows where he will be and what he will be doing by the time you read this. He lives vicariously through his new e-mail address, AmtrakLife@yahoo.com, which says a lot about him. Look for his first novel at a bookstore near you as soon as he finishes writing is, sells it, and gets it published

JAIME CORTEZ is a visual artist, writer, and comic performer based in San Francisco's Mission District. He is the editor of *Virgins, Guerrillas, and Locas: Gay Latinos Writing about Love* (Cleis Press). His work appears in *Queer PAPI Porn* (Cleis Press), *2sexE* (North Atlantic Press), and *Besame Mucho* (Painted Leaf Press), as well as in his own 'zine, *A la Brava*.

JESSE GRANT is a publishing executive living in Los Angeles. He is the editor of *Friction*, volumes *2, 3*, and *4*; and *Men for All Seasons*. He writes using a variety of pseudonyms, and his short fiction, essays, commentary, and reviews have appeared in numerous anthologies, periodicals, and online publications.

DOUG HARRISON has written book reviews, essays, and short stories for *Black Sheets* and *Body Play*. His short stories appear in the anthologies *Men Seeking Men, Best Bisexual Erotica 2000*, and *Still Doing It*. He is currently working on two books, *Erotic Whipping* and *The Jockstrap Book*. In addition, Doug is a Ph.D. engineer who does unusual things on weekends. He has been active for many years in the Modern Primitives movement and the San Francisco leather scene, was Mr. June for the AIDS Emergency Fund's 1999 South of Market Bare Chest Calendar, and appears in straight and gay videos as Brad Chapman. He lives in San Francisco and identifies as a bisexual top/bottom. He can be reached at puma@dnai.com.

SEAN MERIWETHER is working on several projects, including a novel about a young gay man growing up in rural Pennsylvania, and a collection of unflinching short stories entitled *Invisible Children*. He is also the editor of *Outsider Ink,* an online e-zine for niche fiction and poetry (www.outsidermedia.com). His short fiction can be found on and around the Internet and in some small-press magazines (if you look really hard). "For Hire: A Date with John" was taken from a multimedia exhibit that ran at A Different Light Gallery in New York City in fall 1999. Sean lives in New York with his partner, photographer Jack Slomovits, and their two dogs, Sasha and Nik Nak. To the dogs, he adds, "Don't eat this book."

MARSHALL MOORE, a North Carolina native, lives and works in the San Francisco Bay Area. His work has also appeared in *Space and Time, Rebel,* and *The Ghost of Carmen Miranda.* He may be reached at marshallmoore@aol.com

EDDIE MORENO left the red deserts of rural New Mexico for the big city after high school to pursue a career in sex. He's danced on bars from Key West to Bangkok, and shaken his money-maker in Sydney, Amsterdam, and London. His professional wanderings eventually led him to San Francisco, where he currently resides. He dreams someday of owning a dude ranch in the mountains of New Mexico where he can strum his guitar beside a roaring fire and suck big dick till the cows come home. In the meantime he's scouting the globe in search of big-hung cowboys to man his ranch. For more info, visit Eddie's Web site at www.eddiemorenousa.com.

IAN PHILIPS is a merry ol' troll. He's been skulking around the pages of *Best Gay Erotica* since 1999. He also haunts sites of deliciously transgressive writing in cyberspace as well—like www.suspectthoughts.com. He's just gathered "Foucault's Pendulous..." and a dozen other fine specimens of literary filth into a book-sized bestiary called *See Dick Deconstruct: Literotica for the Satirically Bent* (Attagirl Press). He welcomes e-mail at iphilips@aol.com.

FELICE PICANO is a best-selling author of fiction and poetry, as well as memoirs and other nonfiction. Considered a founder of modern gay literature along with six other members of the Violet Quill Club, he also founded and ran the SeaHorse Press and Hay Presses of New York. He writes regularly for *The San Francisco Examiner, The Lesbian/Gay Review, Lambda Book Report,* and Barnes&Noble.com. Felice is best known for coauthoring *The New Joy of Gay Sex* and for writing the award-winning novels *Like People in History* and *The Book of Lies.* His 1981–1983 stories have been reissued by Alyson as *The New York Years,* and his novel *Onyx* will be published in 2001.

ANDREW RAMER is the author of *Two Flutes Playing: A Spiritual Journeybook for Gay Men* (Alamo Square Press) and of *Revelations for a New Millennium* (Harper San Francisco), as well as coauthor of the books *Ask Your Angels* and *Angel Answers: A Joyful Guide to Creating Heaven on Earth.*

THOMAS S. ROCHE'S short stories have appeared in mainstream horror and crime markets as well as the *Best American Erotica* series, the *Best Gay Erotica* series, and the *Mammoth Book of Erotica* series. His books include three volumes in the *Noirotica* series of erotic crime-noir anthologies: *Sons of Darkness, Brothers of the Night,* and the short story collection *Dark Matter.* Visit www.thomasroche.com or send e-mail to thomasroche-announce-subscribe@egroups.com to subscribe to his monthly newsletter, *Razorblade Valentines.*

SANDIP ROY grew up in India and now lives in San Francisco where he works in the software industry when bills are due. When not writing code, he has written for various anthologies like *Men on Men 6, My First Time, Quickies, Quickies 2, Male Lust, Contours of the Heart, Q & A,* and *Chick for a Day.* He won the Katha Prize for Indian American Fiction and an award from the South Asian Journalists Association for an Outstanding Story on South Asians in North America (print media). He also edits *Trikone,* a magazine on GLBT South Asian issues.

SIMON SHEPPARD is the author of *Hotter Than Hell and Other Stories,* due from Alyson Books in late 2001, and is, with M. Christian, coeditor of *Rough Stuff: Tales of Gay Men, Sex, and Power,* also from Alyson. His work appears in some fifty anthologies, including *The Best American Erotica 2000* and all but one of the *Best Gay Erotica* series. His column "Sex Talk" appears on the Web and in queer newspapers nationwide, and he's currently hard at work on a nonfiction book about kink; cute masochists who wish to help him with his research may contact him at smutsmith@aol.com.

MICHAEL V. SMITH writes stories intended to make you fuck more freely. He is a novelist, film-maker, grant-given poet, and celebrated hottie. His fiction can be found in the Arsenal Pulp Press anthologies *Carnal Nation, Contradiction,* and *Quickies I* and *II.* To receive a copy of his raunchy 'zine *Cruising,* write cruisingzine@hotmail.com.

MICHAEL STAMP can't remember a time when he didn't want to be a writer. His earliest influences were the novels of Gordon Merrick and John Preston, so it's not surprising that all of Michael's erotica, even his S/M tales, has a decidedly romantic bent. His stories appear in the anthologies *Casting*

Couch Confessions, Sex Toy Tales, and *Strange Bedfellows,* as well as *Inches* and *In Touch* magazines and the electronic book *Y2KINKY: Erotica for the New Millennium.* He lives in a small New Jersey suburb with an overweight tomcat named Sam Beckett. Romantic that he is, Michael hopes one day to find his soul mate, who will have to like cats and love sex.

MATT BERNSTEIN SYCAMORE is the editor of *Tricks and Treats: Sex Workers Write About Their Clients.* His writing has appeared in numerous publications, including *Best American Erotica 2001, Best American Gay Fiction 3,* and *Best Gay Erotica 2000.* He is currently editing *Dangerous Families: Queer Writing on Surviving Abuse.* He recently finished a novel, *Pulling Taffy,* and can be contacted at tricksandtreats@hotmail.com.

LARRY TOWNSEND is best known for his *Leatherman's Handbooks.* His stories have been published since the late 1960s. At present he has thirty-some novels in print, plus several collections of short stories and articles. He has done a monthly advice column for more than twenty years, first for *Drummer* and currently for *Honcho.* He is also a regular contributor to *Bound & Gagged* magazine. His titles include *Run, Little Leather Boy; CZAR! A Novel of Ivan the Terrible; A Contagious Evil: The Mind of a Serial Killer; Stalked: An Anatomy of Sexual Obsession.* Complete information is available on the author's prize-winning Web site: www.larrytownsend.com.

BOB VICKERY is a regular contributor to various magazines, and his stories can be found in his two anthologies, *Cock Tales* and *Skin Deep.* He also has stories in numerous other anthologies, including *Best Gay Erotica 1999; Best American Erotica 1997* and *2000; Friction, Friction 2,* and *Friction 3;*

and *Queer Dharma*. Two of his short stories, "Southern Boys" and "A New Man," are being made into a motion picture, titled *Love, Lust, and Repetition*, by independent filmmaker Edgar Bravo. Contact Bob at www.bobvickery.com.

KARL VON UHL resides gratefully in the American Midwest. His fiction has appeared in *Bear* and *Powerplay* magazines, *Best Gay Erotica 2000*, and *Rough Stuff*. He is occasionally on the cable-access show *The Life We Lead*, bringing ska and order to the new millennium. Having completed a collection of short stories, he is currently working on a novel. He may be contacted at leathernk@hotmail.com.

BARRY WEBSTER is a classical pianist and writer of both fiction and nonfiction. He has published in *Quickies*, *Quickies 2*, and *The Washington Post*, as well as in *The Globe and Mail, Dandelion, The Dalhousie Review, The Newest Review, Pottersfield Portfolio*, and numerous other Canadian publications. He has received awards from the Toronto Arts Council and the Canadian Authors Association. He is presently finishing *Bicycle Dreams*, his first collection of short stories. He recently moved to Montreal where he's completing his master's degree and learning how to speak French. Contact him at fodxyz@hotmail.com.

About the Editors

RANDY BOYD has been a professional writer his entire adult life. His short stories and essays have appeared in numerous publications, including *Frontiers, Washington Blade, Gay & Lesbian Review, Flesh and the Word 2, Flashpoint, Certain Voices,* and *Friends and Lovers: Gay Men Write About the Families They Create.* His first novel, *Uprising,* was nominated for two Lambda Literary Awards: Best Men's Mystery and Best Small Press Title. His second novel, *Bridge Across the Ocean,* tells the story of what happens when a suburban white family meets a black gay man with HIV during their summer vacation in Cancun, Mexico. *Bridge Across the Ocean* was inspired by a true story. An avid sportsman and longtime fan of his hometown Indiana Pacers, Randy divides his time between California and Indiana and lives with his dog, Boomer, named after the Pacers mascot. Randy started his own publishing company, West Beach Books, to publish his own work as well as that of others. For more information, visit www.westbeachbooks.com.

RICHARD LABONTÉ is a former bookseller who helped found A Different Light Bookstore in Los Angeles in 1979; he stepped down in July 2000 as general manager of its stores in San Francisco, New York City, and West Hollywood. Before book-selling, he worked for more than a decade for a daily newspaper in Ottawa. After book-selling, he is spending a year or two of low-key life in rural Ontario on a 200-acre farm he has owned communally since 1976 with a group of friends who met in college in the late 1960s. He reads a lot but luckily lives with Asa, a man who reads hardly at all (and Percy, a dog that never does), so the word-count karma in his home is well balanced. Richard continues to dabble in the book trade, mostly writing book news and reviews for PlanetOut (www.planetout.com) as well as columns and book-selling commentary for *Q San Francisco* and *Lambda Book Report*. Reach out and touch him at tattyhill@hotmail.com